"Let's go to your place and take it from there."

Gil looked at Clare a few more seconds, trying to decipher the expression in her eyes, but he couldn't. At least she'd made the right choice. They had to finish what they'd begun.

Once inside, he helped her off with her coat. He froze when he brushed against her neck, mesmerized by the memory of the first time he'd touched it. He wanted desperately to stroke her skin and press his lips against her hair.

"Something wrong?"

Clare's words brought him back to life. He whisked her coat off her shoulders and took it to the hall closet. Her footsteps echoed behind him.

"Didn't we try to do this the other day?" she quipped as she came into the room.

He realized what she meant when he saw her nod toward the writing supplies on the table. "Maybe we'll have better luck the second time around."

Dear Reader,

Most of us, at one time or another, have attended a high school or college reunion and have learned that seeing old friends can sometimes be hurtful as well as exhilarating. Going back isn't always easy to do. In fact, it can be downright risky—as Clare Morgan discovers in *Past, Present and a Future*.

Returning to Twin Falls, Connecticut, for the first time in seventeen years is much more than a trip down memory lane for Clare. What started out as a visit to attend the christening of her best friend's new baby becomes a confrontation with Clare's worst memories of her senior year in high school. Betrayal. Distrust. Murder.

And a key player in her memories—Clare's former boyfriend, her first love, Gil Harper—has returned for the christening, as well.

Going back offers Clare an opportunity to put things right—to lay to rest for once and for all the painful memories of her seventeenth summer. Only then, Clare realizes, can a future with Gil Harper be possible.

Enjoy!

Janice Carter

Past, Present and a Future

Janice Carter

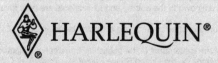

HARLEQUIN®

TORONTO • NEW YORK • LONDON
AMSTERDAM • PARIS • SYDNEY • HAMBURG
STOCKHOLM • ATHENS • TOKYO • MILAN • MADRID
PRAGUE • WARSAW • BUDAPEST • AUCKLAND

ISBN 0-373-71178-6

PAST, PRESENT AND A FUTURE

This edition published by arrangement with Harlequin Books S.A.

® and TM are trademarks of the publisher. Trademarks indicated with
® are registered in the United States Patent and Trademark Office, the
Canadian Trade Marks Office and in other countries.

Visit us at www.eHarlequin.com

Printed in U.S.A.

For Susan Hess, valued friend, great sister-in-law
and terrific brainstormer.
Not to mention the best aunt in the world.

Books by Janice Carter

HARLEQUIN SUPERROMANCE
593—GHOST TIGER
671—A CHRISTMAS BABY
779—THE MAN SHE LEFT BEHIND
887—THE INHERITANCE
995—SUMMER OF JOANNA
1079—THE REAL ALLIE NEWMAN
1144—THE SECOND FAMILY

Don't miss any of our special offers. Write to us at the
following address for information on our newest releases.

Harlequin Reader Service
U.S.: 3010 Walden Ave., P.O. Box 1325, Buffalo, NY 14269
Canadian: P.O. Box 609, Fort Erie, Ont. L2A 5X3

CHAPTER ONE

GOOD NEWS and bad news. Funny how the two often came together. Clare read the e-mail a second time. Her best friend since elementary school was the proud mother of a baby girl named Emma. Clare felt a rush of emotion that was a mix of joy and envy.

The bad news was that Laura wanted her to be the child's godmother, which meant going back home to Twin Falls, Connecticut. And home—somewhere she hadn't visited in the last seventeen years—was the last place on earth Clare Morgan wanted to set foot.

She quickly sent a return congratulatory message, expressing delight at the request but avoiding a definite reply by saying she'd telephone on the weekend. That would give her two days to come up with a plausible excuse to politely decline. She was flattered that Laura had thought of her, but she couldn't see herself in the role of a godmother.

Such as? Clare leaned back in her chair. There was no way she could refuse. Laura Kingsway, nee Dundas, had been her best friend since they'd started school together at Mountview Elementary in Miss Goodfellow's kindergarten class. Their friendship had weathered upheavals such as the divorce of Clare's parents when she was nine, along with boyfriend troubles during their high school years. Though their separation due to college and careers had altered the nature of their relationship to one of phone and e-mail—in fact, the last time Clare had seen Laura

was at her marriage to Dave Kingsway two years ago—
they were still close.

Twin Falls. Clare had difficulty uttering her hometown's name even in her head. She still couldn't believe
that Laura and Dave had chosen to move back there. But
then, Laura hadn't been affected by the whole sordid mess
seventeen years ago in quite the same way that Clare had.

Clare shut down the computer. She was having lunch
with her editor to discuss changes to her upcoming book
tour to promote her second novel. It was an important
meeting and one that Clare had been anticipating for several days. The book had—to Clare's astonishment—recently made the *New York Times* bestseller list a mere
three weeks after its launch. She just hoped today's news
wouldn't diminish her enjoyment of the celebratory luncheon.

"SALUT!" Alix Bennett clinked her champagne flute del-
icately against Clare's.

Clare took her first taste of Cristal, savoring its crisp
fruitiness and thinking she could get used to the trappings
of success.

"So when can we expect the next proposal?" Alix
asked.

"Maybe a couple of weeks?"

Alix nodded. "Try to get it in as soon as possible. It'd
be nice to be able to mention it during some of your
appearances."

"You haven't even offered me a contract yet."

"After the success of *Growing up in Paradise* I'm sure
that won't be a problem. Not after what you've already
told me about this new one."

"Tina really likes it," Clare said, referring to her agent.

"Too bad she couldn't make it for lunch today."

"She's unbelievably busy but promised to make the next one."

"You mean the signing celebration for the new one?" Alix smiled.

Giddiness swept through Clare. She still had difficulty believing that all this heady success was indeed happening to her. "Assuming you buy it," she repeated.

"Given the initial sales of *Growing up in Paradise,* it's a done deal. But don't quote me on that," Alix said with a mischievous grin. She paused while the waiter set down their appetizers. After he left, she asked, "So, what's new in your life these days? Aside from the dizziness of fame?"

Clare smiled. Her editor loved to tease and had a penchant for hyperbole—certainly a plus when it came to pitching a book to the honchos who made the final decisions. "My best friend just had a baby girl. She wants me to be godmother."

"Ahh, that's nice. And a compliment."

"Yes. Laura and I haven't seen each other for a couple of years. Her family lived just down the street from mine in Twin Falls. We met in kindergarten."

"Wow! Not many people can lay claim to that kind of long friendship."

"She married a guy from Twin Falls, too. Dave. They dated briefly in high school, then split up and got back together again in college."

"No kidding? When I think of the guys I dated in high school, no way would I want to end up with any one of them."

Thinking of just such a guy, Clare averted her gaze from Alix to the table. She waited for the usual uneasiness that accompanied thoughts of Gil Harper to surface but when nothing happened, she raised her head with an almost audible sigh of relief.

"You okay? Thought I'd lost you there for a sec."

"Must be the champagne," Clare said. "I'm not used to drinking at lunch."

"Hey, you'd better get used to it. I see lots of celebrations ahead in your future."

"Book sales will be good enough for me, believe me. All of this," she gestured toward the plush interior of the Plaza, "is wonderful but not really my thing."

"Not really mine either, frankly." Alix put a chunk of artichoke into her mouth. "So we should enjoy while the boss is paying."

Clare followed suit, though her appetite had waned at the unbidden memory of Gil Harper. She tried to concentrate on Alix's patter of conversation, but her mind kept going back to the man responsible for her self-imposed exile from Twin Falls. Giving up, Clare pushed her half-eaten salad aside.

"I just had a brilliant idea," Alix piped up as the waiter began to remove their plates.

"What?"

"The book tour's supposed to start in a couple of weeks, right?"

Clare nodded.

"And you said this friend who wants you to be godmother still lives in your hometown?"

Another nod, accompanied by a rising dread.

"So how about an appearance right in Twin Falls? I mean, the symbolism's perfect. A coming-of-age book based on your life in Twin Falls—"

"Loosely based," Clare emphasized.

Alix shrugged. "Whatever. But I bet you're not fooling anyone back home with name changes and a bit of reconstruction."

Clare fiddled with the cutlery in front of her. "Perhaps not, but I didn't intend to market the book as a memoir.

It's a novel. Fiction," she added, reinforcing her argument.

"Doesn't matter. It's the whole human interest angle I like. Small town girl—okay, woman—makes it big writing a novel based *loosely* on her life in said small town. Having a book signing and interviews with local media from say, the town's quaint bookstore—"

"There is no bookstore in Twin Falls. At least, there wasn't one seventeen years ago."

"Hey, things change. If no bookstore, they've got to have a public library. Right?"

"I'm not—" Clare hesitated. She and Alix had a friendly relationship, but they were not friends and definitely not confidantes. How could she adequately explain her reluctance to go along with such an unthinkable scheme without spilling her guts about the event that had wreaked havoc with so many lives so long ago?

"What?"

"Hmm?"

"You started to say something. Sorry, you know me. I get carried away."

"It's just that, I'm not sure if I'm going to take Laura up on her offer of being godmother. It's...it's a big commitment." The excuse, lame to her own ears, left Alix's mouth slightly agape.

"Seriously? But isn't she one of your best friends?"

The arrival of the waiter with their main courses gave Clare a few seconds to put together an explanation that would save her from appearing too coldhearted. When he left, she said, "I guess I'm anxious about confronting some people. You know—people who might be offended by certain parts of the book."

"But as you said, it's fiction, right?"

Clare didn't know which bothered her more: Alix's annoying habit of using the word *right* constantly or her pushiness. But she did know she wanted the lunch to end as pleasantly—and as quickly—as possible. "I'll give it some thought," she demurred and fixed her attention on her pasta.

After a slight pause, Alix picked up her own fork. "I have to pass it through marketing anyway, but think about it."

Two weeks later, Clare's fears were realized. Driving out of New York City in her rental car, she couldn't help but wonder what quirk of fate had plunked her on this inextricable path to her past.

First there had been the tense phone call with Laura, who saw through Clare's reservations about being godmother immediately. "Don't pretend you're too far away to take on the responsibilities of being a godmother to Emma when you and I both know what this is all about," she'd said.

And when Clare had protested otherwise, Laura merely suggested it was time Clare put the past behind her. "All the clichés apply, Clare baby. Face up to it and get over it. Everyone here's talking about your book. It's only for a few days and it'd be so great to see you again."

Guilt had won out in the end. Laura and Dave were her only remaining friends from Twin Falls and she knew she couldn't afford to lose them. The christening and the start of the book tour had synchronized with minor adjustments and Clare had had no credible reason—short of feigning insanity or some terminal illness—not to go.

And yet once out on the highway, she actually began to enjoy the drive. It was a perfect autumn day in mid-October—a brilliant blue sky teamed with a harvest-gold sun and there was just the slightest crispness in the air. As she headed northeast toward Connecticut, the scenery turned postcard perfect with splashes of color set against dark green pines on the distant hills.

Clare had left early, hoping to arrive in Twin Falls shortly before dinner. Emma's christening was set for Sunday morning, so she'd have tonight to visit with Laura and Dave before the book signing Saturday afternoon in—to Clare's surprise—the town's bookstore, Novel Idea. The rest of Sunday she was free to do as she pleased. The next signing wasn't until Monday in Hartford, a mere one-hour drive away.

There had been some disagreement about where she would stay. Laura finally agreed that the local hotel was acceptable given that Clare's publisher was footing the bill.

"Probably for the best," Laura had said with an emphatic sigh. "One of us might as well get some sleep."

"How's she doing?"

Another sigh. "Emma's doing great. Dave and I are the ones slogging around in a zombielike state."

Clare had made the expected sounds of sympathy, then remembered to ask, "Who's the godfather?"

There'd been the slightest pause before Laura mumbled something about Dave not having yet made a decision.

"Dave?"

"We thought it was only fair if I picked the godmother, he should get to choose the godfather. But you know Dave."

"Still having trouble making up his mind?"

"Tell me about it."

They'd laughed together and for a few moments Clare was transported to the old days when she and Laura had shared confidences as well as laughter. When she'd hung up, she realized that due to the isolation induced from finishing her book, it had been a long time since she'd had a giggle with anyone.

Clare popped in a Tori Amos CD and let her mind slip into auto-drive. She'd spent the past two weeks in an increasingly heightened state of anxiety about the visit to Twin Falls. Once the decision to go had finally been made, she had tried to ease her jitters by reminding herself that Gil Harper had left town long before she had and she wasn't likely to bump into him at the local convenience store.

The music kept her free of the past until the first familiar landmarks of Twin Falls appeared—the white bulbous shape of the town's water tower looming over trees and rooftops, the spire of the Catholic church and on the opposite side of the river that bisected the town, the bell tower of the Methodist. Clare eased up on the accelerator.

She could either enter town from the first highway exit or take the winding road that afforded a panoramic view and led directly into the town center. Impulsively, she chose that route, and turned right onto the smaller, two-lane paved road. She stopped at the crest of the hill, pulling over onto the shoulder to survey the town.

Twin Falls lay in the valley below, spanning both sides of the river. From Clare's vantage point, it looked much the same as it had when she'd last seen it.

Tempted to make a quick U-turn and hightail it back to New York, Clare forced herself to focus on the reason for her return—to see her old friend, Laura, and to meet Laura's first child. Returning to Twin Falls wasn't really going back, she reminded herself, but moving forward, to the next generation. Although, she wished the christening could have been held somewhere else. She shifted into Drive and angled back onto the road, pumping the brake as the Jetta made the downhill curve to the stop sign below.

But now the stop was a three-way, accommodating a road leading to what appeared to be new houses. *Good grief. Twin Falls has a subdivision.* Clare didn't know whether to be amused or appalled. The Jetta continued its descent to the two-lane bridge and Clare instinctively turned her head to the right to see the falls that had given the town its name.

The twin watercourses were too narrow and sparse to be famous beyond the scope of the county. Still, their twenty-foot parallel tumble over a granite rock cliff was impressive enough to be an occasional draw for local daredevils or careless youngsters, resulting in a handful of tragic accidents over the years. Clare noticed that a sturdier and higher metal railing had replaced the original wooden one. She also noticed the new traffic lights a few yards past the end of the bridge and slowed to a stop as the amber light turned red.

Clare was surprised at the line of traffic waiting on the other side and wished she'd taken a better look at the Welcome To Twin Falls sign at the top of the hill. The town's population had obviously risen from three thousand.

Navigating Main Street was as slow as it had always been, though, no longer due to the country gawkers, as Clare's father had labeled them. Now traffic crawled because there were more cars.

Clare felt she'd joined the gawker's club herself, with her head turning from side to side. She had expected some changes in Twin Falls, but expansion hadn't been one of them. At least two chain stores had opened branches on Main Street—small ones, granted, but the name brands must have set aflutter the hearts of the town's teenage population. Clare and her friends had had to beg for shopping expeditions to Hartford.

At the end of Main Street, she made a left into the older, residential area where Laura and Dave lived. When Clare was a teenager, she had often walked these streets, wondering what treasures or secrets the grand three-story Victorian homes contained. Set far back on manicured lawns, their elegant verandas and etched-glass front doors had symbolized an era and social class far beyond Clare and her circle of friends.

The neighborhood, known as Riverside Park, had housed the descendants of the town founders, the original settlers who had parlayed their pioneering skills into commercial ventures that became the backbone of the town's economy. After the Second World War, the population of Riverside Park had swelled as sons and daughters returned with their young families for a simpler way of life.

Clare's and Laura's parents were among those who had purchased a postwar bungalow on the outskirts of the town near the highway leading to larger urban areas where many found work. Clare realized that the tract of homes where she grew up—the first subdivision in Twin Falls— must have been met with the same concern by the residents of Riverside Park as she had just felt driving by the new homes on the other side of the bridge.

It was funny, Clare thought, that although she'd spent so many years of her adolescence fantasizing about what went on behind those etched-glass doors, it was Laura— who had always vowed to leave Twin Falls—who eventually moved into one of the stately homes. But Clare could hardly complain. Those same fantasies had inspired her to write the novels that were earning her a living.

As she drove along the street memories flooded her mind. There was the house once owned by the town's doctor and somewhere in the same block—she couldn't recall the number—was the former mayor's home. Judging from the sight of extra meter boxes attached to the sides of some of the homes, there had been a shift from single dwellings to apartments.

The size of the homes diminished slightly as she neared

the end of Riverside Drive. Clare slowed down, looking for Elmwood Drive, the side street where Laura and Dave lived. She hung a right and scanned the front doors for number fifty-four. It was midway along the street, and there was a free parking space right in front. Clare eased into it, turned off the engine and sat for a minute, studying the house.

It was a two-story fieldstone with a small veranda— more modest than the grander homes closer to the center of town, but impressive all the same. Its wood trim had been painted a dove gray that complemented the stone of the exterior. A latticed trellis, painted the same color, was attached to one of the veranda's fieldstone pillars and a thick climbing rose, now boasting clusters of rosehips, spread up and across it. Small clumps of evergreen shrubs filled the gap between veranda and lawn in front of the house.

Clare stared at the glow of lamplight in the front bay window. She inhaled deeply, grabbed hold of the car door and pushed it open. *No turning back now.*

The front door of the house had been flung open by the time Clare had walked up to the sidewalk and Laura was bounding down the veranda steps. She scarcely had a chance to look at her friend before she was enveloped in a bear hug. Then they stood back and smiled at one another.

"You look fabulous," Clare said. "I would never believe you've just had a baby. Have you got highlights in your hair?"

"Yes. Like it?" Laura executed a dainty pivot. Her honey-blond hair was cut in a shoulder-length bob that swirled around her.

"I do! You look great!"

"You have to say that because you're my friend, but thanks anyway." Laura's cheeks dimpled. "Thank goodness for makeup and that stuff that covers up dark circles under the eyes. But look at you! That flaming red hair will never need highlights. You've cut it since I last saw you. I like it.''

"I cut it a while ago, but I haven't seen you in ages.''

"True. Come on, Dave's opening a bottle of wine. I may even get a chance to gobble down dinner before Emma's next feeding.''

"How's the nursing going?''

"Better. It's weird, isn't it? That something so natural should be so damn hard at first?''

Clare smiled. No doubt her friend was tackling motherhood with the same zeal that she'd shown on the cheerleading squad. "I'm sure you'll figure it out,'' was all she said as she walked arm in arm with her up the steps.

Dave greeted them in a small entrance hall. "Congratulations,'' he said, hugging Clare. "At last we know someone famous.''

Clare felt the color rise into her face. "Yeah, right,'' she quipped and they all laughed. As teenagers, Laura and Clare had made a bet to see who would become rich and famous enough to move away from Twin Falls. Little did we know, Clare thought, that moving away required neither fame nor money.

"I like the goatee,'' she said, smiling at Dave.

"Laura hates it, but thanks.'' He shot his wife a told-you-so look that had a tinge of reproof in it.

Clare glanced at Laura's red face. There was an awkward moment that Laura broke by asking, "Do you want to refresh or something?''

"No, I'm fine. I stopped a few miles outside of town for a break.'' Clare followed Laura into a large living room. "This is lovely,'' she said. "You've done a wonderful job, Laura.''

"Sit here, it's the most comfy chair.'' She gestured to

a plump chintz-covered armchair next to a sofa where she herself perched.

"Are things okay between you and Dave?" Clare asked as soon as they sat down.

Laura gave her a reassuring smile. "Don't be alarmed by the sniping you just witnessed. It's the usual husband-and-wife tension after the first child."

"I would've thought a baby would bring you closer."

"She has, but there are other things. Dave isn't happy with his work and we've taken a real pay cut since I decided to stay at home with Emma for a while."

"Are you getting any help from your folks?"

"They're living on a fixed income now so…"

"How are they, anyway?"

"Good. They sold their house last year and moved into a new condo on the edge of town."

"Condos? God, I can't believe how much this place has changed."

"Believe it. Did you notice the subdivision as you came in?"

"Yes! And is it my imagination, or are there twice as many cars on the road?"

"Twin Falls is becoming one of those satellite communities you read about. People working in Hartford want to live in a rural environment." She laughed. "Can you believe it? Twin Falls as a rural environment? Remember how we used to make fun of the farm kids who were bused into school?"

Laura glanced toward the doorway. "Dave must be checking on dinner." She leaned toward Clare. "Your book is fantastic, Clare. I'm almost finished it. But I have to tell you, everyone's been talking about it." She paused a beat. *"You know."*

"Know what?"

"C'mon Clare. This is me, Laura. You don't have to

play dumb. It wasn't very hard to figure out you were writing about Twin Falls. I mean, except for the description of the town and the name changes, it's all there.''

Clare glanced toward the entrance hall, wishing Dave would appear with their drinks. She'd known this moment was going to happen but trust Laura to get to it right away. ''It's not a secret that *some* of it is gleaned from here.''

''But how did you get the nerve? I mean, when you and your mother moved away, you swore to put everything behind you.''

''We both know that none of us can really forget what happened, Laura.''

''Well, I have. Otherwise, I wouldn't have been able to live here.''

''I wondered about that. But then, you weren't really involved—'' Clare broke off when Dave, carrying a tray of glasses and a wine bottle, appeared in the doorway. To her relief, Laura let the subject drop as well, and they made small talk—catching up on the events of the past two years—until dinner.

When dinner was ready, Clare sat at the dining-room table. She watched Dave and Laura bustle back and forth from the kitchen, realizing that she'd never seen Laura in such a domestic context. After high school, they'd gone on to different colleges and settled in different states, keeping sporadic contact with one another via telephone or e-mail. There was a time, Clare thought with some chagrin, when the idea of her best friend cooking a roast-beef dinner with all the trimmings would have amazed her. And, added to this surprising picture of domesticity, was the whole new dimension of motherhood.

A sense of being left behind swept over Clare. She had other friends who were married with children, but none who shared the bond of childhood and adolescence with her. Her friendship with Laura had not been a perfect one, but it had been constant.

Clare was thrilled to see Laura with a new baby and a husband who adored her, but the blissful scene made her own personal life seem so bleak. There was no special man in the picture, much less the prospect of a husband. As for babies…well, maybe in the distant future. Perhaps her life might have followed the same track as Laura's if only she and Gil Harper had not broken up. That sudden thought made her feel even worse.

"Dave, can you bring the veggies?" Laura stood in the doorway of the dining room, calling back into the kitchen.

Clare fixed a cheerful smile on her face, and asked, "Are you sure I can't help with anything?"

Laura continued on into the room and set a platter of roast beef on the table. "Thanks hon, but we're fine. Just plain food tonight, but tomorrow we've got a sitter and reservations at the hot new place in town."

"You mean there's another 'in' place besides The Falls Steak and Grill?"

Laura smiled. "Thank goodness. Twin Falls can now boast a three-star restaurant. It's called Serendipity and the food's wonderful."

"I hope you're going to let me treat."

"We'll discuss that later," Laura said, sitting down across from Clare. Dave returned with the vegetables and began to carve the roast.

Clare stared at her two old friends, feeling she'd been pulled back to her adolescence and another Sunday dinner with Laura's family. An only child, the split-up of Clare's parents and subsequent divorce had been tough. But her friendship with Laura and her acceptance in the Dundas household had been a comforting refuge from loneliness.

During dinner Laura and Dave filled her in on the changes in town and Clare recounted the story—now oft repeated—of her latest book and its huge success. Dave was in the kitchen making coffee when Clare asked, "Has he made up his mind yet about the godfather?"

Laura didn't answer at first. She cocked her head and frowned. "I think I hear Emma."

At the same time, Dave poked his head through the kitchen doorway. "I hear Emma on the intercom."

Laura jumped up. "I'll be back after I've changed and fed her, Clare. And you're not to do any dishes. Not tonight, anyway." She smiled, stooped for a quick hug and dashed from the room.

Clare waited a few more seconds, then got up and began clearing the rest of the dishes. After she and Dave had retreated to the living room with coffee, Laura brought in the baby, holding her proudly in front of Clare.

"This is Emma, your goddaughter."

Clare peered down into the small pink face. "She's so cute! And she's going to be a blonde I bet."

"That's what we think. Dave's hair was pretty fair until he was in high school and even though I give mine some help, my natural color's sort of what they call dishwater blond."

"I never could figure out what that was supposed to mean. Any dishwater I always saw was gray."

Laura giggled. "Anyway, she hasn't got enough hair yet to tell for certain."

"I don't know much about babies, but isn't it too soon to predict hair and eye color?"

"Want to hold her?"

"Oh, well…"

"Come on, don't be scared. Just hold out your arms and I'll tuck her into them."

Clare leaned against the back of the chair. She didn't really want to hold the baby, who seemed awfully small, but suspected such feelings were inappropriate for a godmother. Still, the soft bundle wrapped in a fleecy blanket was surprisingly solid. Emma's dark blue eyes stared unblinkingly up into Clare's face.

"Feels good, doesn't it?"

Clare looked up and grinned at Laura. "Feels different. Warm. And nice, too." But she was ready to hand her back and when Emma scrunched up her tiny face, Clare quickly passed her over to Laura. Then she remembered the question she'd asked earlier. "So Dave, who did you finally decide on for godfather?"

Dave and Laura exchanged a look. "I had a heck of a time," Dave began. "Mainly because my good buddy from college is over in Afghanistan right now, so that ruled him out. Then I was going to go with Cal Rubens. Remember him?"

Clare shook her head.

"He was a year ahead of me at Twin Falls High. He runs a health-food store. I left work early today to ask him, but on the way I happened to bump into someone I haven't seen in a long time." Dave leaned forward on his chair. "I want you to know, Clare, that this was a completely impulsive and last-minute decision on my part. I'm not as organized about these things as Laura is."

"So who is he? Is he coming to dinner tomorrow night?"

"I've asked him, but he wasn't sure. He…uh, said he would pop around tonight though."

"And his name—?" Clare smiled wishing Dave would get to the point.

As if on cue, the doorbell rang, setting Emma into a wail. Dave jumped up and headed for the front hall while Laura walked back and forth, patting Emma on the back. Clare heard the low rumble of male voices.

Dave came back into the room an anxious expression on his face. Behind him stood the last person on earth Clare wanted to see in Twin Falls.

CHAPTER TWO

THE SAME, yet different. That much registered for Clare in the next five seconds as she stared at Gil Harper.

He had already reached his growth potential of six-two seventeen years ago, but he'd been almost eighteen then—lanky and loose-limbed in scruffy Levis and bulky sweatshirts. This Gil with his broader shoulders, wearing pressed jeans, a denim shirt and a black leather jacket, looked like a candidate for *GQ*'s Man of the Year award.

His charcoal-gray eyes stayed on Clare a moment longer before turning their gaze to Laura who was hovering at his left with Emma. He murmured a greeting and peered down at the baby in her arms. "This is the famous Emma, I presume." He gave the baby a tentative smile, but his attention quickly shifted back to Clare. She rose unsteadily from the armchair.

"Hello, Gil."

"Clare," he said with a formal nod. "You've changed as much as the rest of us, I see. Your hair's shorter."

"It's been a while," she said, wondering if her voice sounded as peculiar to everyone else as it did to her at that moment.

"Would you like a brandy, Gil? Clare?" Dave asked.

"I...uh, really can't stay long," Gil said.

"I'll have one," Clare said. *A large one.*

"Glass of milk for me, please," said Laura. "Surely you can stay long enough for a drink, Gil? At least until we go over the plans for Sunday."

He shrugged. "Okay, then."

Dave gestured to the couch, next to Clare's chair. "Have a seat, Gil. I'm sure you and Clare have a bit of catching up to do. Laura, want to help me in the kitchen?"

Laura took the hint and, with the baby, followed Dave from the room. Clare remained standing until she accepted the fact that she hadn't fallen asleep after dinner and awakened in a bad dream. Gil Harper wasn't going to vanish before her eyes no matter how much she wished he would. She sat on the edge of the chair, ready to bolt if necessary.

He loomed in front of her a fraction longer before sitting on the couch. She watched him from the corner of her eye, noting from the rigid way he perched that he was just as uncomfortable as she was.

"I assume this has caught you by surprise, too," she said.

"Definitely. As a matter of fact, I was asked to be godfather at two o'clock this afternoon when I met Dave on Main Street."

"Same old Dave."

"Apparently."

He shifted on the couch turning toward her. "Congratulations on your new book."

"Thank you."

"I just finished it. Very…gripping," he said, after a slight pause.

"You bought a copy?"

"Of course. I have your first one, too—*Frankie and Me*. I liked it very much. You always had promise as a writer."

"Inspired by English class with Miss Stuart."

He smiled for the first time. "Yes. I wonder if she's still teaching."

"Hmmm." Clare wished Dave and Laura would return so they could make plans for Sunday and she could leave.

"I hope you understand that I had no idea you were even in Twin Falls," he went on. "I just got here myself a couple of days ago to clear out my dad's house."

"Has your father moved into a retirement home?"

"No, he…uh, he died of a stroke about three weeks ago."

"Oh, I'm so sorry, Gil. And your mother?"

"Heart attack, five years ago. How about your folks?"

"Mom's in New Jersey with her second husband. Dad's still in California with his second or third wife. Can't recall which."

"Your mother remarried? Good for her."

Clare thought back to the day four years ago when her mother called to announce her upcoming marriage to someone she'd met only a year before. She'd been surprised at the news and at first, had tried to persuade her mother to simply move in with the man.

"I'm still an old-fashioned woman, Clare," her mother had said. "And this is the time of my life when I need companionship more than ever. Besides, the fact is, I love Hank."

Love. One thing to write about, quite another to experience. Clare sneaked a sideways glance at the person she'd once thought she loved. His hands—once so familiar—rested on his knees. She didn't see a wedding ring.

As if reading her mind, he suddenly asked, "What about you, Clare? Are you married or engaged?"

She felt her face redden. "No."

He nodded and conversation skidded to a halt. Clare was about to excuse herself to find Laura when Dave came back into the room with a tray of drinks.

"Sorry to take so long, but Laura wanted to get Emma to sleep. She'll join us in a minute or so." He passed large brandy snifters to Clare and Gil and, taking one for himself, sat opposite them in a wing chair. "Cheers!" he said, raising his snifter. "To old friends."

Clare and Gil raised their glasses, though neither echoed his toast.

Dave cleared his throat. "So, Clare, what time is your book signing tomorrow?"

"Ten o'clock."

"You're having a signing? Where?" Gil asked.

"There's a new bookstore in town—at least, new to me. Called Novel Idea."

"It's been here a couple of years, I think," Dave said. "It's on Spruce Street, near Main."

"I'll have to drop by."

Great, Clare thought. Let's get right into the whole horrible reunion thing.

"We're not sure if we can go," Dave said. "We still have a lot of running around to do for the christening luncheon on Sunday. And speaking of the christening, there's not a lot you two have to do. It'll be at the Methodist church, still in the same place—" he gave a slight laugh "—at eleven. We'll save seats for you at the front. There's another christening that morning, too, so the church may be crowded. Basically all you have to do is follow the pastor's instructions. One of you will hold Emma for the blessing. Then we'll have family and friends come back here for a buffet lunch. There won't be too many people."

"Sounds good," Gil said, standing up and setting his empty glass on the coffee table. "So I'll see you on Sunday morning."

"Are you leaving?" Dave got to his feet, his brow creasing.

"I should. Still have some packing up to do before the cleaners come in tomorrow."

"We were hoping you'd join us for dinner tomorrow night. I've made reservations for four at a new place in town. It'll be like old times," Dave added.

Clare tensed, hoping Gil would decline.

"I don't know, Dave. I really shouldn't."

"Shouldn't what?" Laura asked from the entrance to the living room. She walked over to the table where Dave had placed the drink tray and picked up her glass of milk. "You're not leaving already, Gil?"

"Lots to do, Laura. The cleaners are booked for tomorrow afternoon and I've still got a lot to do."

"But you'll come tomorrow night? It's all arranged."

There was a long silence until Gil murmured, "Sure. That sounds fine."

Clare sighed. There was no stopping Laura when she set her mind to something. She downed the last of her brandy and rose to go.

"Clare, not you, too!" Laura protested.

"I'm sure you and Dave will appreciate an early night, Laura. I'm tired myself and I have to be up early."

"Where did you say you were staying? Want to come here for breakfast?"

Clare smiled at Laura's love of making plans for other people. "I'm at the old Falls View Hotel, can you believe it? Though it's had a bit of a makeover since I lived in town. Thanks for the offer of breakfast, but you'll be busy enough." She headed for the entrance hall and picked up her purse from the small table there. Her suit jacket was slung over a nearby chair and she draped it over her arm.

"Are you driving?" Gil asked, hovering at her elbow.

"Yes. I rented a car in New York."

"How'd you like to give me a lift? I had an errand in town late this afternoon and decided to get some exercise by walking here. I could call a cab but…"

Clare hesitated. They were all looking at her and she

couldn't think of a good excuse. "Sure," she murmured. She hugged Dave and kissed Laura on the cheek. "See you tomorrow."

Laura held on to her by the forearm and whispered, "Are you sure this is okay? I mean, Dave can give Gil a ride."

Clare watched Dave and Gil step out onto the porch. Keeping her voice low, she said, "No, it's okay. I just wish I'd known about this godfather thing."

"I'm sorry, Clare. I didn't know myself until this afternoon just before you arrived. Will you manage? Want me to see if Dave can get out of it? I mean, he's the person responsible."

Clare guessed Gil would jump at the chance to be relieved of his duties. But a change now would be embarrassing for everyone, especially Dave. "No, no. Don't worry. We're both adults now." She went out to the porch.

Both men turned around as she walked past them down the steps and headed straight for her car. She heard Gil following virtually on her heels while calling out a last goodbye. He didn't speak until they were buckling up their seat belts and the engine was running.

"I hope this isn't an inconvenience."

Now he worries about that. Clare mumbled a no and pulled away from the curb, craning back to see Laura and Dave waving from the porch. Her glance took in Gil, staring straight ahead.

His profile was all angles and sharp edges, from the slightly hawkish nose to a jaw more formidable than the one she recalled. He'd always had a dark, broodish air about him and the years had further defined that quality. His long fingers drummed nervously on his kneecaps and for an unsettling second Clare had a vivid memory of those fingers on her, tracing an invisible line up and down the inside of her arm. He used to tease her about how ticklish she was there and liked to hear her beg him to stop.

She felt a sudden chill and clicked on the heat, tempted to also turn on the radio to fill up the tense silence. When he mumbled something about the weather, she was torn between relief that she didn't have to think of anything to say and sadness that small talk was all they now had between them.

When she braked at the first stop sign, Gil asked, "Do you remember how to get to my place?"

"Oh, yes," she said, aware at once of the edge in her voice.

"Will you be staying long?"

No longer than I have to, she wanted to say. "Until Monday. I've another signing in Hartford."

More silence. "Have you gotten any feedback about your book from people here in Twin Falls?"

"Just Dave and Laura. I don't keep in touch with anyone else from the old gang."

"Me, neither."

She drove into the housing tract where she, Laura and Gil had grown up. Gil's house was at the farthest edge of it, just before the Visit Again sign where the road turned into highway. But when she turned onto Glendale Road, expecting to see the rows of bungalows she remembered, Clare was shocked. Scarcely half a dozen remained, including Gil's father's place at the very end.

"Good heavens!" Clare exclaimed, pulling over to the curb.

"Surprised?"

"Shocked." She turned to look at him. "I guess I expected it all to look the same."

"Unfortunately Twin Falls hasn't escaped the tear-down epidemic of the big city. It's a real commuter town now.'' Gil stared out the window at his childhood home. ''I don't anticipate any problems selling the house.''

Struck by the tone in his voice, she asked, ''Isn't that a good thing?''

''I guess. Just that the place is my last link to Twin Falls. Once it goes...''

He didn't need to finish. Clare knew exactly what he meant to say. ''But isn't that also a good thing?'' she asked softly.

His face, turned to hers, was impassive. ''Do you think so?''

Clare's eyes held his a long uncomfortable moment before flicking back to the windshield and the street beyond. She wasn't certain what he meant, but suspected he was veering the talk onto shaky ground and decided to keep quiet. The silence in the car became so stifling she had to put the window down. The engine idled gently at the curb.

''What part of New York do you live in?'' he suddenly asked.

''Chelsea.''

''Oh, yeah? Nice area.''

Another pause. He seemed in no hurry to get out of the car. ''And what about you?'' she asked. ''Where do you live now?''

''New York.''

''New York City?''

His eyes met hers. ''Yes.''

Clare looked away. She couldn't believe the man she'd been trying to forget for the last several years had been living under her nose. Well, sort of. Give or take a few million other people. Still, what perverse hand of fate had led both of them to the same city?

''I've got a condo on the East Side,'' he went on.

When she found her voice, she asked, ''How long have you been there?''

"About five years. I got a job at a law firm in Manhattan a couple years after I was called to the bar."

Clare jerked her head back to him. "You're a *lawyer?*"

A faint smile crossed his face. "Yeah. Ironic, isn't it?" Then he pushed down on the door handle. "Thanks for the lift, Clare. See you tomorrow." His long legs swung out and, without looking back, he closed the door behind him.

Clare sat unmoving until he disappeared inside the small bungalow. How strange life is, she mused. Gil Harper—once suspected of murdering his ex-girlfriend—now a lawyer.

"COFFEE?"

Clare raised her head from the book she was signing. One of the store clerks was standing at her left side. "Yes, please. Double double."

The clerk grinned. "Gotcha," and vanished into the cluster of people milling around the table. Clare smiled at the middle-aged woman waiting in front of her and pushed the novel across the table.

"Thank you very much," the woman said. "I bought it for my daughter. I thought she'd be interested in knowing Twin Falls can boast a real live author. We just moved here from Hartford and she thinks it's like living on another planet."

Clare figured the daughter was closer to the truth than the woman could have imagined. And at that moment, she was feeling neither real nor alive. It was eleven-thirty and she'd only signed about twenty-five books, which wasn't bad for a bookstore in a place the size of Twin Falls, but already her fingers were cramped, her back ached and her stomach was rumbling. Yet how could she complain? Each book she signed contributed to the royalty checks that supported her now that she'd left teaching for a full-time writing career.

The clerk returned with a take-out coffee and set it near her elbow. "Anything else?' she asked.

"Maybe another right hand."

The younger woman smiled and left Clare to it. She signed three more books and, as the line began to dissipate, sipped slowly on the coffee and closed her eyes, waiting for the jolt of caffeine to course through her.

"You look tired."

Clare's eyes flew open at the familiar voice. Gil Harper was standing in front of the table. In his black cords, dove-gray crewneck pullover and leather blazer—all complimenting his ebony hair and dark eyes—he was drawing quite a few glances from nearby women. He held a worn copy of her book and handed it to her when she set her coffee down.

An inscription of some kind was necessary, of course. What would Miss Manners recommend in such a situation? *Thanks for the memories?* Or, *Great while it lasted?* Her pen poised above the dedication page with its "For Old Friends and New." Clare had an inspiration. Writing Gil's name above the dedication line, she simply signed her name below. When she passed the book back to him, he took a second to study the page.

Then he raised his head and quipped, "At least it doesn't read "'Old Friends and Enemies.'"

The smile Clare attempted struggled against her frozen cheek muscles.

"Did Laura mention what time we're supposed to meet tonight?" he asked.

"Tonight?"

"Dinner. At the new restaurant. Can't recall the name. Serenity or something."

The smile tugged harder at the corners of Clare's

mouth. "Ah yes. Serendipity. I…uh…I think reservations are for six."

He nodded, continuing to check her out. "Are you sure you're okay with this?"

She knew what he meant, but played dumb. "What?"

"My coming along. Maybe you'd rather be with them on your own."

She ignored the hook he was dangling before her. No way was she going to get into that debate in a public place. "I think Laura's counting on both of us."

"Well, Laura can't be let down."

Clare caught his fleeting grin and broke into a full smile. "True enough."

Someone jostled him from behind. "See you tonight then," he said before walking away.

She kept her eyes on him until his broad back disappeared in the bustle of shoppers and store clerks. When she turned to take the next book, she saw a young man with notebook and pen in hand standing patiently in front of her.

"Miss Morgan? I'm Jeff Withers from the *Spectator,* the town's newspaper. I wondered if you could spare me some time for an interview."

"Um, sure. I'm finished here in about fifteen minutes."

"There's a diner right across the street. Mitzi's. Why don't I buy you lunch? It looks like you might be all coffeed out."

Clare smiled without any effort this time. "That would be great. I'll meet you over there." What she preferred to do was to head back to her hotel for peace and quiet, but she knew interviews were an important part of a book tour. When the signing wrapped up, she slipped on her suit jacket, assured the effusively appreciative manager that the pleasure was all hers and made her way across Main Street.

The reporter was sitting in a booth facing the door and waved at her. He stood up as she sat down, a courtesy that pleased Clare but made her feel about twenty years older.

"The specials are up on the board," Jeff said, pointing to the wall to her left.

"The food must be good," Clare said. "The place is packed."

"Always is on the weekends. They serve a mean brunch."

A waitress arrived while Clare was skimming the menu so she made a quick decision. "The frittata special please, with salad instead of home fries."

Jeff ordered the same and as soon as the waitress left, set his notepad and pen on the table. "Would you mind if we talked while we ate? I've got a four o'clock deadline."

"Not at all. When will the interview be in print?"

"Tomorrow's Sunday edition. Look in the Lifestyles section. Now," he said, flipping open the notepad, "I know that *Growing up in Paradise* is your second novel."

"That's correct. The first, *Frankie and Me,* was published almost three years ago."

"Is it normal to have such a gap between books?"

Clare smiled patiently. She'd been asked this question many times. "I don't know if there's anything in the world of publishing that could be called normal, but I don't think the gap is unusual."

"And this one made the *New York Times* list so I guess that's all that matters."

She wasn't certain what he meant by the comment. "It's a wonderful recognition, if that's what you mean."

He smiled. "Of course! Now, I understand you were born and raised right here in Twin Falls."

"I was actually born in Greenwich, but I grew up here."

He paused while the waiter brought their drinks and then he placed a small tape recorder on the table. "Do you mind? I'm not the best note taker."

Clare frowned. "All right. I guess there's not much I can tell you that'll come back to haunt me."

He laughed. "Not in Twin Falls. The cover blurb of your book calls it a coming-of-age novel of a young girl growing up in a small town. But I'm curious—is it really based on your personal story?"

Clare tried not to roll her eyes. She'd been asked this question so many times, she had the answer down pat. "My own experiences gave me an informed point of view, of course, and there are some similarities between the heroine, Kenzie, and me, but the story itself is fiction."

He nodded thoughtfully. "Can you summarize the central theme of the book?"

Clare paused while their orders were placed on the table. "I think the title is the clue, right? The notion that small towns may seem like paradise on the surface, but underneath is the same ugliness that can be found in big cities."

"Kind of like the snake in the Garden of Eden?"

"I guess, but mine isn't a spiritual message. Simply that good and evil can be found anywhere, even in an idyllic place like…well, like Twin Falls."

"So *is* the book based on an actual event in Twin Falls?"

Clare put down her fork. "I don't believe I said that, did I?"

His smile didn't seem so charming this time. He cocked his head to one side and as if mulling over her question, switched tactics. "But isn't that basically what we've been playing cat-and-mouse about these last few minutes? And here's what you say in your acknowledgements." He pulled a copy of her novel from his backpack and thumbed through the first couple of pages. "You thank a bunch of people, then make a general statement that certain events may *appear to resemble*—I like that phrase—events that may have occurred elsewhere but any similarities are entirely coincidental." He raised his head, frowning. "Sounds like something a lawyer wrote, doesn't it?"

Perhaps because one did, Clare was thinking. Suddenly she was no longer hungry. She wanted to leave, but she also wanted to clarify her point. "I—"

He interrupted, "Do you think there's a possibility someone here in Twin Falls might find something too close to truth in the book?"

Clare set her fork down. "What are you getting at?"

He leaned forward, fixing his eyes on hers. He was no longer making notes, but the tape recorder whirred away. "Here's my point. The novel centers around the death of a friend of the heroine's. The death is ruled accidental, but there's ambiguity about the finding that has a profound effect on the main character. What was her name again? Kenzie?"

Clare nodded. She knew where he was going now.

"And the death eventually results in Kenzie's leaving forever the town where she grew up. Kind of a *Paradise Lost* idea. Right?"

Clare checked her watch, wondering when there'd be an opportunity to leave. "That's part of the story, yes."

He leaned further across the table. The eyes behind his wire-rimmed glasses glimmered. "And isn't that what happened to *you,* right here in Twin Falls, seventeen years ago? When your friend was murdered and your boyfriend accused of the crime?"

"As I've already told you, what happens in my novel

is fiction. And Rina Thomas was a classmate, rather than a friend. I'm sorry but I have to go.'' Clare stood up.

Startled, he pulled back from the table. "But your lunch."

"Let me pay my share."

He rose from his chair. "No, no. The boss is paying. Listen, could you spare five more minutes? I just want to explore the idea of your novel being based on the Thomas case."

"If you want to discuss my book, fine. However, if your real purpose in talking to me is to discuss something that happened many years ago in Twin Falls, then I'm sorry, I can't help you. You'll have to go to the police for that." She started to move away.

"But the two stories are not so very different, are they?"

"The novel is drawn loosely on my childhood experiences and observations growing up in a small town. I'm sorry but I can't spell it out any other way. Any similarities are—''

"Entirely coincidental," he finished, quoting from the preface. "But off the record, Miss Morgan, which parts are *not* coincidental?"

"It's *all* fiction, Mr. Withers. Goodbye," she said and walked out the door. She brushed past a handful of people lined up to get inside and marched straight to her hotel, a brisk five minutes away.

It wasn't until she was safely locked inside her room that she sank into a chair and succumbed to the trembling that began the instant she left Mitzi's.

CHAPTER THREE

SHE HAD TIMED HER entrance perfectly. Laura and Dave were just sitting down at their table, and judging by the half-finished glass of wine in front of Gil, Clare figured he'd arrived a bit early. She handed her coat to the host and walked toward them, pleased that she had avoided a few moments alone with Gil—something she'd worried about on her walk to the restaurant.

"Clare! You look ravishing," Dave enthused, standing to greet her. "Doesn't she, Laura?"

"Now that she's a celebrity, she has an image to keep up, right, Clare?" Laura winked.

The spotlight wasn't really what she'd been seeking, but Clare struck a pose, hoping she didn't look as awkward as she felt. She cocked her head, her shoulder-length hair swaying to one side, and scanned the room. "What? No paparazzi?" she demanded, smiling. She gave Dave a quick hug and bent down to give Laura a peck on the cheek.

Gil had stood at her arrival as well and was pulling out the chair beside his. Clare hesitated, then acknowledged him with a nod of her head. "Gil," she mumbled and sat down. As he pushed the chair in, his hand brushed across her shoulders and the instant tingle distracted her enough that she missed Laura's next remark.

"I said," Laura repeated seeing the blank look on Clare's face, "that I love your dress. Is it silk?"

"Yes. A celebration splurge."

"It's stunning," Laura went on. "Those earth tones are wonderful with your hair and complexion. Whenever you move, they seem to shimmer in different shades of brown and gold."

"More like copper," Gil added.

"Since when were you such a fashion connoisseur?" asked Dave, grinning across the table.

"I know my colors as well as the next guy," Gil said, grinning. He turned toward Clare. "Laura's right. The dress is perfect for you."

His smile was sincere, Clare thought, but the intense expression in his eyes unreadable. She suddenly felt uncomfortable and gave him a quick smile that felt lopsided, then turned her head toward Laura. "Who's looking after Emma tonight?"

"My mother. She and Dad are heading off to Florida Monday morning so she wanted to spend more time with her."

"Will they stay in Florida the whole winter?"

"They usually do. Though this year, they might brave the weather and come back for Christmas. Unless we go there," Laura said, casting a quick glance at Dave.

A shadow crossed his face. Obviously, he didn't want to discuss the matter right then. Clare quickly said, "Well, wherever you end up, Christmas will be special this year because of Emma."

"You're right, Clare. Emma's what matters," Laura said, giving Dave a pointed look.

A waiter arrived with sparkling wine and four glasses. "I hope you don't mind," Gil said. "I ordered it just before you arrived. Thought the occasion required a toast."

When the wine was poured, Gil raised his glass. "To Laura, Dave and baby Emma."

"And let's not forget old friends," Dave said.

The waiter came to recite the specials and for the next few minutes, attention was devoted to the menu. Once their orders were taken, Dave broke the silence by asking Clare how the book signing had gone.

"Fine, though I wonder if I'll ever get used to these things."

"You better," Laura said. "I've a feeling there are many more in your future."

"There was quite a crowd at the store," Gil added.

"You went?" Laura asked.

"Sure. Got to support the local talent, right?"

Laura's glance switched from Gil to Clare. But if her friend was looking for some sign of how the encounter had turned out, Clare wasn't cooperating. She met Laura's gaze with impassivity and abruptly changed the subject to her interview with Jeff Withers.

"That guy!" Dave grimaced when Clare mentioned the reporter's name.

"Why?" Clare asked, suddenly worried about the interview.

"He's one of those sensationalist reporters. You know the kind—knocking on the doors of families who've just suffered a devastating loss. He's good at pulling the emotional strings of his readers."

Clare understood then Withers's dogged insistence on focusing on the Rina Thomas case, rather than her novel. For the second time that day, she regretted the interview.

"So how did it go?" Gil asked.

She turned his way, saying merely, "Fine." He was the last person she wanted to discuss the interview with, especially its focus on Rina Thomas. The arrival of the waiter with their food prevented her from having to elaborate and after he left, the talk turned to food, restaurants and changes in Twin Falls. On safer ground, Clare began to relax and enjoy the evening.

But two hours later, her relief that the dinner had transpired without serious reference to the past evaporated. The laughter, topical chitchat and catch-up on their current lives had merely been embellishment to her false sense of security, Clare realized. Standing on the sidewalk outside Serendipity—and acknowledging the irony of its name, under the circumstances—Clare was painfully aware of the huge gap between the teenaged Gil Harper she'd adored and his present self. Someone she knew not at all.

Outside the restaurant after dinner, Laura and Dave lingered for a few seconds, reminding them of the time to be at the church the next day. "Sure you don't want a lift back?" Laura asked anxiously, reading all too clearly, Clare thought, the state of her mind.

"My hotel's just a few blocks away," Clare was saying when Gil piped up.

"I'll walk her back," he said to Laura and before Clare could find an excuse, he clasped a hand under her elbow and gently turned her in the direction of the Falls View Hotel, four blocks away. "I insist," he added.

Her first impulse was to shake loose of his grasp, but she was worried the move would seem too inappropriate. She reminded herself that he was simply being polite, a trait she recalled from the adolescent Gil Harper, only the present day Gil Harper seemed nothing like the teenage one she'd adored.

"You're deep in thought," he commented, breaking the silence.

More like deep in history, she thought, but only made an innocuous remark about the evening.

"Yes," he agreed, "the food was great, too. A far cry from the diner we used to hang out at after school. Remember it?"

As if she could forget. Harvey's Diner was where her

history with Gil had begun. Just two blocks away from Twin Falls High, the small family-owned snack bar had been, along with the town's pool hall, one of the few places that tolerated the teenage crowd.

But she refused to be drawn in to reminiscing. "I do. The best hamburgers and fries in town." As if that had been its only claim to memory.

He didn't pursue the point. Conversation ceased then and all that Clare heard were the hollow echoes of their shoes on the sidewalk and the voice in her mind, urging her to say something—anything—to break the strained silence. Yet there was a time when silence between them had been companionable. A bond, rather than an indicator of the way their lives had diverged. Oddly, the thought saddened her.

They were approaching the old movie theater—its facade rebricked and updated—as the audience exited, spilling onto the sidewalk ahead of them. Gil slowed down, letting Clare take the lead through the knots of people. Someone jostled against her and when she turned to her right, Clare saw a thin, middle-aged woman staring at her in astonishment. On the verge of apologizing Clare was met with a glare so hateful that she froze in her tracks. A couple strolled between her and the woman and by the time they'd passed, the woman had been swallowed up in the crowd.

"What is it?" Gil asked, coming up beside her. "Why did you stop?"

"I don't really know," she said, still scanning the place where the woman had been seconds ago. "I bumped into some woman and when I turned to apologize, she glared at me as if I'd done something unbelievably rude."

"What did she look like?"

"In her forties and skinny. Brown hair. She was looking at me as if she knew me," Clare said.

Gil stretched his neck to look over the crowd. He turned back to her. "Maybe it was someone you knew from before."

From before. A curious expression, Clare thought, looking at Gil. *Just as I once knew you—from before. Or thought I did.*

"More likely someone who didn't like my book," she said, laughing it off. She resumed walking, eager to remove herself from his gaze. She tried to keep a distance ahead of him but her heels were no match for his effortless stride.

He caught up to her as she turned onto the side street where her hotel was situated. Clear of Main Street and with fewer shops, the street was much darker. It ran along the river, fenced off by a guardrail and gentle embankment to its edge. On the opposite side rose the steep dark cliffs that snaked around the bend in the river to the falls at its head. Two brilliant spotlights aimed at the falls illuminated their flow down the cliffs.

"I don't recall those lights when I lived here," Gil said.

"No," Clare said, slowing to take in their nighttime splendor. "They were installed a few years ago," she said. "A porter at the hotel told me some drunk driver missed the bend in the road and went over the top. They put up the fence afterward."

"Remember how we used to make jokes about what this place might have been called if the falls weren't here? Like Rivertown?"

"Yes," she said, laughing suddenly at the memory flash. "Laura and I came up with River Crossing and River Forge, but our favorite was Nowhere U.S.A., getting away from the river theme. If the falls weren't here, we decided we'd have to rename most of the town. The high school, this hotel, at least one of the restaurants in town at the time, as well as a couple of the streets."

"Not to mention the town's first shopping mall."

"Really a strip plaza," she said.

"Right." He grinned down at her.

In that unguarded instant, their eyes connected, sharing a memory. It was as if the intervening years hadn't happened at all. She was still seventeen and in love. Clare looked away first. She shivered, bunching her shoulders beneath the trench coat she'd brought for the weekend. "It's getting chilly," she mumbled, "and we have an early morning."

"Not too early," he said, his voice as low as hers.

Was he suggesting something, she wondered, or simply correcting her? Whichever, she decided not to respond.

"Look," he went on, "I'm assuming you feel as uncomfortable about the christening as I do. But obviously, we don't want to spoil the day for Laura and Dave. Can we agree on some kind of truce for tomorrow?"

Clare kept her face impassive. "I wasn't aware that we were involved in some kind of feud. Do we need to agree on neutrality when indifference is really what we're feeling?"

There was a second of confusion in his face, quickly followed by understanding. He took a step back, looking as if she'd struck him.

"We're both adults," she said, trying to soften the bluntness of her remark. "And we've both managed to put the past behind us. Do we need to say more?"

"Apparently not," he replied, his voice almost a whisper. "Good night then, Clare." He turned his back on her and strode briskly toward Main Street.

Clare waited until he disappeared around the corner before she summoned the energy to move. In spite of her belief that what she'd said was perfectly true, she felt mean and ashamed. *What is it about Gil Harper, that prompts such behavior in you?* she asked herself.

She pushed open the front door of the hotel, crossing the deserted lobby on her way to her room. She didn't realize there was a phone message for her until she reached across the nightstand to turn out the lamp.

"Welcome back to Twin Falls, Clare. This is Lisa Stuart, your former English teacher at Twin Falls High. I missed your book signing today but heard via the grapevine that you might be in town a couple more days. I wondered if you'd be interested in visiting the school and giving a short talk to my senior lit class. I hate to impose on what must be a busy schedule, but some of my students have already read your latest novel and we'd all be thrilled to have you visit. If not, then perhaps the two of us could get together over coffee. I'd love to see you and hear all about your success. Call me anytime at 613-8527 and let me know. Looking forward to seeing you, bye for now."

Clare jotted down the number, though she doubted she'd accept the invitation. Twin Falls High definitely wasn't on her list of places to visit. She lay her head down on the pillow, too drained to read. *One more day, then I'm out of here.*

INDIFFERENCE. Gil didn't dare turn around, even though he felt her watching him as he left. But he wanted to. He especially wanted to confront her about that glib remark and to tell her that she hadn't really changed at all. That she was still shutting down, refusing to listen, just as she'd done seventeen years ago when he'd tried to explain why he'd been with Rina Thomas that day.

He slowed his pace when he reached Main Street, grateful for the cool night air and its calming effect. A woman, walking in the direction of the hotel, stopped as he passed her. Gil had the impression she was staring after him— maybe she'd seen something in his face, he thought. His anger and frustration flashing from him like a warning sign. *Stop. Danger from the past just ahead.*

By the time he reached the restaurant he felt more in control. Serendipity. What irony. The coincidence of finding himself linked with Clare Morgan after all these years was more bad luck than serendipity. And in spite of his extreme effort to be cool about the whole thing—to try to convey to her that he felt just as cornered by the christening as she did—she'd deftly turned the tables on him.

Yet to be truthful, it wasn't simply her gibe that had touched a nerve so much as the unexpected jolt he'd felt at it. It wasn't pain, he decided—more like anger quickly followed by sadness. He'd felt the same way when he'd read her book. He hadn't been fooled at all by the name changes, recognizing at once himself, Rina and Clare. Of course, Clare had neatly avoided attaching blame for the death of the Rina character to his counterpart in the novel. That was where fiction and fact diverged. She'd been all too quick to blame him seventeen years ago.

Gil reached his car, parked a block beyond the restaurant, and climbed in. He'd impulsively offered to walk Clare back to her hotel after she turned down a ride from the Kingsways because he'd thought it would be an opportunity to clear the air between them, to straighten things out a bit before the next day. But no such luck.

You said it yourself, buddy. She hasn't really changed. Her hair may have a different look, her golden-brown eyes, more wary, and her skinny teenaged frame has definitely morphed into something any other man would fantasize about, but inside, she was as unchanged as the falls. Self-righteous, inflexible and unforgiving.

Gil turned over the engine of his Mercedes and sat a minute longer, picturing the look in her face when she'd made that damned comment. He'd seen right away that she was trying for indifference but those eyes said it all.

You're a liar and a cheat and you don't mean anything to me anymore. Precisely what she'd flung at him seventeen years ago, right after his release from jail. Words he'd never forget.

He shifted into Drive and edged away from the curb. At least he now knew where he stood. After tomorrow, Clare Morgan would be out of his life once again—which was just as well, for his sake.

CLARE CLOSED the car door behind her and lowered her head onto the steering wheel, its cool surface the perfect balm for the pounding at her temples. The christening ceremony had been relatively brief, for which she was grateful. Holding a squirming two-month-old for more than ten minutes would have been a challenge. Especially under the somewhat bemused gaze of Gil, who hadn't bothered to offer any help. As soon as her part had finished, Clare quickly thrust the baby back into Laura's arms. She thought she heard a low snort from Gil as she did so, but couldn't be certain.

After the service, people clustered outside the church in small groups. In spite of her reluctance to return to Twin Falls, Clare was pleased to see Laura's parents and family members again. She'd had many happy childhood memories with the Dundas family. When Gil came up to ask if she needed a ride to the Kingsways', where the reception was being held, Clare was also grateful that she'd driven her rental car. His very presence seemed to strike a nerve.

Laura and Dave's house was teeming with people when Clare walked in the front door. She placed her christening gift—a hand-smocked designer dress with matching sweater—onto the hall table along with the other presents and was making her way to the dining room where drinks were being served when Gil arrived.

His charcoal-gray designer suit seemed out of place in the small-town crowd but she had to admit, he was breathtakingly attractive in it. He gave a curt nod, clutching the handle of a gift bag. Clare could see the fluffy brown ears of a stuffed animal poking through the tissue paper. Her eyes connected briefly with his before she turned away and made for the dining room.

Dave was pouring mimosas from a tall crystal pitcher, assisted by a slightly older man who bore a striking resemblance to him. "Clare! Here, you must have one of these." He handed her a champagne flute and tilted his head to the other man. "You remember my brother, Rick?"

Clare smiled and nodded. "Kind of. You were a couple of grades ahead of me at school."

"That's right," he said. "I know your name because of your connection to Dave and Laura, but I have to admit I don't recall too many kids from your year." He chuckled, adding, "Well, except for Rina Thomas and I guess *everyone* knew her."

Clare saw Dave give his brother a subtle nudge as he smiled nervously at someone behind her. She turned to see Gil standing in the doorway. The slight pulse at his jaw line—a sign of emotion held in check that Clare recalled all too well—told her immediately that he'd heard. He gave a polite but stiff nod as Dave introduced Rick.

"No, thanks," he said to the offer of alcohol. "Coffee for me." And without another word, headed for the kitchen.

Sensing that Dave was about to explain the faux pas to his brother and unwilling to be part of it, Clare smiled vaguely and, glass in hand, drifted into the living room. Laura shrieked a greeting from across the room.

"Clare!" She was with her older sister, Anne-Marie, whom Clare hadn't seen since Laura's wedding.

They hugged and made small talk for a moment before Anne-Marie asked, "How's your book doing? I haven't read it yet, but I brought my copy with me so don't forget to sign it before we leave."

"Sure," Clare said. "You look great. Life in Greenwich must be agreeable."

"A bit quiet, but it beats Twin Falls for action. I still don't understand why Laura and Dave came back here. Do you like living in New York, Clare?"

"It's great. Always something to do or see."

"Did you know Gil Harper was there, too?" Without waiting for a reply, Anne-Marie ducked her head closer to Clare's. "He's even more to die for than he was as a teenager, isn't he?" Then, realizing what she'd just said, added, "Sorry I wasn't intending any bad pun there, believe me Clare."

Obviously the past was never going to leave her alone, Clare was thinking, as she smiled mutely at Laura and her sister, who wasn't taking the hint. "I know that sounds indiscreet, but the whole business has been resurrected anyway by the article in today's paper."

"What article?" Laura asked.

Jeff Withers's flushed and eager face rose before Clare. *I knew that was going to come back to haunt me.* "The one I mentioned at dinner last night," Clare said. "My interview with Jeff Withers."

Laura blinked. "What did he write? Do you have the paper here?"

"No," Anne-Marie said, "we left it in the motel. Don't you get it delivered?"

"Not anymore, but get to the point—what did he write?"

Anne-Marie's eyes flicked from Laura to Clare. "He was supposed to be interviewing you about your book, right?"

Clare nodded.

"But most of the article is a rehash about the Rina Thomas murder. He basically came right out and said that the whole story is right in your novel. Is that true?"

"Of course not! I've drawn on some of my experiences growing up here. Writers do that, you know. And there is a death in my novel, but an accidental one. The circumstances are very different," she added.

Anne-Marie shrugged. "The article suggests there's a parallel between your novel and what really happened. Withers plays up the notion that the death in your book may have been murder, too."

"This is so frustrating," Clare said. "What kind of journalist is he?"

"Clare, you need to read the article. He even mentioned your own connection to the Rina Thomas case. He implied you had inside information about the actual murder and used some of it in your book."

Fighting to keep her voice even, Clare said, "That's ridiculous!"

"I think it's time to cut the cake and bring out the lunch stuff," Laura cheerily interjected.

"I need to use the washroom," Clare mumbled and charged blindly through the crowded living room and up the stairs.

Someone was already in the bathroom and Clare sagged against the wall outside, gulping in oxygen. The door opened and Gil Harper was suddenly standing next to her, his hand on her arm.

"Clare? What's wrong? You look upset."

She closed her eyes. *Of all the luck.*

"Please don't say nothing is wrong," he went on. "I've a lot of weaknesses, but stupidity isn't one of them."

That drew a faint smile. "No, stupidity was never one." She hesitated, then admitted, "Just something

Laura's sister said. About that damn newspaper interview.''

His brow furled for an instant, then cleared. ''Ah, yes. You were talking about it last night. What did the guy do? Trash your book?''

''If only. I could have handled that. No, he...uh, he tried to link my plot to Rina Thomas's murder.'' Her eyes shifted briefly to the framed print on the opposite wall. He was quiet for so long she thought he wouldn't respond. But to his credit, he didn't evade the issue now that it was out in the open.

''But aren't the story lines somewhat similar?''

It was a fair question from Gil, someone briefly connected to the murder, and he deserved frankness. ''When I wrote the novel,'' she began, ''my intention was to tell a story about growing up in a small town. I lived in the South for a few years after graduation and grew to love the people and their generous hospitality. That's the reason I set the novel in the South.''

''What were you doing down there?''

''Teaching in a four-room country school.'' She smiled, thinking how naive and inexperienced she'd been.

''Quite a challenge,'' he said. ''How long were you there?''

''Four years. Then I went back home to New Jersey for a bit and did some substitute teaching while I took postgrad courses to get my masters.''

''A masters in English lit, I bet.''

She nodded. ''That's when I started writing. I was inspired by what I was learning, I suppose.'' Though she knew otherwise. *More like inspired by demons that wouldn't leave me alone.*

One of the guests appeared on the landing, searching for the bathroom. Gil clasped Clare's elbow and pulled her aside. ''Can we politely make our excuses, do you think, and leave the party early? I'd like to talk to you some more about what you've been doing with your life."

She hesitated only for a fraction of a second. There was the risk of delving into the past with Gil, she realized, but at the same time she was enjoying talking to him. "All right. Laura said they'd decided against speeches or anything formal. There'll be a toast to Emma and as godparents, we'll have to be present for that. And she'll be upset if we don't have any of the lunch."

"True. How about if I meet you outside on the front porch after the toast and a bite to eat?"

"Okay. I'll look for you there."

He nodded, turned and headed back down the stairs. Clare stared at his retreating back. What had she just gotten herself into?

The bathroom door opened again and Clare, smiling at the woman exiting, took her turn. By the time she'd refreshed and was back downstairs, people were congregating in the dining room around the table, now laden with food.

Dave stood at the entrance to the dining room with Laura and Emma beside him. Gil was off to the side. When Dave spotted Clare, he addressed the guests. "Does everyone have a glass of something for a toast? Laura and I want to thank all of you for coming to share this very special day with us. It's even more special with the presence of family and old friends." He smiled directly at Clare and Gil. Then, raising his wineglass, he said, "Join us in wishing Emma a healthy, safe and long life."

Everyone raised their glasses and said, "To Emma."

Dave raised his glass a second time. "And to our dear friends—Clare Morgan and Gil Harper—Emma's godparents. Thank you both and God bless."

Clare felt her face heat up as all eyes turned her way. As soon as the toast was finished, she set her wineglass down and, paper plate in hand, picked a couple of morsels from the buffet table. Then she moved toward Laura, who was passing Emma to her mother.

"Do you mind if I leave early, Laura? I've a headache coming on and Gil suggested a walk to get some fresh air."

"Are you upset because of what Anne-Marie said? 'Cause I'm sorry, Clare. You know how she is. She didn't mean any harm."

"No, no. I know Anne-Marie too well to take her the wrong way. But I have the signing tomorrow in Hartford and I'm still a bit tired from the one yesterday." Her voice trailed off. Laura was too smart to be fooled by such lame excuses but she didn't say anything. Clare popped an olive into her mouth.

"Can you come by for breakfast in the morning, before you leave?"

"Actually Lisa Stuart—remember her, senior English class?—called and invited me to speak to one of her classes in the morning." Clare munched on a red pepper strip and scanned the room for Gil. Had he already left?

Laura's face cleared. "Oh, that's wonderful. Those kids would love to see and hear a real live author, especially one from here."

Clare ignored a tug of guilt, knowing she'd made the decision to visit the class only at that moment. "I was honored to be asked," she said. "How about if I call you tonight?" She set her paper plate down on the hall table and headed for the front door, Laura at her heels.

"Want to come for dinner tonight?" Laura asked. "We're just ordering in and my parents will be here, but at least we could have a bit of a chat."

Guilt won out. "Perhaps. I'll call you later this afternoon."

"Okay. And…have a nice walk with Gil," Laura said.

Clare saw the curiosity in her friend's face and would have explained the situation but a quick glance through the glass-paned door behind her registered Gil, waiting for her at the foot of the stairs. ''Talk to you later,'' she said and walked out onto the porch.

CHAPTER FOUR

HE DIDN'T SAY a word until they reached the end of the sidewalk. "My car or yours?"

Clare hesitated. "Maybe we should just forget about this."

Gil sent her a look—a challenge. "Is that really what you want?" He didn't pause long enough for a reply. "How about meeting in the park across from town hall? We'd still be taking a walk, getting fresh air and no one has to feel bad about skipping out on the christening reception."

"We were there for the important part," she added.

"Definitely," he said. "I'll see you at John Calvin's statue in about ten minutes?"

He walked to his car before she could change her mind again and call a halt to the plan. Clare muttered to herself during the short drive to the park, wondering why she'd agreed to his suggestion. There were plenty of parking spaces around Riverside Park although several families were taking advantage of the balmy day to visit the town's scenic center. She quickly spotted Gil, lounging against the statue of the town's founder.

"Looks like we weren't the only ones thinking of the park today," he commented as she approached.

Clare nodded. "The children's play area over there must be a draw," she said. "Too bad we didn't have anything like that when we were kids."

"We hung out at the school playground then. Remember?"

She did. They'd attended one of two elementary schools in town and the whole class had moved to Twin Falls High afterward. There'd been no escape from any of her classmates, Clare remembered. No place else to go, except out of town. Some students, mostly those in a higher economic bracket, had gone to various private schools in or near Hartford.

"Shall we take the river trail?" Gil asked.

"Sure," she said, knowing how indifferent she sounded but not really caring.

He led the way to the strip of asphalt running along the top of the riverbank. "I think I liked this trail better when it was just gravel," Gil commented. "It seemed more natural. This makes me feel like I'm in one of those theme parks."

Clare smiled to herself. She bet Gil had never stepped foot in a theme park. "I think it would take more than an asphalt walkway to qualify."

"I guess it's my age showing—I hate seeing so many changes."

"But a lot of the changes in town look to be good ones," she said. "They show growth and economic stability."

"True enough. I remember a time when I was a kid that my folks seemed real worried about making a go of it here. Especially after the lumber mill closed down."

She'd forgotten about that. By then, her parents had divorced and her mother was working at the bank. "I don't remember where your father ended up after the mill closed."

"He took some computer courses at night school in Hartford and eventually managed to get a job in the administration department at town hall. He stayed there 'til retirement.''

"When was that?''

"Five years ago. He was seventy when he had his stroke.''

"I always liked your father.''

They walked in silence a few more yards until Gil said, a bit gruffly, "Yeah, and he always liked you, too.'' He motioned to a bench ahead. "Want to sit for a minute?''

She hesitated, sensing the stop might lead to more reminiscing and she wasn't sure she wanted that to happen. But she was reluctant to decline, especially right after talking about his father. Plus, she and Gil had been friends—more than friends—long ago.

"Sure,'' she said and sank onto the wooden seat. A line of trees were strung along the other side of the trail and through them, she could make out the wooden footbridge spanning the river and the steep embankment leading up from it. Her eyes moved up to its high point. "I see there's a guardrail over there, too.''

Her gaze shifted slightly to the left and she noticed the distant rooftop of Twin Falls High. She bit down on her tongue as she realized what she was looking at. They were sitting directly across the river from the place where Rina Thomas's body had been found.

Gil noticed where she was looking and, after a moment, said, "I imagine they put it up after Rina died. Maybe to discourage kids from using the shortcut.''

She turned his way but he was still staring at the opposite side of the river. When he finally spoke, his voice was so low she could hardly hear. "It's taken me a while to be able to refer to Rina with equanimity, but I've managed to put the whole thing behind me.'' His eyes fixed on hers. "And I suggest you try to do the same, Clare.

Otherwise, comments like the ones we both heard today will always bother you.''

Blood rushed to her head. ''I don't know what you're talking about. I was upset because…because some people have focused on a single aspect of my book.''

''Maybe your reaction shows that you're unsure about your intentions in writing the book. Not that I'm saying you purposely set out to produce a tell-all kind of book. But I do know that the Clare Morgan I remember had a tougher shell than the one I saw today at the christening.''

Clare leaped to her feet. ''You amaze me, you really do. I mean, we haven't seen or spoken for seventeen years and you have the nerve to think you still know me. It's almost laughable.'' She folded her arms across her chest and stepped away from the bench, keeping her eyes on the view ahead. She heard him get up and for a tense instant, thought he was going to move closer and place a hand on her shoulder. But he didn't. She spun around.

''In fact,'' she went on, ''you don't know me any better now than you did then.'' She forced her eyes on his, challenging his set, impassive expression to reveal some emotion. *Any* emotion. But his gaze, coolly resting on her flushed face for no more than a second, shifted to some distant point beyond her.

''You're right about that, Clare. I thought I knew you then, but I was wrong.'' He moved farther away from where she was standing. ''Good luck with your signing in Hartford tomorrow and…all the best with your book tour.'' He turned his back on her and walked steadfastly toward the center of the park.

She watched him go until she accepted the fact that he wasn't going to change his mind and turn around. Slowly, her heart rate slowed to normal and the pounding in her head decelerated to a faint pulsing.

Clare picked up her purse from the bench and headed

for her car on the far side of the park. When she passed John Calvin's statue, she noticed the small bench to its right and a rush of memory overwhelmed her. It was the exact spot where she and Gil had parted company two nights after Rina Thomas was killed. The irony didn't escape her. But it did fill her with a surge of sadness that she knew only time and distance from Twin Falls would vanquish.

"I WAS SO HAPPY when you called to say you could make it after all tonight," Laura gushed as soon as she opened the front door. When Clare stepped into the hallway, Laura added, "You don't have to worry about any indiscreet remarks, either, because only my folks are here and they're totally engrossed in Emma." Then she whispered, "But did you get a copy of the paper?"

"Yes, I did, as soon as I got back to the hotel. I agree with Anne-Marie. The article was completely off topic. If I wasn't leaving tomorrow I'd lodge a complaint. But—" she shrugged and worked her face into a big smile "—who's going to be reading the *Spectator* outside Twin Falls anyway?"

"Point taken," Laura laughed. She looped her arm through Clare's. "Come and get a drink. The food's on its way and I've nothing to do but get caught up on the last couple of years."

When the deliveryman arrived with cartons of Thai food, they gathered around the dining-room table and talked as they ate. After Laura's parents left, Laura pulled Clare by the arm into the living room.

"Dave promised to put Emma to bed so we can have a little chat. More coffee?"

"Heavens, no. I'll be up all night." Clare sat in the armchair while Laura curled up on the couch across from her.

"So," Laura said with a big smile, "how did your walk with Gil go?"

Clare laughed nervously. "You get right to the point, don't you?"

"I always have. You know that. I don't mince my words. But I was surprised that you took off with him. I mean, after the way you acted Friday night and then last night at dinner—"

"What's that supposed to mean? *The way I acted?* Considering the shock of his appearance on your doorstep Friday night, I think I behaved very well. We were polite and courteous. We got through the ceremony without drawing blood."

Laura laughed. "You both acted as if you were meeting for the first time. I wish you could have seen your face when he walked into the room. Dave was totally oblivious to the electricity zinging around, but I wasn't."

"You always tended to exaggerate, Laura. I doubt even a spark could be generated from any contact I might have with Gil Harper."

"Ouch!" Laura grinned. "I take it the walk was polite and courteous then?"

Clare knew a fishing expedition when she saw one. "For the most part. At any rate, we said goodbye and…well, that's that." Clare shifted her attention to the table in front of the bay window where some of Emma's gifts were on display. "I see Emma got some lovely things."

Laura followed her gaze. "Yes. And thank you again for the beautiful dress. I noticed the label. It must have cost a fortune."

Clare flushed. "Only fitting I think, from the god-mother."

"Gil gave her the sweetest teddy bear, as well as a silver locket that can hold a tiny photograph. I was surprised. I mean, he didn't have much warning about being godfather."

Gil again. Clare peered down at her watch, hoping Laura would take the hint. "I should go, Laura. Early start in the morning."

"Oh, yes, you're visiting the school. How did Miss Stuart sound on the phone?"

"The same. Though I've a feeling she's married now or at least in a relationship. A man answered the phone."

"That's nice. Gee, it'll be strange for you to be back at Twin Falls High, walking those corridors again. What time are you on for?"

"Nine-thirty. I have to leave by ten-thirty to get to Hartford before noon."

"Did you tell me what bookstore in Hartford you're going to be signing at?" Laura asked.

"A place called The Dust Jacket."

"I've heard of that. It's supposed to be an amazing store. Dave's taken the day off tomorrow, otherwise I'd get him to pop by."

Clare smiled, trying to picture Dave doing just that on a busy workday. She stood up. "I really should go, Laura."

"I know. You've got glamorous things to do tomorrow while I'll be nursing a baby and doing laundry."

There was a wistful note in her voice that surprised Clare. "And doting on your beautiful baby. Don't forget that!"

"Oh, no. Trust me, now I'll never be able to see myself in any other role. It's just that I never expected to… well…settle down like this without doing all the things I once dreamed of. Isn't it ironic how we both have kind of exchanged places?"

"What do you mean?"

"Remember when we were in our last year at Twin

Falls High, dreaming of going off to college and starting new, exciting lives for ourselves?''

Clare smiled. "I do."

"I distinctly recall one sleepover being entirely devoted to what we wished for in our future. I wanted to be rich, famous and travel the world. But what shocked me—at the ripe old age of seventeen—was that you said you wanted to marry Gil Harper and live in Twin Falls for the rest of your life."

Clare's smile froze. "I don't remember that at all," she said.

Laura held up a hand. "Now don't get all worked up, Clare Morgan. But you did say it."

Clare leaned over to pick up her purse, slung over the arm of her chair. Laura had an uncanny knack for calling up the most embarrassing moments in one's life, she thought. *But she did remember.* Her ridiculous wish was uttered a scarce six months after she'd started dating Gil—when she was still madly in love with him. She draped her purse over her shoulder. "If you say so, Laura. You obviously have a much better memory than I."

Laura cued in to the stiffness in Clare's voice. She stammered out an explanation. "I was just thinking…you know…how funny it is that I married my high-school sweetheart and bought a house in Twin Falls while you went on to become rich and famous."

Clare saw the worry in Laura's face. Neither, she knew, wanted the weekend to finish on a sour note. She reached out and affectionately tapped the end of Laura's nose. "Not rich or really famous yet but…hopefully…getting there." When she laughed, Laura's face creased in relief.

They smiled at one another for a long moment before Laura said, "Thanks ever so much for coming, Clare. I know how hard it must have been for you and I want you to know how much I appreciate it. Promise not to wait another two years before we see each other again?''

"Yes," Clare said, reaching out to embrace her. "And when you've finished nursing Emma and are feeling like you need a break, let me know. I'd love some company."

"Oh, I'll take you up on that one for sure!" She walked Clare to the door. "Say hello to Miss Stuart for me."

Clare waved goodbye and headed for her car. As she pulled away from the curb, she craned around to see Laura waving goodbye from the doorstep. Her adolescent wish from years ago surfaced again. *If life had played out the way you'd expected, that would be you at home with a baby.* That was the scenario she'd fantasized about while dating Gil, scrawling "Mrs. Clare Harper" over and over in her notebook during Chemistry class.

Instead, she'd led mainly a solitary life, finding fulfillment in teaching and later, success in writing. Success that had come at a price. Her hard work over the past few years had pretty much excluded a personal life. At least, one that sustained love and the promise of a long-term partnership. Now the notion of marriage and children was not only daunting, but completely mind-boggling.

"IT WAS SO WONDERFUL of you to come," Lisa Stuart said to Clare as her twelfth-grade English class scrambled out the door.

Clare smiled at the woman who had been not only her favorite teacher in high school, but who'd inspired her to major in English at college. She was struck again by how little her teacher had changed over the years. But then, she reminded herself, seventeen years ago Lisa Stuart had been a new teacher and probably not much older than her students. It was odd how once you passed thirty, the age gap seemed to shrink.

"I just hope they weren't too bored," Clare said.

"Heavens, no! Did you notice how quiet it was in here when you were speaking? They hung on to every word."

"Especially the ones referring to royalties," Clare quipped.

"Yes, very typical of young people these days to get to the bottom line." She sighed. "If there's no money attached to something, it seems there's no value in it. Are you sure you don't want to come up to the staff room for a coffee?"

"I really need to get on the road. I'm due in Hartford at noon."

Lisa nodded. "Thanks again, Clare. It was very nice to be able to brag about you. Teachers don't always have success stories like yours. And it was lovely of you to attribute some of that success to me, though I think you were far too generous."

"Not at all, Miss Stuart. You weren't just *my* favorite. All the kids loved you. By the way, Laura Dundas sends her regards. Remember her? She married Dave Kingsway."

"Please call me Lisa, Clare. And yes, I remember Laura very well. I saw the birth announcement in the *Spectator*. She and her husband must be thrilled."

"They are." Clare began to pack the sample books she'd brought into her canvas bag. She glanced around her.

"Missing something?"

"My new book. I passed it around but I don't see it anywhere."

Lisa frowned. "It's got to be here." She walked around the room. "There it is. Someone's left it on a desk. Kids never seem to listen." She brought it to Clare. "And thanks for signing my personal copy."

Clare tucked the book into the bag. "Well thank you for buying a copy. I was going to give you one."

"You can't give them away, Clare. Every cent of royalty counts. Have you had a chance while you were in town to see many of your old high-school friends?"

Clare wondered how much her former teacher had been aware of her students' personal lives. "Not really," she evaded. "Most have moved out of Twin Falls."

"I read yesterday's article in the *Spectator*," Lisa said.

Clare fiddled with the clasp on her purse. "Oh, yes? What did you think of it?"

"Typical of that reporter's usual fare. An attempt to be sensational. To incite public speculation. I hate it when journalists pretend to be writing one thing but really have an agenda all their own. He starts off by claiming to review your novel and suddenly shifts into something that happened years ago. I haven't finished your book yet, but I found his claims about the similarities between the two to be exaggerated."

"I'm afraid people will think I was merely rewriting history and camouflaging it as fiction."

"Well, obviously you drew on your experiences in a small town with your heroine but I never actually thought the story was based on real life."

Clare swallowed hard, resisting the urge to admit that one or two incidents had actually occurred. "Plus the death in my novel wasn't a murder."

"Exactly. I thought Withers was stretching it to focus on the Rina Thomas murder the way he did. Anyway, it happened so long ago I doubt a lot of readers even know about the case."

"Unfortunately, they do now." Clare sighed.

"Don't let people like Withers get to you, Clare. As I said, he was more interested in producing a bit of sensationalism than in giving an honest review."

"Thanks for that. And thanks, too, for the opportunity

this morning. It's been a while since I faced a group of teenagers in a classroom."

"Your teacher training was very evident, believe me," Lisa said. "I've encouraged some of the kids to read the book for their novel study this term."

Clare slipped on her coat, picked up the canvas book bag and her purse and walked with Lisa to the door. There, she impulsively hugged her. "Thanks again, Lisa. For everything."

She hastened along the corridor to the exit nearest the parking lot. Her low heels clipped along the tile floor, echoing in the muted quiet as classes droned on behind closed doors. She had a sudden flash to another day when she had rushed along this same hall, eager to meet Gil on the playing field after his baseball practice.

She reached the exit and pushed down on the bar of the door, stepping outside. The field stretched ahead of her. It looked the same, she noted, though was now enhanced by tiers of bleachers for spectators.

Clare stared at it, remembering with sudden, vivid clarity the sight of Gil Harper embracing Rina Thomas out there. She had stared in disbelief from the very place where she was now poised, watching Gil and Rina walk arm in arm toward the ravine and the shortcut to the footbridge spanning the river. It was the last time she ever saw Rina Thomas.

Clare took a shaky breath. *Relax, Clare. It's all over and done with. And in a few minutes, you're out of here.*

She rounded the corner of the school to the parking lot, just as she had that day, only this time tears weren't blinding her way. Striding to her car, she determined to put as much distance between the past and the present as quickly as possible. By the time she reached the sprawling outskirts of Hartford, Clare was thinking only of her book signing.

She parked in the lane behind the store, which was tucked into a beautifully renovated section of the old town. Clare took the canvas bag with some promotional bookmarks and posters and hoped that the shipment of books her publisher had ordered for the event had arrived. A clerk on standby at the rear of the building opened the door for her, greeting her enthusiastically.

There was already a small crowd milling about, in spite of the fact that it was a Monday. The manager took her coat, brought her coffee and a bottle of water, and ushered her to a solid and comfortable armchair behind the table. By the time Clare began, asking the name of the first person in line, she'd already pushed from her mind the morning visit to Twin Falls High.

This was the part of her new role in life that she loved—chatting to ordinary people who not only liked to read, but who liked to read *her books*. She still had difficulty accepting the idea that complete strangers would want to read something she wrote. She was sipping the last of her coffee when a man's voice caught her attention and she looked up over the rim of her cup.

"Mr. Wolochuk?" she asked, squinting at the man in front of the table.

He gave a quick nod. "Nice to see you, Clare. And nice to see you remember me."

"Of course I do. I—I struggled through your chemistry class in senior year."

His tentative smile revealed an uneven set of tobacco-stained teeth. The years had obviously not been kind to Stanley Wolochuk, Clare thought. Stoop-shouldered with limp, graying hair, he looked close to retirement, although Clare guessed he must only be in his early fifties.

"If I recall correctly, you passed my course. And it appears you've gone on to bigger and better things." He gestured to the stack of books on the table.

"I've been very lucky," she said, knowing luck had been a small part of the process.

"Well… uh…when I saw the notice in the paper here about the signing, I thought I should come and say hello. And buy a book, too," he added with a strained laugh. His long, sallow face creased into deep ridges. He nudged a copy of her novel toward her.

Clare flipped to the title page, her mind racing for an appropriate inscription. It was so much easier to write something innocuous to a stranger. Acquaintances and friends demanded more personal attention. She felt his eyes on her while she lowered her head to write. Scrawling something about having more success at writing than chemistry, she flipped over the cover when she'd finished.

"So are you still teaching, Mr. Wolochuk?"

"No, had to go on disability a few years ago." He paused. "Heart condition."

"Oh, I'm sorry to hear that." Clare didn't know what more to say. There was only one woman left in line behind him and she was thumbing through a book, apparently in no hurry. "I did a signing in Twin Falls yesterday," she said, "and this morning, I paid a visit to the high school. Lisa Stuart asked me to speak to her senior English class."

His eyes narrowed with interest. "Oh? How did that go?"

"Very well, or so Lisa assured me. Lots of questions from the kids at the end, which is always a good sign. Though most of them had to do with the money and fame aspects of publishing."

"And…uh…" he paused, noisily clearing his throat, "did you have a chance to see any of your old friends?"

"One or two," she said, keeping vague in order to cut short the conversation. The woman still in line was now looking up.

But Mr. Wolochuk seemed in no hurry. "Were you in town long?"

Clare shook her head. "Just for the weekend. Are you still living there?"

A flicker of some emotion Clare couldn't read crossed his face. After a moment, he said, "No. Left there quite a while ago. I live here now."

"Oh." Clare saw the woman check her watch. "Well, it was very nice to see you again, Mr. Wolochuk, and thank you for buying my book."

He gave a slight nod but stayed rooted in place. The woman behind him coughed and Wolochuk suddenly woke up to the fact that someone was waiting. He picked up the book and moved aside for the woman.

Clare smiled at her next customer and, just before inquiring about a name, glanced at Mr. Wolochuk. "Thanks again," she said brightly.

"Yes. Goodbye then, and good luck." He turned and walked away.

When Clare raised her head again, she caught a glimpse of the back of his faded denim jacket as he went out the front door. She saw him hesitate briefly on the sidewalk, as if he were thinking about coming back inside. Then he resumed walking and disappeared from view.

Clare blew a sigh of relief. Two former teachers in one day and both so very different. She'd always thought her chemistry teacher to be a bit odd. Now he seemed almost sad, as if life had been sucked right out of him.

Clare was packing her things when the store clerk rushed over to say there was an urgent phone call for her. "You can take it in the manager's office," the clerk was saying as she led the way.

Thoughts of who it could be flooded Clare's mind— her mother, her agent? The one voice she wasn't expecting to hear on the other end of the line was Laura's.

CHAPTER FIVE

"CLARE! I'm so sorry to interrupt your signing but something has happened."

"Laura! You sound terrible! What is it? What's happened? Not Emma?"

"No, not Emma, thank God. It's Dave. He was up on the roof this morning cleaning out the eavestrough and he fell off the ladder."

"Oh, no! Is he okay?"

"He's in surgery. A compound leg fracture."

"God, that sounds horrible."

"It could have been worse. The doctor says he's a lucky man. But…but the thing is, Clare…" Laura's voice wobbled and suddenly broke off.

Clare could hear her breathing heavily on the other end, trying to compose herself. "It's all right, Laura. Take your time."

"He has to be in hospital for at least a few more days and then when he comes home, he'll be off work for a while longer. And the thing is, I just can't manage on my own. I know I should be able to, but Emma's still getting up at night and I haven't had a full night's sleep since she was born."

Clare ignored the faint alarm bell going off in her head. Laura was calling for advice. That was all. "Well, isn't there someone who can help out? Your parents or Dave's?"

"Mine have already left for Florida, remember? And I

hate to call them back. Dave's mother's in a nursing home and his older sister has her own problems.'' There was a frustrated sigh. ''The only friends I have here are all working, including Anne-Marie. *There's no one*.'' Her voice pitched in despair.

Clare's hand tightened on the receiver. She sensed what was coming.

''Could you…I mean, this is a horrible thing to have to ask but I was wondering if you could come back and stay with me? Just for a couple of days while I try to find someone in town. You said you had a gap in your book tour, didn't you?''

Clare closed her eyes, her imagined fear now out in the open. ''Laura, I—I don't think I'd be any help to you at all. I mean, I don't know a thing about babies.''

''I just need someone to watch her while I go back and forth to the hospital. You know—well, I guess you don't—but it's so hard to pack up a baby and take her everywhere. Her schedule will be completely thrown off. Besides, I don't know if they'd even let babies onto Dave's ward.'' She paused to catch her breath. ''The other thing is, I just need another person around. I don't know if it's the hormones or what, but I can't stand being alone.''

The rush of words told Clare that Laura was in no shape to take charge of the situation. ''Okay, Laura. I'm finished here and I suppose I can afford a couple of days.''

''Oh, Clare, thank you so much. I don't know what I'd do without you. I've been frantic here.''

Clare had a feeling that in other circumstances, her normally take-charge friend would have managed quite well. But perhaps the undercurrent of tension she'd picked up between Dave and Laura over the weekend was a sign of things not being normal in the Kingsway household. Whatever the reason, Clare knew she couldn't refuse. She hung up the phone and stood for a long moment, thinking about the commitment she'd just made.

Rearranging her book tour wouldn't be a problem. Her next signing wasn't until the end of the month. Still, staying on longer in Twin Falls meant postponing following up on her recent book proposal with her editor. She'd submitted it just before leaving for Twin Falls and was looking forward to getting back to work on the project. But the note of desperation in Laura's voice was impossible to ignore. Her friend needed her. The Dundas family had been there for Clare years ago, and now she had the opportunity to repay that debt. If she had any luck left at all—and she was starting to wonder about that—she'd be able to put in her two or three days and leave again without having to bump into Gil.

An hour and a half later, when the front door of the Kingsway home flew open at her knock, she knew luck had deserted her.

"Clare!"

"Gil. What are you doing here?"

"You heard about Dave?"

"Laura called me at the bookstore. Where I was signing," she explained at the confusion in his face. It wasn't only his unshaven face that added to his disheveled appearance, she was thinking. He was wearing jeans and a dark green plaid flannel shirt, tails out and unbuttoned to reveal a white T-shirt. His hair looked as though someone had been running fingers through it. Under any other circumstances, Clare might have thought there was a woman inside with him. But a sudden sharp wail from deep within the house told her the only female on the premises was baby Emma. A very unhappy baby Emma.

Clare brushed past Gil and stepped inside. "Is Laura home yet?"

"Still at the hospital. But she called a few minutes ago to say she'd be home in an hour or so."

Thank heavens. "Did she call you to come over after it happened?"

He nodded. "I was cleaning out my dad's garage at the time. The baby was asleep when I got here so I told Laura to go with Dave."

Another long wail. His head jerked up, toward the stairs. "I think she's awake now."

"Sounds like it," Clare said. "Maybe you should go get her."

"Me?"

She smiled at the incredulity in his voice. "Aren't you the baby-sitter?"

"Well, uh, isn't that what you're here for?" When she failed to reply, he said, "Then I'll leave you to it," and made for the door.

"Wait! You can't leave yet."

"I've an appointment in half an hour with a real-estate agent at my dad's place. I was about to call and cancel, but fortunately for me, you arrived in time."

Clare frowned. "But I don't know anything. I mean, Laura didn't give me any instructions about Emma."

"She didn't give me any, either. Only that the diapers were on the change table in her room and...and there were a couple of bottles of...uh, breast milk in the fridge." His face flushed and his eyes flicked back to the staircase.

Clare wondered what he was looking for. Baby Emma to come down all on her own? The wails increased in volume and as one, they both moved automatically to the stairs.

"Only one of us needs to go get her," Gil said.

He sounded a tad snappish, she thought. "Then you go and I'll heat up the bottle of milk in the microwave."

He seemed to like that idea until her reminder about

diapers slowed his ascent. Clare hurried into the kitchen, dropped her purse and coat on a chair and opened the refrigerator. There were two small bottles of milk on a shelf. Probably left from Saturday night when the baby-sitter came. Clare wondered how long the milk would be good for. Did breast milk have a shorter expiry date than whatever other milk babies drank? She'd no idea, which confirmed once again how useless she'd be helping Laura.

Still, she couldn't help smiling at how out of his league Gil was. The dashing big-city lawyer look had certainly taken a dive. When he showed up in the kitchen minutes later, trying to contain a squirming and teary Emma, his face had an unhealthy pallor.

"I think something must be wrong with her," he said.

Clare gave Emma a second look. "Why?"

He merely shook his head. "I don't see how such a cute baby could produce what…well, what she produced up there."

Grateful she'd been on bottle duty, Clare summoned a sympathetic smile. "I'm sure it's all perfectly normal. Anyway, she doesn't look sick. Shall I take her while you wash up?"

"Please." He handed Emma over before Clare had a chance to sit and vanished from the kitchen. Clare removed the bottle from the microwave and sat down, gingerly arranging Emma in the crook of her left arm. She'd remembered that much from her limited baby-sitting experience, along with the need to test the milk's temperature. That proved to be more challenging. As soon as Emma saw the bottle, she started kicking her legs. While Clare was trying to sprinkle some milk onto her wrist, Emma began to wail again.

"Shh," Clare whispered. "I'm working as fast as I can." The milk felt warm but not hot so she lowered the nipple to Emma's mouth and was shocked at how voraciously she latched onto it. By the time Gil reappeared, the kitchen was silent except for the occasional gurgle from the bottle and Emma's contented sucking.

"You look like you've done that before," he observed.

"Maybe once, a long time ago. I have a feeling this is the easiest part of baby-care."

He nodded, but didn't say anything. His stare was unnerving so Clare asked, "You have to be somewhere?"

"Huh? Oh, yes. I've an agent coming to the house with an offer on it."

"That sounds like good news for you."

"I hope so. I booked off a week to pack up and sell but if the offer's too low, I may have to take a few extra days."

Emma detached her mouth from the bottle to come up for air.

"Don't you have to burp her or something?" Gil asked.

"I know." She wondered where he'd picked up that bit of information. They'd both been only children and she doubted he'd ever baby-sat in his life. Clare slowly raised Emma and carefully placed her up against her left shoulder. A loud gas bubble echoed in the room and they both laughed.

"Sounds a bit like Dave working on his third beer," quipped Gil.

"Yes. Well, with Laura as a mom I'm sure Emma will develop more ladylike habits as she grows older."

"I bet."

Except for Emma's contented sounds, the room was silent. But now Clare wasn't as uncomfortable with Gil hovering at the counter opposite the kitchen table. He was obviously in no hurry to leave, despite his appointment with the real estate agent. In fact, he seemed very content to just stare at her as she fed Emma. Feeling a need to fill the silence, she asked, "What kind of law did you say you practiced in New York?"

"Corporate. I've just been made an associate of the firm." He paused, adding, "I really wanted to get into criminal law, but when I graduated I had a massive debt to pay off and the success ladder in the criminal branch looked a bit higher. Besides, I had a contact in the firm who helped me get my articling position there while I was studying for the bar."

Emma started squirming. Clare lowered her back into the crook of her arm so she could finish the bottle. "Well, it appears you've done well for yourself," she said to Gil, for want of any other comment.

"Considering the rough start I got, I think I did."

Rough start. The slight edge in his voice hinted at the specific start he was referring to—beginning freshman year under a cloud of suspicion after Rina's death. Clare sighed. *Every conversation seemed to get back to this. It's always going to be between us.* The thought was oddly depressing. Yet why should she care, after all these years? The problem was, she did. For some inexplicable reason, she wanted him to think well of her.

He must have sensed her reaction to his comment for after a slight pause, he said, "Guess I'd better go then. Good luck with Emma. I hope for your sake Laura gets home soon."

Clare pursed her lips. "Yeah, me, too."

Gil hesitated a minute longer, ran a hand through his hair and said goodbye as he left the kitchen. Seconds later Clare heard the front door close behind him. She exhaled a mouthful of air, uncertain if what she was feeling was relief or disappointment that he'd left without another word.

She looked down at the baby cradled in her arms, and wondered what to do next. For the first time, she felt a new respect for Laura, wondering how she got anything done. By the time Laura arrived, almost an hour later, Clare was ready to hand the baby over and head for the hotel.

But Laura would have none of it. "I need someone here in the house," she explained patiently, as if Clare were a teenage baby-sitter. "What if they call me to the hospital in the middle of the night?"

Clare gritted her teeth. "How likely is that? Dave's only got a broken leg."

"Not only, Clare. It's a compound fracture and a nasty one. He'll be in a cast for weeks." Laura slumped into the sofa cushions. "I don't know how he's going to manage the stairs."

"You'll have to make up a bed in the den. At least you've got a downstairs bathroom."

Laura sighed and forked her hand through her hair. "Of course. I'm not even thinking straight. See, that's another reason why I need you! It's only until I can get someone to come and stay."

Clare saw the anxiety in her friend's face and knew she had no counterargument. She'd agreed to help and now she was stuck with her decision. Later that night, after they'd ordered a pizza for dinner, fed Emma again and got her off to bed—with Clare watching to see how it was done—Clare eagerly turned back the covers in the guest room and climbed into bed. It wasn't quite ten o'clock, but felt like midnight. First thing in the morning, she vowed, she'd start looking for help for Laura.

Morning arrived a lot sooner than she'd anticipated. Emma's wails started just before five and were stifled as soon as Laura got up to feed her. Clare tried to go back to sleep, but even Laura's tiptoeing around upstairs kept her awake. Finally she gave up and joined her in the kitchen.

"Coffee's over there," Laura said, nodding toward the counter opposite where she sat, nursing Emma.

"I thought you fed her already," Clare said, shuffling toward the coffeemaker. "I heard her wake up about an hour ago."

"She only nursed on one side and then fell asleep. Now she's ready for the other side."

Coffee mug in hand, Clare sagged into a chair opposite Laura. "I don't know why I feel so tired when you're the one who had to get up in the night."

"Actually, Emma slept from eleven 'til five. That's the longest stretch ever."

"Six hours. I can barely function with eight."

A ghost of a smile crossed Laura's face. "I used to be the same but you have to make changes when a new baby comes into your life."

There was a wistful tone in her voice that Clare couldn't ignore. "I've read that relationships between husbands and wives change a lot then, too."

"Believe it. I think that's the biggest change—other than not going into work every day."

"Do you miss not working?"

"I do, but not enough to want to turn Emma over to a stranger." She sighed. "That's a bone of contention between Dave and me. He thinks I should go back to work when my maternity leave is up because we need both salaries to knock down our mortgage."

"And you—"

"Want to wait. Even a year. I get six months so it would only be another six months without pay. My boss is willing to give me the time."

Clare sipped her coffee. She couldn't think of anything to say other than the obvious. "I guess you and Dave will have to talk about it some more."

Laura kissed Emma's forehead while she nursed. When

she raised her face back to Clare, her smile was a bit wobbly. "I guess we'll have plenty of opportunity to do that now that he's going to be home from work for a few weeks." Her chin trembled. "And then I'll have *two* people to look after." Her eyes filled up.

Clare guessed what she was thinking. *Who's going to look after me?* She leaned across the table to pat Laura's forearm. "Well, I'll be here for a couple of days and we're going to look for someone to give you a hand. So, what's on the agenda for today? I suppose you'll be going to see Dave?"

"Yes. What about you?"

Clare didn't have to think long. "I'm going to call that reporter and give him a piece of my mind."

As soon as she'd finished tidying up the breakfast dishes for Laura, she did exactly that.

"Personally, I thought it was a great article and wonderful publicity for your book. I can't see what you're complaining about," Jeff Withers said after Clare's opening complaint.

Clare's hand clenched tighter around the receiver. She reminded herself that making an enemy of a reporter—even one in poky old Twin Falls—wasn't a smart thing to do, and calmly replied.

"Of course I appreciate your warm comments about the book. The few that you made. However, I'm worried that some readers will be unable to make the distinction between my *novel* and a real-life murder case. Your attempt to link the two is very self-serving, Mr. Withers. I think you were more interested in selling papers than actually reviewing a book."

He cleared his throat. "Well, I happen to think there is a link between your book and Rina Thomas's murder, Ms. Morgan. It can't be a coincidence that you've made the mysterious death of your heroine's best friend a pivotal part of your story when you yourself played a part in a real life murder here in Twin Falls.''

Blood rushed into Clare's head while her resolve to set the record straight took a nosedive. Dry-mouthed, she said, ''I haven't the faintest idea what you're talking about, Mr. Withers. I had no part in the Rina Thomas case.''

''That's not what I've heard. My source told me that you pointed the police in the direction of someone you were dating at the time. I forget the guy's name. Uh, just a sec while I—''

''His name was Gil Harper and the police questioned him briefly as part of their investigation. He was released. That's it.''

''But Rina's killer was never found so I don't think the story has officially ended, do you?''

Clare sighed, refusing to take the bait, ''I'm sorry you were unable to differentiate between a novel and an old murder case. And even more, I'm sorry I agreed to the interview. I won't make that mistake again. Goodbye, Mr. Withers.''

''Wait, wait. Hold on a minute. You may think I can't tell the difference but there are some people here in town who can't, either.''

''I don't know what you're talking about.''

''Have you heard from the manager of the bookstore where you had your signing on Saturday?''

''No. Why?''

''Just that sometime later that day someone vandalized the posters advertising your book. Scrawled across them with permanent marker and obliterated your name.'' He paused. ''Now why do you think someone would do that, Ms. Morgan?''

When Clare found her voice, it didn't sound like hers at all. ''I haven't heard a thing about this.''

"Do you think the graffiti artist might be someone who had the same difficulty I had in believing your book was purely fiction? Or was it only a coincidence?"

"Goodbye, Mr. Withers," she said, hanging up. She rested her head against her hand. "What a mistake."

"What's that?" Laura's voice rang out from the den where she was making up a bed for Dave.

Clare heard her walking along the hall back to the kitchen and wished she'd made the phone call later, when Laura was at the hospital.

"Are you okay? You look like death warmed over, as the saying goes." Laura observed from the doorway.

"I feel worse than I look. That…that Withers creep. I wish I'd never called him. I should have just let the matter drop."

"Why? What happened?"

"Basically he refused to see my point. Then he said he had some source who'd given him information about the Thomas case. And he managed to get the last word by telling me that someone had vandalized my posters at Novel Idea and implied that it happened because of my book."

"That's crazy." Laura sat down across from Clare. "It was probably some kid trying to prove something. They write graffiti everywhere for heaven's sake."

"Yeah, but mine were the only posters damaged apparently."

"Well, maybe whoever did it didn't have a chance to get to the others. And what was that about a source of information about the murder? What kind of information?"

Clare looked away. "I don't know."

"Come on, Clare. You do know. That's why you're so upset."

"Because he knew something that...well, only a few people could know."

"Which is?" Laura asked, her voice gentle and coaxing.

She'll find out anyway, Clare thought. "The reason the police took Gil in for questioning was because...well, because I told them that I'd seen him walk toward the ravine with Rina. That afternoon." She turned her head to Laura. "I was the one who told on him."

"Omigod," Laura whispered. "So was that why you two split up?

"Part of it. A big part." Clare shook her head. "The only people who know that are the police and Gil and I. Or so I thought."

"You know what, Clare? I think you should forget about this. The guy's stirring you up, that's all. Maybe he wants to write a follow-up article."

"I shouldn't have called him." Clare covered her face with her hands. When Clare removed her hands, Laura was still staring at her. "What do you think I should do?"

"Frankly, forget about it." Laura peered at her watch. "Look, Emma's due to wake up any second. After I feed her, I'll head over to the hospital. Right now, why don't you call the bookstore? At least you'll feel like you're doing something. I'll try to get Emma back down again, but it may not work. She's awake for longer stretches of time now. Is that okay? You could put her in her carriage and take her for a walk."

"Okay." The prospect of exercise and fresh air was, after talking to Withers, very appealing. "And thanks for the loan of the jeans, Laura. I didn't bring a lot of clothes with me."

"Thank you! Here you were expecting to come for a weekend and you end up staying on to baby-sit."

Clare patted Laura on the shoulder and as soon as

she left the room to tend to Emma, Clare telephoned Novel Idea.

The manager apologized profusely and told Clare that the police had been called but could do little. "Unfortunately," she said, "the store security camera wasn't focused on the particular spot where the display of your books was located. But at least none of the books themselves were damaged."

"Do you think kids were responsible?"

The manager sighed. "That's what the police are suggesting, though we've never had anything like this happen before. And I don't know why teenagers would target just your display."

It was exactly what Clare had concluded, as well. She reassured the manager that there'd been no way to prevent such an act and hung up. Then she went upstairs to change for her walk with Emma. She pulled on her own black cords, pairing them with Laura's black turtleneck. Although the day had begun balmy, the temperature had dropped to its usual autumn crispness after noon. Leaving the room, she brushed against a chair holding the books and notes she'd taken for her talk with Miss Stuart's English class. The copy of her novel toppled to the floor and as it landed, a folded piece of paper flew out from it. Clare stooped to pick it up, noting the bleed marks of writing inside. She unfolded it and stared, her mind not instantly registering the block printing in red magic marker:

"Your a troublemaker."

CHAPTER SIX

GIL COULDN'T believe his eyes. It had to be her, he thought, with that sun-burnished hair. Pushing Emma's baby carriage, no doubt.

The sight of Clare Morgan taking care of a baby was both unbelievable and wondrous at the same time. He'd felt that yesterday as she fed Emma at the kitchen table. He knew she'd had little baby-sitting experience, yet she'd looked so natural holding Emma and smiling down at her. He'd had a sudden, blinding fantasy of her cradling their own child.

It had been one of those crazy what-if moments. What if he'd never been implicated in Rina's death? What if they'd never had that last, horrible fight? What if, instead, the daydreams they'd shared about college and marriage had all come true? He took a deep breath, shook his head clear of pointless speculation about a future that never happened, and jogged up behind her.

"Hi there," he said, more casually than he felt.

She jumped, as he'd expected. The instant her tawny eyes focused on him he knew that she was less than thrilled to see him. Color rose in her face. "I didn't know you jogged," she blurted.

He couldn't stifle the grin. "Why would you know?"

The flush deepened. "Laura's gone to see Dave," she went on, gesturing to a sleeping Emma inside the carriage. "I'm hoping to keep her this way until she gets back, though I may have to cover the whole town to do it," she said with a slightly nervous laugh.

"Mind if I join you for a bit?"

She gave a halfhearted shrug as he strolled along with her. "So what's the latest word on Dave?" he asked.

"Laura called the hospital this morning and he was doing fine. He's been fitted with crutches. Should be home in another day or so."

"That should make you happy."

Her eyes flashed at him. "You make me sound petty. I really don't mind helping out a friend."

"Sorry, Clare. That wasn't my intention. I just mean that you and I both seem to be uncomfortable around babies. I'd be counting the seconds, if it were me looking after her."

"I guess we're a pretty poor choice for godparents."

"I meant to ask, but never got around to it. What are godparents supposed to do, anyway?"

She smiled, catching her lower lip between her teeth. A gesture he recalled all too well. "I've no idea," she said, "though I suspect the job involves birthday and Christmas presents."

"Hmm. Well, I guess I can handle that. Or at least, make calendar notes for my assistant."

"Occasional visits may be expected, too," she said.

Gil frowned. "That won't be as easy. I'm usually very busy. In fact, this is the first time off I've had in a couple of years."

"Really? And you can hardly call it a holiday what with having to clean out and sell your father's place." She glanced his way again. "How did things go yesterday?"

"They made me an offer but it was too low so I presented them with a counteroffer. I decided I'd rather take the extra few days than to see my parents' house go for nothing. They put too much love and work into it.'' He didn't add that learning Clare Morgan was going to be in Twin Falls at least another couple of days had had some bearing on his decision. "How about you? Is this going to disrupt your book tour very much?''

"Not really. There are a few more signings in New York and the suburbs, then in New Jersey. Fortunately, most were already slated for early November. I may be a celebrity here in Twin Falls, but elsewhere…'' Her voice trailed off.

He wanted to point out that anyone making the *Times* bestseller list was indeed a celebrity but decided she still wasn't used to all the attention her book had garnered. Maybe she hadn't changed too much after all. Oddly, that pleased him, though he couldn't have explained why he cared. He was studying her profile so intently that it took him a moment to realize she was still talking. And about something upsetting, from the quaver in her voice.

"What was that?'' he interrupted. "Go back to what you just said.''

"I said I doubt that I'm well liked by everyone here, judging from the damage to my promotional posters. That was bad enough. Finding an anonymous note in one of my books was a lot more upsetting.''

"What do you mean?'' He stopped and placed a hand on her arm.

"Someone defaced my posters on display at Novel Idea, the store where I had my signing on Saturday. Then just as I was getting ready to take Emma for a walk, I found this note in one of the books I'd taken to Miss Stuart's English class.''

"What? Let me see it,'' said Gil. "Look, Emma's sleeping. Why don't we go sit on that bench over there for a minute?''

Clare peered down into the baby carriage, then raised

her eyes to Gil. "Okay," she said and wheeled the carriage to the bench.

He sat down beside her and took his time looking at the note.

"I just shoved it in my pocket," she explained, "on my way out the door with Emma. I haven't even shown it to Laura yet. She was all set to leave for the hospital and I didn't want to hold her back."

"Not a good speller, that's for sure" he said. "Let me get this straight. You passed the copy of your novel around the class while you were speaking?"

"Yes. I read a section from it and then someone asked a question about the cover blurb so I passed the book around."

"So it was some kid who wrote this."

"I guess. Though I can't understand why a kid would write a note like that. I can see them writing some comment about the book or its cover art or whatever, but why call me a troublemaker?"

Gil gave the note back to her. "First your posters in the bookstore and now this. Both events occurring right after that newspaper interview. It can't be a coincidence. Someone's obviously very upset about your book."

She chewed at the edge of her lower lip for a moment before saying, "I came to the same conclusion on my way over here. But I still don't understand why. And why a kid?"

"I know you insist the book is pure fiction, but even I thought some of it clearly paralleled Rina's murder when I read it. That was the point of that newspaper article, wasn't it?"

"You read it? You never said a word about it yesterday when I saw you at Laura's."

He could hardly tell her the article had ticked him off so much he wanted to go down to the paper and punch the guy. A bit excessive, he granted. But the guy's intent was so obvious it was insulting. He obviously didn't give a damn about reviewing the merits of the book itself, but only wanted to cause a stir by dredging up Rina Thomas.

"It was trashy journalism," he said. "Not a book review at all. And I didn't mention it, because I figured you wouldn't want to talk about it."

"You're right," she conceded. "I wouldn't have. What's the point?"

He sensed that in spite of her apparent dismissal of the article, she was still disturbed by it. Time to change the subject he thought. But she surprised him by going back to the book.

"Of course some of my own recollections are in the book. It happens…you know…when an author is writing about something that is similar to events in his or her personal life. The only reason I put the death in," she rushed on, "was because Rina Thomas's murder impacted on all of us. I wanted to use my own emotions at that time to give credibility to my character. To make her more real. Basically all I used from the real case was the death of a classmate."

But she'd left something out of her plot line and he couldn't let it pass. "There was one other fact, wasn't there, that differed from the real case?"

Her eyes shifted downward. When she raised them again, looking at him through her thick lashes, the misery he saw in them tugged at him. Suddenly he was a teenager again and in helpless thrall to Clare Morgan. He clenched his jaw, wishing he wasn't so easily taken in by those big eyes.

Color rushed up into her face. "You know there is," she said softly, "if you've read the book."

Gil waited, wanting her to say it.

"I had Marianne—the girl who died—leave school that day with her friend Kenzie's boyfriend."

Just as I left with Rina. The throbbing that had begun in Gil's head as Clare spoke was now reverberating throughout his whole body. She'd finally come out with it.

"But the boyfriend is never accused of murder—the idea of his being responsible is…well, is only in Kenzie's mind," she quickly added, as if wanting to justify herself somehow.

"And that would be another part you *didn't* change?"

She paled, catching the bite in his voice. "I guess not. I mean, in the book no one else suspects the boyfriend except for Kenzie."

"So she never informed on him?"

"No," she whispered.

"So that's definitely a part that you changed."

She glanced away, obviously embarrassed, and he could have kicked himself. What was he thinking? That finally getting her to confess her betrayal of him would make things better?

"Let me explain this time—please," she said, turning her head back to him.

Her eyes were moist. Gil wanted to tell her to forget everything—all of it—and wrap his arms around her, but he couldn't. "Go ahead," he said.

"The book is supposed to be about how Kenzie realizes that the town she grew up in—the quintessential small town—is not the paradise she'd thought. When I was writing it, my mind kept going back to Rina Thomas and how her death split apart our class. That's what I wanted to show in the novel. How a single tragic event can change so many lives. So I invented a slightly different scenario." She paused, her gaze steadily fixed on his face. "Different because I don't have the same suspicions that Kenzie had.''

The look in her eyes implored him to believe her and part of him wanted to. Still, he couldn't help focusing on a word in her last sentence. *Don't. As in, not anymore.* Certainly it didn't mean she'd never harbored suspicions about him because they both knew better. He backed away from the retort he was tempted to make. Better to try to give her some advice than dwell any longer on a past that could never be changed. He took a deep breath and looked at Emma sleeping in her baby carriage.

"I think the first thing you need to do is to go see Miss Stuart again and show her that note. See what she has to say about it," he said, avoiding her face.

"I don't know if she'll be able to help—I mean, it's not as if she'd recognize the handwriting."

"Still worth a try."

The energy created by the talk seconds ago had vanished, leaving behind a tension that was almost palpable. *Where do we go from here,* Gil wondered? *Or have we reached another dead end, just as we did seventeen years ago?*

She gave a vague nod, as if she were thinking about something else. He guessed she was expecting him to go on about the book but he didn't know what else to say. She'd admitted the thinly disguised reference to him and Rina in the book. In spite of his claim earlier that day that he'd put the past behind him, Gil knew he'd been referring to only part of that past. He still carried with him the part that had centered on Clare Morgan. So he breathed a small sigh of relief when she stood up to go.

"I should probably get Emma back home," she said. "Thanks for the advice about the note."

Gil got to his feet. "Give me a call if you find out anything from Miss Stuart."

"At your dad's place?"

"Oh, right. The phone's been disconnected. Here." He took his wallet out of his nylon windbreaker and handed her a business card. "My cell phone number's on there."

She took the card and pocketed it, keeping her eyes on his. "Thanks," she said and turned to leave.

"Clare!"

She swung around.

"Take care and…uh…all the best. In case I don't see you before you leave."

She nodded. He jogged away before he could change his mind and take her into his arms, whispering that the past was done with. At last.

CLARE SHUT the driver-side door of the Jetta and, after a second's deliberation, locked it before she marched briskly through the parking lot at the side of the school around to the front entrance. The bell must have just rung because groups of students, jostling and shouting at one another, were spilling out the doors.

The memory surge she'd experienced on Monday returned as she took the main staircase to Lisa's classroom on the second floor. Rows of lockers, except for a different coat of paint, were as dilapidated as they'd been in her time. The same types of posters advertising dances and other social events were plastered on the same shabby-looking walls. It wasn't until she noticed a boy scowl at her as he passed that she was reminded of the note. Laura had been shocked to hear about the note when she'd come home from the hospital and had insisted that Clare call Lisa Stuart immediately. No argument there, Clare had thought. Discussion about the note had also saved Clare from having to give a detailed account of her encounter with Gil in the park.

The door to Lisa's classroom was open and Clare stuck her head in. "Hi!"

Lisa looked up from a paper she was grading. "Hey there! What a nice surprise. Come and pull up a chair."

Clare dragged a chair closer to the desk. "Sorry to disturb you," she began. "But I needed to see you as soon as possible."

"What is it? It sounded urgent on the phone."

"When I was speaking to your class on Monday, I passed around a copy of my novel and—"

"God, don't tell me one of my students wrote in it."

Clare shook her head. "Something worse, I'm afraid. I found this in it." She opened her purse and handed Lisa the note.

Lisa frowned as she studied it and when she raised her face to Clare, she was angry and upset. "This is horrible. I don't understand. Are you sure someone from my class wrote this?"

"I haven't opened the book at all since that day. And it's only been in my possession, both before the class and after."

"I don't know what to say, except I'm so sorry." She stared at the paper a moment longer. "I don't understand why anyone would write this. What does it mean?"

Clare shrugged. "I've no idea. I was hoping you might recognize something about it—the writing or the paper."

"Unfortunately, even the bad spelling isn't a clue. It could have been written by any one of half a dozen kids in my class."

"Don't worry about it. Maybe someone thought he—or she—was being cool. Who knows? As for the message, I probably shouldn't read too much into it."

"Are you worried about it? Do you think you should go to the police?"

"Maybe I will." She stood up. "I won't take any more of your time Lisa."

The teacher handed the paper back to Clare. "If I get any brainwaves about this, I'll let you know. Are you still at the hotel?"

"No, actually I'm staying with my friend—Laura Kingsway."

"Oh, yes. You mentioned her the other day. Then if I need to get in touch, I'll look up her number."

Clare nodded and, turning to leave, noticed a boy standing in the doorway. The same boy she'd seen earlier in the hall. The scowler. He didn't look any happier now, she thought.

"Can I help you, Jason?" Lisa asked looking beyond Clare to the door.

"Just wanted to tell you I'd be bringing in my paper tomorrow."

Lisa frowned. "That's a day late, Jason. We've talked about this before. You promised you'd make a better effort."

"Yeah well, things came up."

There was a tense silence until Lisa replied, "Very well. Tomorrow at the latest. And this is the last time!" she called after he'd swung round and disappeared. "Sorry about that," she said, turning back to Clare. "He's having a bad year and I think, judging by his lack of cooperation, it's just going to get worse."

"Hmm." Clare was thinking it might be her imagination, but the look he'd shot her had been uglier than the one he'd given Lisa.

"Anyway, thanks again for coming in on Monday. I know the kids enjoyed your talk—at least, all but the anonymous note writer." She sighed. "I feel bad about that, Clare. It was so generous of you to give us some of your time. I think you're right about the intention. Probably someone goofing around, trying to be a hotshot.''

"Yes. Probably. Oh, by the way, I bumped into another one of my teachers at the signing in Hartford.''

"Oh?"

"Mr. Wolochuk. I don't know if you remember him. He taught chemistry and physics.''

"Of course I remember him. As a matter of fact—and this is a weird coincidence—that was his son who was just here.''

"What? The boy about the late term paper? The one in the doorway?''

Lisa nodded. "The same. He's in my senior English class—the one you spoke to.''

"I can't believe it. Mr. Wolochuk and that boy. Isn't he too old to have a son that young?''

"Stan is older than his wife. And from what I've heard, he's aged even more in the last couple of years. A heart condition or something.''

"Mr. Wolochuk said he was living in Hartford now.'' Clare was having difficulty connecting the surly teenager to her chemistry teacher.

"He is. Unfortunately, Stan and his wife divorced when Jason was just a toddler.'' Lisa pursed her lips and fell silent for a moment. "Stan's wife assumed custody and Stan moved to Hartford. Did he say if he was still teaching or not?''

"No. He said he was on disability.''

"Well, the whole thing was a shame. Stan was such a good teacher and they'd wanted a child for years. I don't know why they divorced, but these things happen, I suppose.''

Thinking of Laura and Dave, Clare could only nod. "I'll go, then. It was nice to see you again, Lisa.''

"Good luck with the writing. I hope you won't be too successful to come back to Twin Falls for another visit."

Clare smiled and waved goodbye. When she reached the ground floor landing, she was aware of someone descending the staircase behind her. She opened the door and held on to it a second longer in case the person behind was also leaving the school. But no one followed through so she let the door swing shut.

She used the remote to open the Jetta and climbed in. The impromptu visit hadn't revealed anything significant and Clare was beginning to accept that the note had simply been the work of a mischief-maker and not some psycho fan. She turned on the engine and was shifting into Drive when she noticed someone leaning against the side of the school, watching her.

Jason Wolochuk. They stared at one another until Clare took her foot off the brake and drove out of the lot. As she stopped to yield to oncoming traffic, Clare checked her rearview mirror. Jason had moved away from the exterior school wall and was now in the middle of the drive into the lot. His arms were casually folded across the front of his nylon windbreaker as he watched her drive out onto the street.

"BUT I LOVE being home with Emma," Laura said, her voice pitching. "And I'm dreading the day I have to go back to work."

"I guess it must be hard," Clare began, "to give your first baby over to someone else's care. Though plenty of women do it."

"Of course they do. But I'm not other women and I don't want to do it.'

"Have you thought about going freelance? Consulting from here, rather than commuting to Hartford?"

"I could. A lot of tax specialists do. There'd be a drop

in pay, but I'd save on transportation, clothes and business lunches.'' Laura straightened in her chair. Her eyes shone with excitement.

"You could even write off your mortgage payments," said Clare.

"Who's the tax specialist here? I thought you spent economics class penning love notes to Gil."

Clare laughed. "I did, but some of Mr. Oliver's droning lectures must have filtered into my subconscious mind."

"Do you ever think about what might have happened if—you know—you and Gil hadn't split up?"

Clare averted her eyes from Laura's intent gaze across the kitchen table. When the silence in the room began to feel uncomfortable, she finally admitted, "I used to, but not anymore." After a moment, she shrugged and defiantly turned her face back to Laura. "What would be the point?"

"What about kids? Ever thought of having any yourself?"

"Some day." Clare laughed uneasily. "If I can find that certain someone…"

"Gil seems to be pretty good with babies."

"Gil?" She cleared her throat and tried to change the subject. "Anyway, I still can't understand why you studied business."

"I wanted to follow in Dave's footsteps. Go to the same college he did and be in the same faculty."

"At least you didn't become an actuary, too. That I could never have comprehended."

"Me, neither." Laura hesitated, then added, "Sorry for bringing all that up with Gil, Clare, but you two seem to be getting along better and I just thought—"

Clare refused to end the sentence for her. Better to let the matter drop than playing the "what-if" game about Gil. "Anyway," she said, "you've still got four months of maternity left, haven't you? Plenty of time to get something organized.''

Laura nodded. ''True. You know, I'm going to follow up your idea. If I can get someone to come to the house, even three days a week, I might be able to bring in enough money to offset the expenses I have had going into the office.''

''And you'd be here, too, so you could pop in to see Emma whenever you wanted.''

''That might be a problem. I'd want to see her all the time.''

''Maybe by then you won't be so obsessed with her,'' Clare teased.

''I'm not obsessed with her! It's normal to want to be with your child all the time. I admit I'll have to work at not being an overprotective mother because I had parents who wouldn't let me go anywhere by myself for ages. But then, after your parents were divorced, it was just you and your mother. That must have been hard.''

''Only at first. I think high school was the hardest, with the emphasis on fitting in.''

''Do you think that's why you and Gil linked up?''

Clare frowned. It seemed the subject of Gil wasn't about to go away. ''How so?''

''You felt that you didn't fit in at times and he seemed to be an outsider in some ways.''

''Gil fit in. He was the captain of the football team. The big star!''

''But if Gil hadn't gotten that scholarship, he'd never have been able to go to Yale. His family couldn't have afforded it.''

''Gil said his father got a job at City Hall after the lumber mills closed.''

''Yes, the summer you moved to New Jersey. But that

was strange, don't you think? His father getting a job at City Hall?"

"Why?"

"Jobs at City Hall were hard to get. People who got them usually had some kind of pull. You know how it works."

Clare did. She also knew there'd been enough talk about Gil Harper. "Speaking of high school, remember I told you I saw Mr. Wolochuk at the book signing in Hartford?"

"Yeah?"

"He has a son—in Lisa Stuart's English class."

"No kidding. I knew he and his wife had a child after we left for college. So the kid would be about, what? Seventeen?"

"Yes. He's the same age we were when all that stuff happened." Clare fell silent. "Lisa said Mr. Wolochuk and his wife divorced when their son was just little."

"I heard about that a few years ago. Mom told me. Apparently the wife went a bit strange."

Clare recalled what Lisa had said about Jason having problems. "I saw the son today. He came to see Lisa about something while I was there."

"What did he look like?"

"Nothing like his father. I'd never have guessed. Bleached blond hair all gelled up, you know the way some kids wear it. Skinny. Bad complexion."

"Guess he lives with his mother."

"That's what Lisa said."

"Poor kid," Laura said. "That would be tough, on top of the rest of it." She pushed away from the table. "Dave may be able to come home tomorrow." She was partway to the door when she stopped. "Oh, one more thing. Gil may come around sometime in the morning. He called while you were seeing Miss Stuart to ask if he could help out with anything so I did ask a favor of him.''

"What?''

"That ladder Dave was using on Monday morning when he fell is still propped against the house. Gil said he'd put it away for us, back into the garage. I hope you don't mind.''

"Why should I mind?''

"You had a tight look on your face when you told me during dinner about meeting him in the park this afternoon. I wanted to ask more about it but I could tell right away the subject was taboo.''

Clare swallowed her irritation. "That's not how I felt at all, Laura. There was simply nothing more to tell. We met in the park and I told him about the posters and the note I found. Period.''

"Okay, okay. You don't have to get so bugged about it.''

Clare took a deep breath. No point in causing a rift between her and Laura over Gil Harper. "I'm not. Don't worry about how I'm feeling about Gil. You have enough on your plate.'' She patted Laura on the arm, wanting to show her she wasn't upset.

"All right. I'll pick up a video for tonight, okay? A chick flick.''

Clare smiled. "Great. And get some junk food, too.''

Laura paused in the doorway. "Sort of like old times,'' she said, her face brightening.

"Sort of.''

But as soon as Laura left the room, Clare sagged back into her chair, folded her arms on the table and lowered her head onto them.

CHAPTER SEVEN

HE HESITATED only a second, his hand poised inches from
the front door. He figured Laura had gone to the hospital
because the only vehicles in the drive were Clare's rental
and Dave's SUV. Laura had told him she'd leave her car
out of the garage so he could get the extension ladder
inside. All of which meant that Clare was alone with the
baby and instinct told Gil that being alone with Clare so
soon after yesterday was probably not a good thing.

Of course, he could head for the back of the house, get
the ladder straightened away and leave without Clare
knowing he'd come at all. The idea was tempting. But
doing so might look as if he were trying to avoid her. And
he couldn't deny that he did want to see her. He gave the
door a firm, loud rap.

The door flew open. He'd barely pulled his hand away
before he was staring down into a pale face.

"Oh," Clare said, holding onto a wriggling Emma. "I
thought you might be Laura. Come in." She turned away
before he could ask why Laura would knock on her own
front door. He followed her and Emma inside.

"I don't know what to do with her," Clare was saying
as he walked into the living room behind her. "I've
changed her and given her some of the bottle Laura left
but she doesn't seem to want to go back to sleep."

"Is she supposed to?"

Her eyes narrowed as if she thought he was being sar-
castic. "I don't know!"

Gil stifled a smile. The plaintive tone in her voice defied any kind of flippant remark. "I came to put the ladder in the garage for Dave," he said, wanting to establish right away that he wasn't there for a follow-up to yesterday.

"Yes, Laura told me you were coming."

He watched her juggling the baby from one arm to the next. "She looks happy enough," he said.

"Who? Laura?"

"*Laura?* I meant Emma. She doesn't seem upset or anything."

Clare peered down at Emma. "I guess not. I suppose I could put her in that chair thing she has."

He nodded, knowing he didn't have any advice to offer.

"Here, you take her while I go get it from the kitchen." She thrust Emma at him.

"What? Hey, I didn't mean—" Gil watched Clare dash from the room, then lowered his gaze to Emma. She gave him a big smile that he found himself automatically returning. He felt his arms relaxing, adjusting to the sensation of the baby's weight.

Solid, but not heavy. Nice and warm. She had Laura's coloring and he wondered which parent she'd most resemble when she grew up. If she was lucky, she'd have a combination of the best of both of them. The prospect of being a godfather didn't seem quite so daunting at that moment. Maybe when she was old enough—whatever age that might be—she and her parents could visit him in New York. He could take her to a Yankees game.

A small bubble popped out of Emma's rosebud mouth. "You like that idea, Emma? A baseball game with your godfather?" He raised one eyebrow up and down and winked at her. A soft coo and gurgle was her response. He laughed aloud. He would have tried another of his limited repertoire of parlor tricks but a slight movement in the room alerted him. Gil jerked his head up and to the right. Clare was watching him from the doorway, a peculiar expression on her face. Heat rose up into his own.

"Got the chair?" he asked, though he could see it hanging from her left hand.

She extended the arm holding the chair. Gil had a feeling she wanted to say something about what she'd just witnessed—him gaga over a baby—but was restraining herself. Clare set the chair on the floor next to the couch and Gil carried Emma over to it, bending down on one knee to slip her into it.

"I think you have to do up those straps, in case she falls out."

"Oh, right." His fingers fumbled with the plastic snap locks. He wished Clare would move away so he could concentrate on the task, rather than on the heady scent wafting from her. When he stood up, she was standing so close he brushed against her and lost his balance. His hand shot out to steady himself, landing on her upper arm perilously close to her breast. He held it there a second longer than he needed to, as if the sweater she was wearing had some kind of magnetic pull.

But when his eyes connected with hers, he removed his hand and mumbled a halfhearted apology. "I should get at that ladder," he added, backing toward the front hall.

She smiled. Enjoying his plunge into stammering adolescence, he wondered? Then she completely took him by surprise.

"When you're finished, come back inside for coffee. If you like."

"Sure. That'd be great."

Outside he found himself rushing to lower the extension ladder and lug it into the garage. He propped it along the interior wall rather than trying to hang it back onto the wall hooks that Laura had mentioned. No doubt he'd be visiting again when Dave was back from the hospital. He could finish the job properly then.

When Clare opened the kitchen door at the side of the house for him, he could smell freshly brewed coffee and baked goods. Emma was perched in her chair in the center of the table, playing happily with the plastic rings and toys hanging from the chair's handle.

Gil stepped inside. "Smells good in here." He cocked his head at Clare. "Did you bake?"

She flushed at the surprise in his voice. Or maybe the color was merely from the heat emanating from the opened oven door. "I made brownies—from a mix. Laura and I are having a video night tonight. When I saw the package in the cupboard, I thought it would be like old times."

"Yeah? I guess girls have different 'old times' than guys," he commented, pulling out a chair. "Our video nights were all about action movies and lots of junk food. If we were lucky, someone might have nipped a few beers from the family fridge."

Clare poured two mugs of coffee and brought them to the table. "I must confess beer entered our video nights on one or two occasions. I do recall a contraband bottle of vodka once. Only once, though. None of us wanted to repeat the experience."

Her laugh was exactly the laugh that Gil remembered. A deep, throaty eruption. When he was seventeen, he'd thought it was the sexiest sound he'd ever heard. The realization that he still did made him pause.

She brought a plate of brownies over to the table and sat down. He took one and bit into it, savoring the jolt of dark chocolate. Sitting across from Clare Morgan in a kitchen brimming with intoxicating scents made Gil feel that he'd died and gone to heaven. It was a snapshot of domestic bliss right out of a Norman Rockwell painting and Gil loved it. But two bites into the brownie, he knew the fantasy was about to burst.

"I took your advice," she said as she nibbled on a brownie. "I went to see Lisa Stuart and showed her the note," she went on to say. "She couldn't tell who might have done it, but I found out something kind of interesting."

"Oh, what was that?"

"Remember Mr. Wolochuk? He taught chemistry and physics."

"Yeah, though I never had him as a teacher. Why?"

"He turned up at my book signing in Hartford. Apparently he lives there now and is retired from teaching. On disability. Anyway—" she paused to sip from her mug "—he and his wife had a child. A son, just after we graduated."

"Uh-huh?" He didn't have a clue where she was going with the story, but the pleasure of sitting across a table from her, watching her every move and not arguing with her about some ridiculous thing, was enough. He drank some coffee and toyed with the idea of another brownie.

"The son's name is Jason." She leaned forward. The look on her face suggested she was about to surprise him. "He's in Lisa Stuart's senior English class. The class I spoke to on Monday morning."

"No kidding. I always thought Wolochuk was an old man."

She laughed again, lower and deeper this time. He felt a glow inside and wished he was the kind of person who could toss off jokes. Anything to hear that laugh one more time.

"Apparently his wife was much younger. Unfortunately they divorced when Jason was a toddler." She ran an index finger around the rim of her coffee mug, as if contemplating what she wanted to say next. Finally she came out with it. "Talking about Wolochuk must have triggered a memory. On the way home I remembered something from…from that day."

Gil's stomach gave a small lurch. Suddenly he could see the cozy coffee klatch fading away. "Oh, yeah? Like what?"

"I had missed one of my chemistry labs and Mr. Wolochuk let me make it up after school."

"Yes, I remember," was all he said. He didn't feel like going back to that day right then but she wasn't to be stopped.

"While I was writing up my experiment I saw Rina Thomas go into Mr. Wolochuk's office. His office was walled off with these windows so you could see inside but not really hear anything. There was some kind of argument. Rina was furious. All red in the face and shouting at him. I don't know what it was about but I'd never seen her behave like that to a teacher. Especially one as mild-mannered as Mr. Wolochuk. Then she stormed out of his office, slamming the door behind her. Mr. Wolochuk put his head down on his desk. I went back to my write-up then because I was afraid he'd catch me looking."

She picked up her coffee and sipped slowly, jiggling some of the toys attached to Emma's infant seat. Gil knew he didn't have to say anything. He could let the talk go onto something else, which was what he wanted. But perhaps she'd be satisfied hearing part of what he knew if not all.

"I know why she was ticked off at him," he said. Clare's face turned his way. She let go of the brightly colored plastic toy. "Rina found out she'd failed a big assignment," he continued. "It meant she wouldn't get a good grade in chemistry which also meant her chance at getting into the program she wanted to in college was in jeopardy. She went there to persuade him to let her rewrite it. He refused.''

''Oh.'' Clare thought for a moment. ''I guess that explains her anger that day.''

She didn't speak for a long time. Gil thought he saw tears shining in her eyes and he bit down on his lips, wishing he hadn't clarified the scene she'd witnessed that day. She was probably asking herself why he and Rina were still close enough for such a confidence. Most of all, why he hadn't told her before. But the whole thing was complicated enough back then. How could he make her understand the peculiar bond he'd once had with Rina— both of them outsiders in a small-town high school.

Emma began to fuss. Her face scrunched up in a wail of frustration and fortunately for Gil, Clare focused on making Emma happy. She got up to retrieve the half-empty bottle of milk from the counter, then removed Emma from her chair.

''You're getting good at that,'' Gil commented as Clare cradled Emma in her arms.

Clare pursed her lips. Obviously still unhappy about his revelation, Gil guessed. The room fell silent, expect for Emma's contented noises as she drank from the bottle.

But after a moment, Clare said, ''Lisa Stuart suggested I should go to the police about the note.'' She paused a beat. ''What do you think?''

''Considering the vandalism at the bookstore, that might not be a bad idea. At the worst, you'll come away feeling slightly foolish.''

''I already do. Maybe I should just forget about it. I'm sure I won't be here longer than another couple of days. I think Dave comes home tomorrow.''

Gil's stomach gave a lurch. He heard a car pull into the drive. ''Sounds like Laura's back,'' he said and stood up. ''I should get going.'' He hesitated, hoping she might extend some offer. Either to stay or to see him again. But she didn't.

"Thanks for the coffee. Oh, and tell Laura I'll come round to see Dave sometime soon." He made for the kitchen door, sensing Clare's eyes on him as he walked out. But other than a low goodbye, she didn't say another word.

IT WAS JUST AFTER TEN by the time Clare and Laura clicked off the TV. Laura had brought home two movies but they'd both been too tired to watch the second. Video night at age thirty-four was a huge leap from sixteen, Clare realized. While Laura checked on Emma, Clare tidied up in the kitchen. Then she turned out the downstairs lights and went up to her room.

Force of habit compelled her to attempt a couple of pages of the novel she was reading. She had just turned out her lamp when she heard a loud metallic noise outside. Laura had warned Clare that raccoons might try to get into the garbage cans she had placed at the end of the drive for pickup next morning. Dismissing the sound as foraging raccoons, she sank under the covers.

She and Laura had enjoyed reminiscing about school and some of their adventures. They'd sidestepped more serious memories about Twin Falls High and Clare was grateful that Laura hadn't peppered her with questions about Gil's visit that morning. In fact, other than raising her eyebrows because Gil had slipped out the back door, Laura had simply expressed relief that the ladder had been stored away.

But Gil's visit was exactly what Clare wanted to contemplate when she was alone in her room later that night. When he'd arrived, she'd been determined to be polite but detached. She wanted to let him know that they could be friends, in spite of their parting the day before. *The past*

was over and done with so let's get on with the present.
Isn't that what he'd implied himself? And it was good
advice, too, even if she and Gil seemed unable to follow
it.

When she'd walked into the living room that afternoon
to find Gil making faces at Emma, Clare knew she'd seen
a side of Gil she'd never dreamed of. Her seventeen-year-
old self could never have envisioned his naked delight at
Emma's smile. She wondered what other layers of Gil
Harper were left to discover and wished suddenly that she
could have had the opportunity to find out. If she could
rewrite the past, Gil might be standing in their own living
room, pulling funny faces at their own baby.

Clare rolled onto her side, staring into the darkness. The
past couldn't be revised no matter how much she wanted
it to be. The fact that Rina was still coming between them
after all these years proved that. She snuggled deeper under the covers, reminding herself that she'd have to try
harder to keep their conversations in the present, when a
clatter outside had her leaping from bed to the window.

Her room looked out to the garage and driveway and
Clare saw that both garbage cans had been knocked over.
She was about to go back to bed when a sudden movement in the hedge separating the drive from the neighbor's
property caught her attention. Clare pressed her face
against the window and saw a figure dart from the hedge
and disappear into the neighbor's backyard.

She hesitated only a second before deciding to check
if the kitchen door had been locked. On the way downstairs, she thought about waking Laura but decided against
it. She had enough to worry about already. The kitchen
was lit only by the reflection of a crescent moon but Clare
didn't turn on the light in case the prowler was still
nearby.

Seeing that the door was securely locked, Clare peered

through the window to the driveway and the side of the yard. Whoever had been lurking around the house seemed to have gone. She waited a moment longer and glanced at the fluorescent clock on the microwave. Midnight. Not many pedestrians about in a residential area at that time, she thought, and the figure she'd seen had definitely not been walking a dog. After a few minutes, she tiptoed back upstairs and slipped into bed. She lay awake for a long time, listening for any more noises from outside. Her last thought, as she eventually drifted off to sleep, was relief that Gil had removed the extension ladder propped against the side of the house.

GIL SWIPED his forearm across his brow, soaking up the beads of perspiration accumulated from almost three hours of carrying cardboard boxes up from the basement, then sorting the detritus of a lifetime into several piles that were now scattered around the small living room.

The real estate agent was going to be getting back to him tomorrow on his counteroffer to the people interested in buying his parents' house. He figured they'd accept his price, even though they were probably going to tear down the house and rebuild. Standing in the center of the room where he'd spent many hours as a kid, Gil was struck with an unexpected longing to go back to those days. Life was so much simpler then. Before Clare Morgan became something more than the girl who sat three seats behind him and one row over in English class.

Of course, she'd been in the same group of kids who'd followed each other all through elementary school and most of high school. But her circle of friends had not been his and they'd scarcely acknowledged each other, except in a formal and distant way. Until a day when he seemed to see her for the very first time.

She'd been called on to answer a question and, judging

by her stammer and rosy complexion, had likely been day-dreaming. It was midmorning on a frosty winter day and the sun had thrown a strip of light straight down the center of the room, spotlighting Clare as she stood to answer. Or try to answer.

Her hair was a flame of color in that drab wintry class-room and she'd tossed it out of her eyes as she got to her feet. Her long milky-white fingers played nervously with the pull cord on her hooded sweatshirt and two rosy cir-cles daubed her pale cheeks. She didn't know the answer and surprisingly, Gil did. If she'd been closer, he'd have whispered it to her. Instead he had to watch her painful embarrassment. Painful because he knew, as did the rest of the class, that she was the top student in that course. But something other than Shakespeare had captured her thoughts that day and her usual quick, articulate response wilted to an apologetic mumble.

On the way out of class, Gil zigzagged ahead of the others to catch up with her. He didn't have the faintest idea what he was going to say. Asking for her phone number right away wasn't a good strategy. Instead, he quipped, "Enjoy your trip?"

She'd turned a blank face toward him. They'd scarcely spoken more than a few words to each other that senior year, even though they'd both been on the fringes of in-tersecting groups throughout their high school years.

"I assume you went south to escape the cold."

A frown this time. He remembered sweating then, guessing he was adding to his idiot-ranking with every word. But he had to finish, however much he regretted his pathetic attempt to be funny. "During English class?"

And to his relief she'd burst into laughter. He ended up walking her to her next class and had her phone number before the next bell.

Gil stood back to survey the room. Time for a break,

he thought. He headed for the kitchen, made some coffee
and took a cup to the living room. He still had to deal
with all the piles that speckled the floor, but what he was
itching to do was to find a reason to go back to the Kingsway home and see Clare. Dave was being discharged from
the hospital after lunch so the handy excuse was there,
waiting for him. The problem was, he wasn't sure if it
was a good idea. Would Clare think he was trying to start
something up again? More to the point, *was he?*

He took a sip of coffee and plunked the mug down
onto the well-used coffee table near the front window.
Clearing out a house was a hell of a job, he decided.
Especially when, at the end, you knew you were losing a
major chunk of your childhood. Not to mention your parents' lives together. There'd only been the three of them,
in spite of his parents' dreams of having more children.
Perhaps that had been a good thing after all, given how
much both had struggled to keep the family afloat after
the lumber mill closed.

The shabbiness of the furniture in this very room was
a sign of that struggle, Gil thought. After his mother had
died, his father had let things go even more. His parents
had been older than those of other kids he'd chummed
with, and in a different social and economic bracket. In
spite of his skill at athletics, he'd never been part of the
in crowd.

That had been one of the links between him and Rina
Thomas. She'd lived on a farm about fifteen miles outside
of town and was bused into school. Gil had been well
aware of the label a lot of the town kids plastered on those
who lived outside. *Country kids.* He suspected the only
real thing separating him from that label had been an address in town. So when Rina Thomas struck up a friendship with him at the end of junior year, he'd been flattered
and grateful. Flattered, because she was one of the most

beautiful girls in the entire school. Grateful, because having a girlfriend meant not worrying about which crowd accepted you. They'd dated just a few months but had remained friends.

Gil finished his coffee. *Enough reminiscing.* He chose a pile at random and began to sort through stacks of receipts and warranties for various appliances long gone. He'd known his parents had been pack rats, but this was unbelievable. He barely glanced at the sheaves of paper he was shoving into a large garbage bag, but one business-size airmail envelope caught his eye. The penmanship on the outside seemed from another era and he noted that the return address belonged to his grandparents. The date stamp was even more interesting. About a month after Gil had been born. He pulled out a single piece of paper written in the same hand as the envelope.

Dear Marion and Desmond,
Mother and I were so happy after we got your telephone call about young Gilbert's birth. Most of all, my pride and joy at having my first and only grandson named after me is immeasurable. I don't think I deserve the honor, but am pleased to accept it. If young Gilbert is half the man his father is, he will be very special indeed. We look forward to seeing him very soon.

Love, Dad

Gil read the letter once more before tucking it back into the envelope. Then he set it on the coffee table and sat down in the chair next to it. He could barely remember his paternal grandfather, who'd died when Gil was only five years old, and wished he could have seen the letter when he'd been a teenager. He'd always hated his name. Being one of the biggest boys at school and a skilled athlete had prevented a lot of ribbing about the name, but still there'd been some. Now he was used to his name and though he didn't like it a whole lot more, at least the letter would make carrying it easier.

He forced himself to get back to work, knowing a plunge into nostalgia would put him seriously behind schedule. He worked steadily until lunch, a hastily prepared sandwich and a can of cola. The room was almost clear when he came upon a large stuffed manila envelope in the last heap. Figuring the envelope more than likely contained old bank statements or tax receipts, Gil almost tossed it into the garbage. But curiosity, and a fear of throwing away even one thing of his parents' that might be important, stopped him. Gil opened the flap and emptied the contents onto the floor.

Newspaper clippings, letters and an assortment of scraps of paper fluttered out. Part of a headline grabbed his attention, pulling him to the floor where he sat, cross-legged, to sift through the collection. The headline read: Local Boy Questioned in Murder Investigation.

Gil's hands trembled. A rush of queasiness struck as he realized that he was looking at a complete history of the worst days of his life.

CHAPTER EIGHT

"TRUST ME, I don't have the magic touch. It's just a co-incidence. She's probably just all cried out," Gil whispered, cradling Emma.

"Whatever you say," Clare whispered back. She raked her fingers through her hair, pushing it away from her face. She was exhausted—she'd have loved to be doing what Emma was doing at that moment. Sleeping peacefully. *Finally.* "Can you put her down carefully in her playpen? It's set up in the living room."

She led Gil from the kitchen to the front of the house and watched anxiously while he gently deposited Emma onto the mattress. Then Clare pulled a blanket over her and they tiptoed from the room. Back in the kitchen, Clare sagged onto a chair and put her head in her hands. "Thank heavens. She's been sobbing for an hour. I fed her, changed her, rocked her, sang to her—you name it."

"*Sang* to her?"

"Out of desperation. I think I just made her cry harder." Clare drank from a glass of water sitting on the table. "You arrived in the nick of time, Gil. I was about to load Emma into my car and drive her to her parents at the hospital."

"I thought Dave would be home by now."

"He was supposed to be but something got delayed. Paperwork or whatever. I was planning to cook dinner for them but—" she looked over her shoulder at the counter where assorted vegetables and packages of food were lined up ''—I'm way too beat now.''

''Maybe the two of us can put something together,'' he suggested.

The offer was tempting but she thought she ought to refuse. If he helped to cook, then surely he'd expect to stay to eat. And the prospect of a whole evening around Gil Harper was daunting. Still, Laura shouldn't have to worry about getting dinner ready by the time she and Dave arrived home.

She quickly made up her mind. ''I think I'll take you up on your offer. I know there are three steaks in the fridge and I saw another in the freezer.''

''I brought a bottle of wine as a welcome home present for Dave,'' Gil said. ''I left it in the car. I'll go get it.'' He was out the door before she could change her mind.

Clare finished off the water and debated whether she ought to check on Emma or not. Maybe give her another five minutes, she decided. She doubted she could handle the stress of looking after an infant full-time. Gil, on the other hand, was proving to be amazingly adept. She really was about to take the baby to Laura when Gil's face had appeared on the other side of the kitchen door, saving her the humiliation.

She pushed her chair away from the table and went to the counter to start preparing a salad. When Gil returned with the wine, he went right to the freezer compartment of the fridge and rummaged through it until he found the other steak.

''I'll defrost this in the microwave,'' he said, ''then if you like, I can wash and peel those vegetables for you.''

Clare was impressed by his efficiency in the kitchen, though not completely surprised by it. The Gil she remembered had been very organized in his schoolwork and she bet the same trait made him a good lawyer. They worked quietly together as if, Clare thought, they'd done this many times before. What she especially liked was the silence. It was the kind of silence she recalled from the days when they did their homework together after school. A comfortable hum of quiet in which neither felt a need to talk.

Still, she doubted they'd been quite this companionable when they were dating. What she remembered most about that period was the incredible awakening of her sexual self. Their first—and last—lovemaking had been fraught with inexperience and breathtaking fear. Clare vividly recalled how worried she'd been afterward about getting pregnant—or worse—losing Gil's respect. But the next day she'd discovered that he had felt the same and they'd made a vow to be careful with this new aspect of their relationship. Even then they'd realized the importance of taking things slowly and of developing an awareness of each other while exploring their sexuality.

Unfortunately, that side of herself had lain dormant far too long over the past few years. Which must have been the reason, Clare decided later, for her sudden trembling when her hand connected with Gil's as she passed him a chopping board.

"Are you all right?" he quickly asked, grasping her fingers in his. "You're shaking."

She tried to laugh it off. "Too much coffee today."

He didn't let go. His eyes zeroed in on her and she knew he didn't believe her. "Sure it's not something else?" he asked softly.

The memory of how her hand felt in his surged through her. Except his hands back then had often been callused and he'd had a habit of biting his fingernails. Not any longer, she thought. She stared down at the strong but well-groomed fingers wrapped around hers and gently slipped free of his grasp. "Maybe lack of sleep," she said.

"You haven't been sleeping well?"

Wrong thing to say. "I hear Laura up with Emma in the night." She looked down at the counter. "Is this enough for a salad?"

He didn't answer right away. She could feel his eyes burning into the back of her neck. "I just thought you might have been worried about the note and the vandalism of your posters."

Clare set down the chopping knife and turned around. "They bothered me, but I feel more frightened by what happened last night."

"What about last night?"

"I heard a noise outside. At first I thought it was a raccoon after the garbage, but when it happened again, I got out of bed to have a look. I saw someone running into the hedge between this place and the neighbor's." The apprehension she'd felt last night returned.

"What did Laura think?"

"I haven't told her yet. I didn't want to disturb her last night—she gets precious little sleep as it is. And this morning she was busy getting things ready for Dave."

"Do you think someone was purposely prowling around the house?"

"I thought that last night, but now I'm not so sure."

"Taken on its own, last night could be nothing at all. But when you add it to what happened at the bookstore and the note in your book…" He paused, adding, "Personally I think you should to go to the police. There should be something on record about this, in case the person comes back and continues to bother Dave and Laura."

"But maybe I'm the one being targeted."

"Whoever's doing this may not know that you've left town and may come back. You can't just drop the matter."

She wanted to, but sensed he was right.

"Look," he said, holding on to her upper arm, "I can see that you're more worried about this than you're letting on. That's why you should do something about it. You have friends here, and we'll help you."

Her eyes flicked upward. There was nothing more in his face than an earnest desire to have her believe him. The fact that he'd used the words *friend* and *we* together was what convinced her. That was why, after a pleasantly surprised Dave and Laura had been wined and dined, Clare didn't protest at all when Gil told them about the night visitor.

"As you said, it might be nothing but I don't like the idea of someone creeping about our house at night," Laura said right away.

Dave agreed. "The new deputy sheriff is a Twin Falls High grad. I'll give him a call in the morning."

"Who is he?" Gil asked.

"Vince Carelli. Remember him? His father used to be president of First National Bank over on Main Street."

"He was my mother's boss at the bank," Clare said. "Vince was a year behind us, I think." She tried to put a name with the face.

"Yes," said Laura. "Tall and chubby with a bad complexion."

"Still that but no more acne," Dave said. "He just got the job about six months ago. I hear he's hoping to make sheriff when Kyle Davis retires."

"It'd be great if you gave him a call, Dave," Gil said, pushing his chair away from the dining-room table. He reached down to collect the dinner plates.

"I'll clean up. You two made the meal for heaven's sake," Laura said, jumping to her feet.

"And we should finish the job," Clare said. "Why don't you help Dave get settled? It's been a long day for both of you."

She saw the protest forming in Laura's face until Dave spoke up. "I wouldn't mind hitting the sack early tonight. Thank you for everything. Clare, for sticking around to help Laura when I know you had to juggle some things to do so. And Gil, for added support—especially getting the ladder away for me."

"It was a good thing the ladder was in the garage last night. I hate to think what might have happened if it was still leaning up against the back of the house," Laura said.

Her comment cast a momentary pall over the room. "How about if I come with you to the sheriff's office tomorrow, Clare?" Gil suggested. "Dave, call me after you've talked to—Carelli?—and let me know the time."

Clare watched as the two arranged her schedule for her and bit back her irritation. After Gil helped Laura escort Dave to the den, he joined Clare in the kitchen where she was loading the dishwasher.

"I hope you don't mind if I tag along," he said. "But I know how intimidating the law can sometimes be when you're...well, feeling vulnerable."

Clare had her back to him and she froze in place at his remark. Was he referring to his own experience seventeen years ago? Likely. She was afraid to turn around, fearing what she might see in his face. When she failed to respond, he gave a slight cough and went on to say, "I'll see you sometime in the morning then."

"Fine," she said and didn't move until the door leading out to the garage and driveway closed behind him.

Slowly sinking into a chair she wiped the dampness in her eyes with the back of her hand and hoped that Laura wouldn't come back to the kitchen for a bit.

What's happening to you? You're not a teenager again. No longer insecure or uncertain about yourself. And you didn't do anything wrong. You only told the truth. What

*you saw. Most of it, anyway. What happened to Gil wasn't
your fault.*

If only she could believe that.

SHE WAS WAITING at the end of the drive when Gil drove
up to the curb. But he'd seen her half a block away, pacing back and forth as the wind tossed her bright coppery
hair. She was wearing the same black cords and turtleneck
she'd worn the night they had coffee together. It was eerie
how she seemed to have taken on her seventeen-year-old
persona after only a week in Twin Falls.

The first night he'd seen her at Dave and Laura's, she'd
looked very much the successful big-city type. Her suit
was stylish but not a couturier design. He supposed clothing like that might come later, with greater financial success. Not that he was an expert on what celebrity authors
wore and judging from the limited wardrobe he'd seen on
her thus far, neither was she. Though to be fair, she hadn't
planned to stay more than a weekend in town.

Maybe the old adage was right about scratching the
surface just a bit to find the original model. Gil figured
that applied to him. Take away the custom-made business
suits and the Wall Street accessories plus a few years of
hard-earned life experience and what did you have? A
confused, scared and angry seventeen-year-old who'd just
discovered the girl of his dreams had feet of clay after all.
Gil sighed. He'd never make a writer, that was for sure.
But he could figure things out as well as the next guy
when it came to betrayals. Which might explain in part
his impetuous comment about the police last night.

He knew at once how she'd taken it, but it wasn't until
he was halfway home that he questioned his rash behavior. Had he simply blurted it out without thinking or had
his unconscious somehow intervened, wanting to get a dig

in? He sincerely hoped not the latter. He hoped that he'd outgrown a need for revenge.

The car idled at the curb while Clare strode toward it. Her normally milky skin was even paler today, highlighting the remnants of childhood freckles sprinkled across the bridge of her nose and upper cheeks. Gil winced as she yanked the car door open, climbed in and slammed it behind her. All without a word.

As he shifted into Drive and took his foot off the brake, she muttered, "I think this is probably a waste of time. Besides, I'm leaving soon anyway. Laura's found a teenager to help her after school. She starts Monday. So I was thinking of leaving…uh, maybe tomorrow."

Gil jerked the steering wheel to the left as he looked sharply her way. She was staring out the passenger window. *"Tomorrow?"* he asked.

Her face turned toward him, her tawny eyes unruffled by the surprise in his voice. "Probably," she murmured. "Laura can manage for the weekend. I have a lot to catch up on at home. I've put aside a lot of projects that can't be ignored any longer, plus there's the rest of my tour. Besides," she said, turning back to the window, "I've been in Twin Falls long enough."

Gil was at a loss for words. His own stay in town was drawing to a close, as well, now that his counteroffer on the house had been accepted. All he had to do was to stick around while they confirmed mortgage approval, sign a few more papers and lock the front door. End of a lifetime in Twin Falls. He'd spent most of the night contemplating that fact and feeling damned ambivalent about it. Especially when he realized his final goodbye would inevitably include Clare Morgan.

That was why he'd toyed with a crazy idea sometime in the middle of the night—an idea he hoped to pitch to Clare after their visit to the sheriff's office. Something that would help chase away the demons of the past, and keep Clare in his life just a bit longer. Gil shot her another look, noting the crescent of pale blue beneath her eyes. The strain of helping Laura with Emma was evident. Unless she wasn't sleeping well for some other reason. He berated himself again for his harsh treatment of her. Although he'd smugly claimed that he'd put the past behind him, he had to admit that he hadn't.

If she were to leave now, he realized, he'd never have a chance to make things right between them. And certainly he'd have no hope of any kind of future with her. He considered telling her about his idea right then, but decided she was far too tense. Better to wait and see how the talk with Deputy Carelli played out.

"I GOTTA ADMIT, I was damn surprised when Dave Kingsway called to tell me you were coming in to see me this morning. Course, I already knew about your success, Clare, being that the town makes a big deal out of any celebrity, especially artists."

Vince Carelli scrunched up his jowly face as he directed his attention to Gil. "I had no idea you were a hotshot lawyer in the Big Apple, Harper. You likely don't recall me 'cause I was a year behind you two. But some of us who didn't make the team back then sure remember guys like you. *The stars.*"

Clare squirmed in her chair. Vince Carelli's affable manner carried a definite edge, she thought. At least where Gil was concerned. She didn't want to spend any more time reminiscing and decided to prompt the deputy sheriff. "This is the note I received," she said, handing over the piece of paper.

"Oh, right." Carelli reached for it. He took his time reading and then lay it on the desk. "So tell me where, when, and how this came into your possession."

Clare tried not to smile. He made it sound as though she'd received stolen goods or contraband. "It was put in a copy of my novel during my talk to a senior English class at Twin Falls High. Then the other night, I saw someone sneaking around the house."

"Get a good look at the guy?"

"Not really. It was quite late and windy that night. Lots of shadows from tree branches bouncing around. The person—I think it was a male, but can't be sure—was wearing one of those hooded sweatshirts, with the hood up."

The deputy leaned forward in his chair, resting his elbows on the desk. "So where'd this guy go when he ran away?"

"Through the hedge along the drive into the neighbor's yard."

He thought for a moment. "Dave also said someone vandalized your posters at the bookstore. One of my officers took that call." He picked up the note again and stared at it for a moment before glancing up at Clare and Gil.

"Frankly, I think the vandalism at the store was the work of some crackpot. Maybe someone who didn't like your book, Clare." He laughed, looking from her to Gil, then back to the note. When they didn't speak, he went on to say, "The note was probably some kid in that class you visited being smart. As to the prowler, there's nothing to suggest he's connected to any of the other. Know what I mean?"

Clare nodded. Coming here was a mistake, she thought.

Carelli heaved a sigh. "Well, I'll get a case file going anyway. But the chance of finding a link to all of this is slight, know what I mean? If either of you decides to leave town before I can get back to you, just give the secretary out there—" he cocked his head toward his closed office door ''—your phone number in New York. If I come up with anything, I'll give you a buzz.''

"What about interviewing the kids in the English class? Someone could have noticed another student writing the note and slipping it inside the book."

Carelli briefly thought over Gil's suggestion and then shook his head. "I could send an officer out to talk to them, sure. But I doubt anyone would spill the beans. You know how kids hate to rat on each other." His impassive face turned from Gil to Clare.

She dropped her eyes to her hands clasped on her lap. Was it her imagination that this last phrase had been directed at her rather than Gil? She inhaled slowly, forcing such paranoia from her mind.

Carelli pushed his chair back from his desk and stood up. He hoisted up his belt buckle half-hidden beneath a bulging abdomen. "As I said, we'll make some inquiries and let you know. It was real nice seeing you two again. It's been a long time, hasn't it?"

Clare nodded. A long time, she was thinking, and a waste of time, too. Just as she'd predicted. She and Gil got up to leave.

"Don't forget to give my secretary that phone number," Carelli reminded her as Clare turned away. "And good luck with the book."

Clare saw Gil open the office door. She managed a polite but faint smile. "Thanks."

"I haven't got a copy yet, but folks around here say it's pretty good." He paused. "Is it true what the newspaper said?"

Clare's head swung sharply around. "What?"

"The piece in the *Spectator*. It said your book was really the story about Rina Thomas. That true?"

She flushed, biting down hard on her lip. His genial face gave no sign of provocation. Relax, she told herself.

He's just repeating what everyone else has asked since the article was published.

"It's just a novel, Vince. But some events in the book are loosely based on my own memories and experiences."

He nodded thoughtfully. "Well, guess I should buy myself a copy and check it out." He came from behind his desk and walked Clare to where Gil was waiting.

"Thanks again," Clare said.

Carelli tipped his index finger to his forehead in a good-bye salute and shut the door behind them.

"You were right," Gil whispered as soon as the door closed. "That was a waste of time."

Clare blew out a mouthful of air. Now wasn't the time for the I-told-you-so remark she felt like making. She and Gil walked silently along the hall to the reception area at the front of the building. The sheriff's office door, farther down the hall from Vince Carelli's, was closed.

As they passed it, Gil said, "Maybe we should talk to the sheriff, too."

Clare frowned. "That would look bad, wouldn't it? As if we didn't trust Vince to do his job."

"Frankly, I don't. The guy looks like the type who'd say anything to get rid of us and then just go back to whatever he was doing before we interrupted him."

"Perhaps he's right, though. Maybe the chances of finding anything out are slim."

Gil shrugged. "Maybe. Anyway, it's your call. There's the secretary," he said, pointing to a woman sitting at a computer in a small partitioned corner of the reception area.

They walked up to the counter and when the woman looked up, a big warm smile crossed her face. "Gil Harper! I thought that might be you when you came in a few minutes ago, but I was busy on the phone and didn't get a chance to say hi." Her eyes twinkled. "Don't you remember me? Come on, I haven't changed that much. Other than a few extra pounds.''

Clare had been thinking the woman looked familiar. She glanced at Gil, who was returning the smile. "Hey! Beth Moffatt?''

"Not Moffatt anymore. I married Joey Silverstein. He was in my year, too, so maybe you don't know him." She looked at Clare. "Nice to see you, too, Clare. I was a year ahead of you and Gil, but we go way back. Don't we, Gil?''

Clare smiled and turned her gaze to Gil, who explained, "Beth's father and mine worked together at the lumber mill. Our parents played euchre together every Saturday night for years.''

Gil leaned on the counter. "How is your family, by the way? Your brother? Your parents?''

"My mom's in a retirement condo in Hartford." Beth's face sobered. "Dad passed away a year or so ago. Eddie's fine. Has a family of his own now and lives in Greenwich." She paused. "I was sorry to hear about your father, Gil. He was such a nice man.''

Gil pursed his lips and gave a quick nod. "Thanks. So, Vince Carelli asked Clare to leave her home phone number with you. He's checking out an incident for her.''

"Okay." Beth reached for a pad and pen.

Clare gave her the number and wandered toward the front door while Gil and Beth continued to chat a bit more. Finally he joined her and, after calling out another goodbye to Beth, placed his hand in the center of Clare's lower back as he guided her out the door.

"Small world," he commented as they emerged onto the sidewalk.

"Small town," Clare said.

"You said it. Listen," he said, stopping in the middle

of the sidewalk, "would you like to go somewhere for a coffee?"

The invitation took her aback after the coolness that had sprung up between them since last night. "I've had enough coffee today, thanks Gil. But what about a walk? It's such a nice day. Maybe we could go by the bookstore and see if the manager has found out anything more about the vandalism thing."

His smile brought an unexpected shiver. "Lead the way," he said, cupping her elbow with his hand.

The sensation of his touch was both familiar and oddly reassuring. The short walk to the store was made in silence, but this time, it was a companionable one. Clare felt herself relax, enjoying the faint warmth of the autumn sun on her face and the comforting pressure of Gil's hand on her arm. The day was going to be just fine after all, she was thinking as she preceded Gil into Novel Idea.

But the first face she saw inside chased away that notion. Jeff Withers glanced up at her from a book he was perusing and smiled.

CHAPTER NINE

SHE FROZE midstep. Then, regaining her composure, Clare smiled back at Withers and continued on to the rear of the bookstore. As Gil caught up with her, he bent his head down to whisper, "Who was that?"

"Hmm?" Clare peered about for the manager while the only sales clerk she saw rang up an order for a customer.

"The guy that stopped you in your tracks back there. The one with the Cheshire grin."

"Jeff Withers," Clare said. "The reporter who interviewed me last Saturday."

"Ahh. That explains it."

"Explains what?"

"Why his smile hit the floor when you walked past him. I'd have liked to have seen *your* face."

Clare grinned. "I gave him the look I honed in a classroom of rebellious adolescents."

"Brrr. I can feel a chill just imagining it."

She laughed, catching her lower lip in her teeth. Their eyes met and for a breathtaking instant, Clare found herself back in time. But the moment vanished as the clerk finished her task and came toward them.

"Can I help you?" she asked.

"Is the manager in today?"

"She is, but she had to pop out for a minute. She may be back in ten or fifteen minutes. Can I take a message or something?" The young girl frowned slightly, then smiled. "Aren't you Clare Morgan? The author who was in here last Saturday for the book signing?"

"Yes."

The frown returned. "I'm so sorry about what happened with your posters. Nothing like that has ever happened before. It's so awful. We all felt real bad."

Clare nodded. "I was wondering if you still have the posters. I thought I'd take them to the police."

"Oh the police already saw them," the clerk said, waving a dismissive hand. "They said we might as well throw them out. I hope that was okay," she said anxiously, looking from Clare to Gil and back to Clare again. "I mean, we all thought you'd left town until you called the other day, but by then it was too late."

"Was it the deputy sheriff who came around?" Gil asked, thinking of Vince Carelli's casual dismissal of the incident.

"I can't say. I wasn't on shift then. I just heard about it."

Clare turned to Gil and shrugged. "Nothing we can do here, I guess. Shall we go?"

Gil nodded.

As Clare neared Jeff Withers, he reached out a hand to stop her. "Miss Morgan? Sorry to interrupt, but I wondered if I could ask you a few more questions sometime about your book."

He was really too much, she thought. "Sorry, Mr. Withers. Once burned, twice shy as the saying goes." She followed Gil to the door.

But Withers wasn't taking no for an answer. He tagged along behind her, saying, "I'm sorry about that. My editor went to work on the piece to make it a bit more...well, sensational, you might say. I didn't approve at all of some of the changes, but hey, I'm the low man on the totem pole in the newsroom. I just wanted you to know that I've decided to write my own book about the Rina Thomas case.''

Clare stopped walking, half turning his way.

Pressing his advantage, Withers continued. ''Your...uh, novel has piqued my curiosity. A small-town murder that never got solved. That could mean the murderer is still around, right? So I wondered if you'd have any real memories of the case you might share with me.'' He uttered a slight laugh. ''As opposed to the fictional memories in your book, that is.''

''Sorry, but I'm leaving town tomorrow.'' She pushed open the door and stepped out onto the sidewalk where Gil was waiting. Puzzled by the expression on her face, moved toward her.

The door opened again as Withers came out behind her. ''Maybe you could give me your phone number in New York or are you in the phone book?''

''I said I wasn't interested, Mr. Withers, and I've no intention of giving you my phone number.''

Gil spoke up. ''What's going on here?''

Withers turned to Gil. ''And you would be—?''

''A friend of Clare and personally, I think Clare is being far too kind even to talk to you, Mr. Withers. I suggest you leave us alone.'' He linked his arm through Clare's and pulled her away from the bookstore.

''I've got a source for the book anyway. Someone who was there on the scene, so to speak,'' Withers called after them. ''Oh, one more thing, Miss Morgan. Have you ever asked your mother the real reason why you both left Twin Falls that summer after Rina's murder?''

Clare slowed down. She glanced up at Gil and murmured, ''What's he talking about now? Should I go back and find out what he means?''

Gil shook his head. He turned around and said, in a

clipped low voice that carried easily all the way to Withers, "We've been polite too long. Get lost."

Withers took a step backward. "Just ask your mother, Miss Morgan, the next time you're talking to her. And if you change your mind, you know where to find me." He spun around and headed along the sidewalk in the other direction.

Clare's legs felt too heavy to move. She took a deep breath, trying to calm herself. "I don't know why I let that guy get to me. He really is obnoxious."

"Let's go over there and sit for a minute," Gil said, pointing to a small park across the street. Without waiting for her reply, he led her to a bench. "You okay?" he asked quietly, sitting next to her.

She nodded.

Gil placed his hand on top of hers. "Look, you're not very convincing at pretending this hasn't upset you. What was all that about your mother?"

"I've no idea, Gil. I really don't. We moved to New Jersey so Mom could be closer to me while I was at college. What worries me is this book idea he has. I wonder who the so-called source is. Who could it be?"

"Maybe it was all a lie. A ploy to get you to talk."

"Perhaps." She stared down at Gil's hand resting lightly on hers. It felt warm and reassuring and she had no inclination at all to remove hers. "I guess it's a good thing I'm leaving. If I encountered Withers again, I'd be afraid I'd punch him or something."

Gil gave a hard laugh. "If I didn't do it first." He looked down, too, as if realizing for the first time that his hand still covered hers. He slowly pulled his away. Clare wanted to clasp onto his fingers before they left, but lacked the nerve. How would he interpret a move like that, she wondered?

"Listen," Gil said, bringing the hand that seconds ago

had been on hers up to his mouth, "there's something I want to suggest to you and in light of what's just happened, you may be interested."

Clare silently watched him rub his index finger along his upper lip an instant longer before dropping his hand to his side. She suddenly recalled him doing something similar years ago, the first time they'd held hands on the way home from school. Then, he'd brought her fingers up to his lips and ever so quickly kissed them before releasing her hand. She'd been so charmed by the action. Now, she was puzzled. He seemed to be sending out all kinds of mixed messages.

"I was sorting through some stuff at my parents' house the other day," he went on, oblivious to her watchful stare, "and came across something that was kind of disturbing. At least, I was surprised at how bothered I was about it."

"What?"

He cleared his throat. "Apparently, my parents kept all these newspaper clippings about the murder. Especially the ones about my being questioned. If you recall, I was never actually named in the papers but everyone in town knew who the local boy under investigation was." He stopped for a moment, staring off into space.

"The clippings were with some anonymous letters that my parents must have received at the time." He grimaced. "Nasty, crude notes advising my parents to leave town, et cetera. You can imagine the contents and the mentality of the people who sent them."

She could, but what really struck her was the vulnerability in his face. "That must have been awful for your parents," she whispered.

"I'm sure. I just don't understand why they kept them. I'd have burnt everything."

"Maybe they expected to find out who'd written them

someday. Or maybe they just wanted to keep you from finding out about them and hid them away, then forgot about them," she added. She wasn't sure if she believed any of those scenarios, but knew she had to say something.

Gil shrugged. "Maybe. I guess there's no point trying to come up with a reason now. But there is something I can do."

"What?"

"I know I said the other day that I've put this mess behind me and for the most part, I have, but when I found that stuff, I realized for the first time the impact it must have had on my parents. How it must have affected their everyday lives in a way I never imagined. I was so caught up in my own part in everything and going off to college and so on, that I just didn't think about them."

Clare wondered if she'd been part of that "so on" he'd mentioned. Their breakup had happened just after his release from questioning. She kept her eyes on his, sensing that to look away would be cowardly. The pain he must have experienced then still glimmered there. Not knowing what to say, she kept silent.

After a long moment, he said, "I've decided to do some investigating into the case myself."

She couldn't believe what she was hearing. Had he lost his mind? Clare felt her lips move soundlessly.

"I know." He rushed on to say, "It sounds crazy, but I spent a lot of time last night going over this. I'm never going to really get rid of this particular demon unless I face it head-on. And I want to do it for my parents. I want to publicly prove to everyone in Twin Falls who remembers the case or any of the creeps who wrote those letters to know who really killed Rina Thomas."

"I—I don't know how you expect to find that out, Gil. I mean, it's been seventeen years. And you're not a police officer or a private detective or anything like that. How would you go about this?''

''I'll start by doing some research, then asking a lot of questions. You're right. I don't know anything about police work, but I sure as hell know how to ask questions. I called my office this morning and extended my leave. The closing date on the house isn't for another month so I've got a place to stay.'' He stretched out a hand to hers again. ''This is what I want to know—are you interested in helping me out with this?''

''Me?'' Clare heard herself sputtering.

''You must have some unresolved feelings about this case.''

''I...what kind of feelings?''

''Curiosity, for one. Maybe some anger.''

''Anger? About what?''

He hesitated, as if uncertain whether he ought to say what was on his mind. ''Maybe anger because Rina's death was the end of a lot of other things, too. The pall over graduation itself was bad enough, but there was no grad prom, remember? And then there was...well, what happened to us.''

Clare turned her face aside. Here it comes, she was thinking. The hurtful rebuke. The pent-up anger. ''I'm not following you, Gil,'' she finally said, looking back at him.

''Do you think we'd still have split up if Rina Thomas hadn't been killed?''

Yes, I do. Because I saw the two of you very cozy to-gether on the football field that day. The urge to get up and leave was overwhelming, but Clare forced herself to maintain eye contact. She took a deep breath but still her voice quavered when she answered. ''There's no point speculating about what might have happened back then, Gil. It's too late.''

He pulled back as if she'd struck him. After a moment,

he said, "Too late for us, perhaps. But never too late to find out the truth. And I mean to do just that." He stood up. "I should go. If you want a ride back to Dave's place…"

Clare shook her head. "No, I'll walk from here. Thanks for coming with me this morning."

He paused a moment longer. "If you decide you're interested after all, let me know," he said and walked across the street.

She watched him disappear down the street toward his parked car and waited until she felt able to navigate on legs that felt very rubbery. On the walk to Dave and Laura's, Clare made two decisions. First, that she would not postpone her plans to leave Twin Falls in the morning. And second, that she would phone her mother. As much as she hated to admit it, she knew she couldn't wait until she got back to New York to find out what Jeff Withers had been insinuating.

"Hi, Mom."

"Clare? This is a surprise. Is anything wrong? Where are you calling from?"

"I'm still at Laura and Dave's place, in Twin Falls."

"How was the christening? And the baby? Is she adorable?"

"Very. And it all went well."

"I thought you were only staying for the weekend. Why are you still there?"

"Last Monday, when I was doing the book signing in Hartford, Dave fell off a ladder and broke his leg. He's okay, but Laura needed someone to help her out and stay with Emma when she was at the hospital."

"Good heavens! And that person was *you?*"

Clare pictured the expression on her mother's face. "I know, as incredible as that seems."

"So how did it go? Make you want to reconsider having children?"

"Not at all. In fact, I needed help myself."

"What about Laura's parents? Are they still around?"

"Gone to Florida for the winter."

"I see. So when do your duties wrap up there?"

"I plan to leave tomorrow. But there's one thing, Mom. Last weekend I was interviewed by a reporter for the *Spectator*—"

"How nice!"

"Not really. The guy made a big deal of the similarities between my book and the Rina Thomas murder."

There was a slight pause. "But didn't you expect that might happen, dear? I mean, did you really think that people who knew about that case wouldn't make the comparison?"

Clare closed her eyes, tired of the question. "I know, Mom, I know. But today I met the reporter again and he said something very odd. Something I didn't understand at all."

"Oh? What was it?"

"He...uh, he told me to ask you the real reason for our moving away from Twin Falls that summer. After Rina was killed." She waited a long time for her mother to respond. "Mom? Are you there?"

There was a light clearing of throat, followed by her mother's voice, thinly distant. "Yes, dear. I'm here. I'm...uh, not sure why he would say that. What was the context?"

Clare thought for a moment. She'd hoped not to have to tell her mother all about the notes and the vandalism. Her mother was a worrier and would only be upset. "He's going to write a book about the case, apparently, and he'd asked me if I would answer some questions for him."

"What kind of questions? You don't know any more about what happened than anyone else, surely."

"Exactly. Anyway, I kind of told him to get lost and then just before he left, he made that comment about you."

Another pause. "I see."

"So what did he mean, Mom? I always assumed we moved so you could live near me while I was at college."

"Yes, there was that, dear." Her mother lowered her voice. "But there was something else, too, that made leaving necessary. I had hoped not to have to tell you about it, but if you think it's important…"

Clare frowned, unsure where the conversation was going. "If you'd rather not tell me, it's fine. It's not as if I intend to see the guy again."

"Just a minute, dear, while I close the bedroom door."

Clare waited for her mother to return. She probably should never have brought up the matter, but now that her curiosity was aroused she couldn't drop it. After a moment, her mother came back to the phone.

"It's not a long story, but messy, I'm afraid. Right around the time that girl was murdered, some money went missing from the bank. Because I was in charge of the special accounts like some of the trust funds, the inquiry focused on me. Of course I was shocked, and even more horrified that my boss would even suspect I might have had something to do with it."

"So what happened? Did they find out who took the money?"

"No, and things got very unpleasant. People started whispering about me behind my back. Eventually I was shifted into another department. It was made to seem like a lateral move, but we all knew it wasn't. Finally, I was offered the choice to leave with six months' severance or to undergo a full audit with the possibility of a criminal charge.''

Clare couldn't speak at first. She tried to imagine how her mother—a single parent with a daughter about to head off to college—had coped. ''That's awful, Mom. I—I'm so sorry you had to go through that. Why didn't you tell me?''

''Darling, you had your own difficulties at the time. Remember? The murder, breaking up with Gil—was a hard time for all of us. Most of all, for that poor girl's parents. Did you ever hear what happened to them?''

Clare's head was spinning. She wanted to get back to the bank story. ''I'm not sure. I think Laura told me once that one of Rina's parents died shortly after the murder and that the farm was sold.''

''So tragic for them. So sad.''

Clare waited a moment longer, then said. ''Mom, this bank thing sounds very suspicious to me. I mean, if someone there was defrauding the bank why wouldn't the manager go to the police right away? It doesn't make sense.''

''He told me he wanted to spare me. That he'd be satisfied if I just left town.''

''But that's crazy. You didn't do anything.'' She heard a sigh come across the line.

''I know, dear. But I couldn't prove my innocence. I'd been working overtime a few nights alone. I had access to the funds and Mr. Carelli, the manager, knew I had a lot of debts. I felt completely powerless. I'd never been so frightened in all my life.''

''It sounds to me like he was intimidating you.''

''Not at all. He was very upset about the whole thing, too. He said because of my good record that he wanted to give me the benefit of the doubt. That he knew I had you to take care of, and he was willing to cover the missing funds through some special insurance he had.'' There was a brief silence and then she said, "But at the same time, he felt that however much he believed me, he had to consider the other employees. There was a matter of trust."

Clare shook her head in disbelief. She couldn't understand how her mother could have let herself be coerced into such an agreement. When she was able to speak, she asked, "Did they ever find out who took the money?"

"I don't think so. One of the tellers—her name was Fran Dutton—kept in touch with me for a while after our move to New Jersey. She said the mystery was never solved. Also, that the funds stopped disappearing." Her mother's voice cracked. "That made it worse, you know. Because the money stopped going missing after I left. I just don't understand it myself."

"I think it's obvious. Someone was framing you."

"Framing me? Good heavens, you sound like someone in a TV show."

"But Mom, think about it. That has to be the explanation. For some reason, someone wanted to get you into trouble."

A heavy sigh. "Dear, there was no reason for that. I mean, I had no social life at the time, and I doubt I had any enemies at work. Until this happened, I'd always considered myself to be liked by everyone. Why would anyone want to make me out to be a thief? That's what doesn't make sense."

"So why didn't you just quit the bank and look for work somewhere else in town?"

"Honestly, I couldn't bear to be in town after what happened. I would worry about every second glance, or think people were whispering about me. You know how people talk."

She certainly did. Now the sudden decision to move and the quick sale of their house made sense to her.

"Well, Mom, I don't know what to say. I'm so sorry that you had to go through all that by yourself."

"I know, dear. But it's all in the past and frankly, best left there."

"So you've no interest in trying to find out what happened and why?"

"Not at all. I've made a new life for myself here, and I'm perfectly happy with it." She was quiet for a moment, then added, "Though I resent the fact that some people in Twin Falls think I'm a thief. Still, there's nothing I can do about it after all these years."

An idea was taking shape in Clare's mind. "Maybe not you, but perhaps I could make some inquiries while I'm here in town."

"I thought you were leaving tomorrow?"

"I may change my plans."

"Darling, there's nothing you can do. Really. Mr. Carelli is dead, I believe. What's the point of dredging it all up now?"

"Because I have a feeling that's going to happen regardless. Especially if this reporter goes through with his idea of writing a book."

"You know yourself not many people actually follow through on these ideas, Clare. I'd drop the matter, if I were you."

"Perhaps," Clare demurred. "Anyway, thanks for being so honest with me."

"I should have told you years ago, but once we were in New Jersey, I had the feeling we both wanted to start all over."

True enough, Clare was thinking. She thanked her mother, promising to call when she was back in New York, and switched off her cell phone. In spite of her mother's advice to let the matter stay in the past, Clare was beginning to think otherwise. She remembered what

Gil had said that afternoon, about discovering the truth for his parents. A way of making up to them, in some small way, for the pain that the whole case had brought them.

She got up from the bed and began to search through her purse for the business card Gil had given her the other day. When she found it, she sat down to think through exactly what she wanted to say. Then she picked up her cell phone again and punched in his number.

FOR A SECOND, Gil thought he was still dreaming. He'd been holding Clare in his arms, trying to persuade her to go to the prom with him, and the next instant her low, urgent voice was at his ear. He sat up, dropping the pillow he'd been clutching when his cell phone had rung.

"Don't tell me I woke you? It's not eleven yet."

"Hmm? Uh, no…no. But I was about to hit the sack. I finished the last of the packing after dinner and got everything ready for the pickup tomorrow."

"Pickup?"

"I'm sending most of the stuff to one of those charities that sells it to secondhand stores. Some outfit in Hartford. Has…uh…something come up there? With Dave?"

"No, everything's fine. Just that I called my mother tonight."

"Oh yeah? How is she?" Gil rubbed a hand across his bleary eyes, wondering where she was heading with this totally out of the blue call. He couldn't even remember the last time Clare Morgan had phoned him. Back sometime when the future still looked promising.

She didn't answer for a moment. "Do you remember what that reporter said today about my mother?"

He did, but what was really etched in his mind was the look on her face at the end of their talk on the bench. When he'd made the remark about things being too late for them. Not that they both didn't know he was right, but he saw at once that she'd taken it as yet another reminder of her rejection of him years ago. She was probably thinking he'd never let her forget that she'd told on him to the police. Gil had his own burden to carry from that time. Betraying him, he suspected, was Clare's.

"Something about why you two left town."

"Right. He told me to ask Mom why we left so quickly that summer." There was a slight catch in her voice then and she paused. "That comment was bugging me all day so tonight I called my mother and…well, she told me something strange, but interesting."

Gil sat up farther against the headboard of his childhood bed. "What did she say?"

"She told me that some money had gone missing in the bank in the days before or after Rina was killed. I'm not sure exactly when. Suspicion was directed at Mom because she was the person who checked all the debits and credits every day, and she had access to some special accounts."

Gil frowned. He had a feeling where this was going. "And what happened?"

"Her boss, Mr. Carelli, assured her that he believed her when she denied taking any money but felt he had to do something about it."

"Did he call the police?"

"No, that was the strange part. He said he knew she had to support me on her own and didn't want to create any extra hardship for her. So he offered her the chance to quit and leave town, with the promise that she wouldn't talk about it to anyone."

"No bank manager in his right mind would do that. Did she realize that her leaving would be an implicit admission of guilt?"

When Clare finally spoke, her voice was wobbly. "I'm

sure she did. I think she felt she had no options. She certainly couldn't have afforded a lawyer to file a wrongful dismissal suit and Mr. Carelli showed her the evidence he had. She simply had no explanation for as to how the money disappeared and all fingers—literally—pointed to her.''

She stopped talking for a long moment, and Gil thought he heard her blowing her nose. He wished he could be there to wrap his arms around her and comfort her, though with their history, she would probably brush him off.

''I'm very sorry, Clare. It must have been awful for your mother.'' He didn't know what more to say, still unsure of her reason for calling.

''It was. She kept insisting it was all behind her but, I could hear something in her voice when she was talking about it. Hurt and that frustration you have when you know you're innocent but no one believes you.''

Gil wondered if she recognized the irony in what she'd just said. He was tempted to quip that yes, he could relate to all of the above, especially the part where no one believes you. *It's even worse,* he thought, *when* that no one is someone you love. But that would be a sure way of eliminating Clare Morgan permanently from his life. So he said nothing at all, figuring she'd eventually get around to the real purpose of the phone call.

She did, a minute later. ''Remember when you said today that you wanted to find out the truth behind Rina's murder so that you could restore your parents' good name in the community? At least, that's how I interpreted what you said.''

''That's exactly it. Why?'' He swung his legs over the side of the bed. Some premonition of what she was about to say set his heart pounding.

''After I got off the phone with Mom, I decided that I wanted to do the same thing for her. She still carries this…this burden of doubt around with her. That's probably why she's never wanted to come back here for even a visit. So, I've decided to take you up on your proposal.''

For a second, Gil wondered what proposal he'd actually made that day. Maybe this was still part of his crazy dream.

"Did you hear what I said?'' she was asking.

"Uh, yes, I did. Just that I'm a bit surprised and… well…maybe confused, too. You sure about this? What about the rest of your book tour? Getting back to the city?''

"I'm calling my publisher first thing in the morning. I didn't have anything else booked until the end of the month anyway. I—I just wanted to call you right away to find out if you still meant it. About the two of us looking for Rina's killer.''

Said like that, the idea chilled him. *Had they both lost their minds?* Too late to back off now. Besides, the prospect of being around Clare another few days was very appealing.

"That's great. Listen, how about if we get together in the morning? Someplace private is better. We don't want anyone overhearing. And it may be best not to tell Dave and Laura right away. What do you think?''

After a slight pause, she said, "I agree. There's a lot we have to discuss and a public place isn't suitable. But where?''

"Do you want to come over here?''

A longer pause. She hadn't been in his house since the night before Rina Thomas was murdered. "Sure. Okay. I'll bring coffee. See you about—?''

"Nine,'' he quickly said. "You'll be up early anyway, because of Emma.''

"Right you are. See you then. And...thanks Gil, for letting me change my mind." She hung up.

Gil sat on the edge of the bed for another few minutes, just to convince himself that he was awake and not still dreaming.

CHAPTER TEN

"I THOUGHT YOU were leaving today." Laura was perplexed.

Clare couldn't think of a credible explanation for her friend. In spite of Gil's suggestion that they keep their plan a secret, Clare knew she couldn't deceive Laura and Dave. Besides, experience had taught her that one lie usually led to another.

"Sit down, Laura. I have to meet Gil at nine o'clock," she said, ignoring Laura's widening eyes, "and this may take a few minutes." Then she gave a brief summary of the encounter with Jeff Withers and the subsequent phone call to her mother.

Laura's face got redder with each new detail. "This is unbelievable," she kept repeating. When Clare finished, Laura said, "I can't believe any of this."

"Believe it," Clare muttered. "So after I talked to Mom, I knew I had to do for her what Gil was doing for his parents. I thought about this all last night, after I called Gil. It's about time the record was set straight. You know?"

Laura nodded. "I can understand that, but Clare, you and Gil aren't private detectives. What makes you so sure people will speak to you? And what makes you so sure you and Gil…I mean…I can't see the two of you working together as if you didn't have a past."

She'd been waiting for Laura to bring that up. "I understand what you're saying. But we're adults now—I think we can make an effort to keep the present and the past separate. Anyway, we're going to try. Searching for information is going to be a challenge, but I know how to research, and Gil has contacts in law enforcement.''

"Here? In Twin Falls?"

"Well, in New York."

Laura held up her hands in a there-you-go kind of gesture. "Frankly, I've seen a lot of tension between you two over the last couple of days. Are you sure you know what you're doing?"

Clare gave her friend a little smile, "Not exactly. But I'm hoping Gil and I can put aside our...issues with one another while we do this."

"*Issues?* Now you're sounding like one of those so-called experts on a talk show. I'd say you two have more than just issues between you."

Clare felt her face heat up, but she refused to back down. "We have a painful and unresolved history, Laura. I'm not naive enough to think this is going to result in some miraculous change but I'm hoping—since we're both Emma's godparents—that we can come to some kind of friendly understanding."

Laura shook her head. "Psychobabble, Clare. Don't kid yourself. The plain truth is, you and Gil haven't forgiven one another. Until you do, you're never going to reach that *friends* state. And frankly, Clare," she added, "I don't want to see you get hurt."

Laura's bluntness was a trait that Clare had always both admired and feared. She knew there was no point arguing with her and besides, an inner voice told her Laura was right. Forgiveness. A simple word for such a complex act.

"Promise you and Dave won't breathe a word of this to anyone," she went on to say, putting an end to any further talk about her and Gil.

"Of course we won't."

"Not even to Anne-Marie."

"No one, Clare. God!" Laura rolled her eyes.

"Okay. I should go now." Clare got up and collected her purse and coat from the chair next to hers. She stared out the window in the kitchen door. "What a miserable day."

"Tell me about it," Laura moaned. "I was hoping to take Emma for a big walk today. But we can't complain— the weather's been great so far this fall."

Clare slipped into her coat and was about to walk out when Laura asked, "So what are your plans for staying on? Are you giving yourself a deadline?"

"I don't know about Gil, but I'll have to have one. I've already scheduled too many things."

"You're going to stay here, though, aren't you?"

Clare hesitated. She hadn't considered where she would stay. "Isn't the student who's helping you going to be living with you during the week?"

"Yes, but she doesn't come until tomorrow afternoon."

"Then I'll go to a hotel."

"Oh, Clare! I hate to think of you spending all that money on a hotel. Maybe we can work something out."

Clare buttoned up her coat and grinned. "Now you sound like my mother."

"Yeah, well, someone has to do the job when the real one is unavailable."

"I think Emma needs one hundred per cent of you, Laura honey. I'll give you a call if I'm going to be here for dinner. Is that okay? Maybe we can order in—my treat."

She waved a goodbye and went out the door. Her car was behind Laura's in the drive, almost at the sidewalk. She clutched her coat tightly around her neck and ducked her head against the rain. While she was fumbling for her keys, she noticed a movement at her right, from the side of the house. She spun around to see a boy in a nylon windbreaker with a hood over his head dashing toward the street.

"Hey!" she hollered. She dropped her purse onto the hood of the car and took off after him.

He headed for the nearest intersection and was about to run across the street when a car pulled in front of him, forcing him to a halt. His head swerved her way and as Clare got closer, she recognized him. Jason Wolochuk. As soon as the car made its turn, Jason sprinted across and rounded the corner. There was no way she'd catch up to him, but at least she knew whom to confront when the time was right.

Clare ran back to the car, got her purse and climbed inside. She waited, her heart pounding, while the engine warmed up. It was obvious that the boy had been sneaking around, maybe spying on her and Laura in the kitchen. Clare shivered. At least it wasn't the middle of the night.

Then it hit her. Jason had to be the note sender. He'd been in Lisa's English class. She wondered how he knew where she was staying, but then remembered that the day she'd gone back to see Lisa Stuart, Jason had appeared in the classroom door. He could have been out in the hall listening in the whole time. Hadn't Clare mentioned to Lisa that she was staying with Laura and Dave Kingsway? He could have easily looked up their address in the phone book. What she couldn't figure out was his motive for doing such a thing.

She reversed onto the street and headed for Gil's house. Maybe he'd have an idea. As it turned out, Gil had a suggestion instead.

"Why don't we just go see him and find out?" he asked as soon as she filled him in on what had happened.

They were standing in the middle of the tiny front hall of his parents' bungalow. Taped cartons were stacked along the wall and Clare could see more in the living room to her left. "Sure," she said, looking around her. "But why don't we make some plans first? I mean, we want to know what we want to ask him."

"I know exactly what I want to say to him," Gil muttered.

The grimness in his face startled her. He seems to be taking this a lot more seriously than I am, she thought. She moved past him toward the living room. "You've got everything packed up, I see."

"Almost. I'm giving the rest of the furniture and appliances to the local Rotary Club for distribution to people in the area. The rest is being picked up on Monday by an outfit in Hartford."

"So you told me." The room now looked very different from the one she remembered. When they were dating, Gil's house had been a second home for Clare—a place to hang out after school. Gil's mother didn't work and always had a supply of homemade cookies or other treats on hand. Clare and Gil would chat in the kitchen with her, load up plates of goodies and head off to his bedroom or the living room to listen to music and do their homework. The lack of frills in the Harper household was more than compensated for by the warmth. It had always been a stark contrast to Clare's own home and single mother struggling to maintain a certain lifestyle.

For the first time, Clare realized how the bank manager might have automatically suspected her mother of embezzlement. She had worked a lot of overtime and always had bills to pay. But then, her mother's love of clothes and other luxuries ate up a lot of her hard-earned money. "_ place doesn't seem the same, does it? Without _ people, I mean."

Clare turned to Gil, standing at her side. "Not at all. But I suppose the people are what make a house a home."

"Nicely put," he said with a smile. "Just like a writer."

"I hope my writing isn't as corny."

"Corny is okay sometimes," he murmured.

He was so close to her she could detect a faint scent of aftershave. She felt light-headed suddenly and stepped farther into the room, away from him. "So where will we be working?"

"I thought the kitchen. I've still got the table and a couple of chairs. Plus, the coffeemaker." He looked at her for a moment before turning on his heel and heading for the kitchen, at the end of the front hall.

Clare watched him go, thinking he was such a contradiction of emotions. One minute interested in her and the next, coolly aloof. But then, wasn't she herself behaving the same way? Liking the feel of him close to her, then feeling giddy by his presence? She took off her coat and draped it over an armchair in the living room, then proceeded on to the kitchen. When she got there, he was making coffee.

"Oops! I said I'd bring coffee but that little incident with Jason completely distracted me. Sorry."

"No problem. I've kept a small store of items for the next few days." He flicked on the machine and said, "Take a seat."

Two pens and pads of paper lay in the center of the table. "You're all set, I see," Clare said. Suddenly she questioned what they were doing. It seemed so amateurish, like something kids would do.

Gil was taking milk from the fridge and when he turned around, he commented, "You look like you're having second thoughts about this."

He'd always had a talent for reading her mind, she realized. Except when it counted the most—the night they'd had their big fight in the park. She shook her head, more

Get FREE BOOKS and a FREE GIFT when you play the...

LAS VEGAS
GAME

Just scratch off the gold box with a coin. Then check below to see the gifts you get!

YES!
I have scratched off the gold Box. Please send me my **2 FREE BOOKS** and **gift for which I qualify**. I understand that I am under no obligation to purchase any books as explained on the back of this card.

336 HDL DVEM   135 HDL DVE3

FIRST NAME	LAST NAME

ADDRESS

APT.#	CITY

STATE/PROV.	ZIP/POSTAL CODE

(H-SR-01/04)

Visit us online at www.eHarlequin.com

7	7	7	Worth TWO FREE BOOKS plus a BONUS Mystery Gift!
🍒	🍒	🍒	Worth TWO FREE BOOKS!
🔔	🔔	☘	TRY AGAIN!

to toss aside thoughts of the past than to reply to his question. "Just that the Jason thing has me a bit rattled. I can't understand why he'd do something like that."

"We don't know yet that he did."

"It must be him. Too much of a coincidence."

"Then as I said, we should go see him." The coffee-maker stopped bubbling. "After a cup of coffee," Gil added. He poured two mugs and brought them to the table, along with the small container of milk. "Sugar?" he asked.

"Please." Clare hung her purse over the back of her chair and reached for the coffee. It was hot and strong, just what she needed.

"I thought we should start by making some notes about the day Rina was killed. Jot down what both of us remember."

Clare raised her eyes from her coffee to his face. There was no avoiding the past any longer, she thought. Perhaps this is why I was having second thoughts when I got here. "Okay," she said. "Should we both jot down things and then compare notes?"

"Fine." He passed a pad of paper across the table to her along with a pen.

And while Gil lowered his head and began to write, Clare stared at her blank paper for a long time. Where to start? How to convey in point-notes the swirl of emotions of that day? She watched as Gil's pen scrawled across the paper. He was obviously having no such qualms about recording his memories.

His head jerked up then, catching her staring. "Sure everything's okay?" he asked softly.

She wanted to say no. To ask how either of them could so blithely write down what happened seventeen years ago, as if mere words could convey the confusion and the pain of betrayal. Clare's eyes fixed on his and he must have seen something in hers for he tossed his pen down and said, "This isn't going to work, is it?"

She shook her head. "There's too much inside," she tried to explain. "Years of…I don't know…blame and doubt. How can we simply write it all down, as if the story belonged to other people and not us?"

Something flickered in his eyes. She saw his jaw tighten, as if he were trying hard to contain an emotion he didn't want expelled into the room right then. Finally, he said, "We can't, Clare. All we can do is articulate the events of that day and if to do that we have to pretend it happened to other people, then so be it. At least the bare bones of the story will come out. As for the rest of it— the part that impacted on you and me—" he stopped, his eyes intent on hers "—I think we should look on that as a work in progress, don't you? Something that will hopefully mend with time and…and perseverance."

Clare nodded, afraid to speak. He sounded as if he intended this fledgling partnership of theirs to go beyond their stay in Twin Falls. And the tiny spark of hope that suddenly flared inside told her that was what she wanted, too. The thought of being able to repair the damage of seventeen years ago and perhaps come up with something new—even just a friendship—was both thrilling and frightening at the same time.

"All right," he said, dropping his gaze. "Let's finish our coffee and look up Jason Wolochuk. I'll go hunt for the phone book. I know there's one around here somewhere." He left the room and Clare slowly lowered her head onto her hands. This, she told herself, *is the craziest thing you've done in years.* And also, she had to admit, the most exciting.

THE WINDSHIELD WIPERS lazily swung back and forth. Gil thought he could turn them off now, since the rain had let up considerably. But there was something soothingly monotonous about their movement. Besides, it was easier to allow himself to be mesmerized by the wipers than to make conversation with Clare, hunched in the passenger seat next to him. He risked a glance.

She was chewing on a fingernail and peering out her window at the unassuming frame bungalow they were parked in front of. Back home in the kitchen, he could have sworn she was going to burst into tears any second. The thought had frightened him. Mainly because he knew he'd have instantly taken her into his arms and from there.... Well, he didn't want to think about that.

Not that he hadn't contemplated such a possibility over the past week. But once he found himself mentally heading in that direction, he stopped himself, reminding himself that until they'd resolved old issues there wasn't a lot of hope for a future between them. And now that he was back in Twin Falls and with Clare again, he realized how much he wanted that. Besides, he needed to stay focused on the murder investigation.

"Ready?" he asked, darting his eyes at her again. She turned her head and gave a husky yes. "Okay, then. Remember what we agreed on? We want information so our approach isn't going to be confrontational as much as inquiring."

"I can imagine you in a courtroom," she said, casting a faint smile.

"More like a boardroom, I'm afraid." Gil reached for the door lever and pressed down. "Let's go."

He led the way up the walk leading to the house and stood at the door until she joined him on the front stoop, then rang the bell. They waited. He pressed the buzzer again. This time, there was a flash of movement in the drapes covering the main front window of the house. Finally, the front door opened a crack.

The upper part of a woman's face appeared. "What do you want?" she asked.

"Mrs. Wolochuk?" Gil ventured.

"I don't want anything," she muttered, about to close the door.

"I wonder if we could speak to you about your son, Jason? It's about some trouble at school."

The door opened, revealing a gaunt woman in her mid-forties. Her long, straggly salt-and-pepper hair was tied back in a loose ponytail and her suspicious eyes peered at them from a sallow face. She gave them a quick once-over, obviously debating whether or not to let them in. Then she mumbled, "Better come in," and leaving the door ajar, turned away into the interior of the house.

Gil glanced at Clare and winked. So far so good. He felt only slightly uneasy about misleading Mrs. Wolochuk, implying they were officials from the school. But he'd assured Clare the ploy was more likely to get them in the door. "Ready?"

Clare nodded and he led the way inside. The house reeked of stale cigarette smoke and Gil tried not to grimace as he entered the living room. Mrs. Wolochuk was curled up on a sofa that had seen better days, a half-filled mug of coffee at her elbow along with an overflowing ashtray. The room was strewn with magazines and newspapers, as well as various articles of clothing.

Gil turned toward the blaring television and frowned. "Do you mind?" he asked.

From the look in her face, she did. Still, she pressed the mute button on the remote. "So what's he done now?" she began as she lit up a cigarette.

Gil heard Clare come into the room behind him and as he craned his head around, Mrs. Wolochuk inhaled sharply.

"I know you!" she snapped. Her deep-set eyes beaded

in on Clare, hovering nervously in the doorway. "You're that writer. Clare Morgan. The one who did the book on Twin Falls."

Gil thought Clare's face paled. She cleared her throat and said, "Yes," without bothering to correct the woman about the novel. He could understand now her frustration at continually having to clarify the book to people.

"What's this about then? She's no teacher." The eyes fell on Gil. "Who are you?"

"No, we're not teachers," he began.

"Then what's going on here?" Her voice rose to an indignant pitch. She didn't invite them to sit and Gil wasn't sure he wanted to, anyway. He saw Clare gingerly perch on the edge of what looked like a dining-table chair. That left a sagging, stained armchair for him. He decided to remain standing.

"We're here about something that happened at school," Gil said. He gave a brief summary of Clare's visit to Lisa Stuart's class, prompting another snort from the woman. When he finished mentioning the note and Jason's hanging around the Kingsway home that morning, the growing fury in the woman's face had begun to abate.

"Jason would never do anything like that," she uttered, obviously offended by the suggestion. She took a long drag on her cigarette. "He's got his share of problems with schoolwork, having a learning disability and all, but he'd never stoop to something like that. Never!"

"I used to be a teacher, Mrs. Wolochuk," Clare said. "And one thing I learned was that one should never say 'never' about kids. They hide a lot more than we think."

The eyes narrowed in on Clare. "And you don't believe in that, do you? Hiding?" she sneered.

"I don't know what you mean."

The lips curled around the cigarette. "Isn't it obvious?

You wrote that book to stir things up here. To make sure the talk started all over again.''

Gil felt a shiver ride up his backbone. He was tempted to intervene, catching the confusion in Clare's face. But he held back, curious to hear for himself what she had to say in response.

''What talk?''

An expression of sheer incredulity crossed Mrs. Wolochuk's face. ''About the murder of that girl. The one in your class.''

Gil intervened. ''Do you know anything about that case, Mrs. Wolochuk?''

Her frowning face pivoted to his. ''Why should I?''

''Just wondering why this has come up when we were simply talking about the note Jason left.''

''You *say* he left.''

''I think it's pretty obvious, don't you? Is he here? Can we talk to him?''

''He's out. I don't know where. He never tells me.''

''Any idea when he might be back?''

''None at all. Like I said, he doesn't inform his mother about his plans.''

The bitterness in her voice said it all, Gil thought. ''What about your husband, Mr. Wolochuk? Is he here?'' He looked over at Clare who was watching him with eyes that were getting bigger every second. ''Wasn't Mr. Wolochuk one of your teachers at Twin Falls High, Clare?''

She nodded, keeping her eyes on his. Then she seemed to realize where he wanted to go and turning to the woman across the room, said, ''He was my chemistry teacher. The best I ever had.''

Gil watched Mrs. Wolochuk's reaction.

''That so? Then you'd be the first to say it. From what

I recall, Stan shoulda spent a lot more time on his teaching.''

Gil frowned. Something in that, he thought. ''What do you mean, Mrs. Wolochuk?''

She sank back into the sofa. ''Nothing,'' she muttered, her face closing up. ''So when Jason shows up, I'll ask him about the note. Get him to write you a little apology.'' She laughed.

Gil bit down on his lip. The woman's bitterness was obviously going to taint any information they might get from her. He looked over at Clare and raised an inquiring eyebrow. She got his message and stood up.

''We should leave then, Mrs. Wolochuk. But you never told us where your husband is. I thought I might see him, talk about the old days.''

That elicited another peal of laughter. ''Go right ahead, dear. We're divorced, in case you hadn't heard. Stanley lives in Hartford now. He's in the phone book. Give him a call.''

Clare turned to leave and Gil followed. They'd just entered the hall when Mrs. Wolochuk cried after them. ''Tell that no-good scumbag he owes me last month's child support while you're at it.''

When Gil closed the door behind him, all he could utter was a relieved, ''Whew!''

Clare was already walking down the sidewalk. ''You're not kidding.''

Gil was just catching up to her when he saw someone crossing the street and heading for the bungalow. A youth in a navy-blue windbreaker. Jason.

BY THE TIME Clare caught up to them, she couldn't tell who was more upset, Gil or Jason. Both were panting heavily after the sprint across the street and around the corner. If Clare hadn't stepped out of the car, Jason might have made it into the house. But as soon as he eyed her and noted Gil striding his way, he'd taken off.

"Maybe you should relax your hold, Gil," she advised.

Gil released his grip on the boy and stepped back. Clare couldn't recall the last time she'd seen such anger in Gil Harper's face.

Yet it wasn't enough to intimidate Jason Wolochuk. "Wadda you want?"

The defiance in his voice was hiding something, Clare thought. Vulnerability? "Jason, I'm sure you remember me from Miss Stuart's class. This is a friend of mine and we want to know why you left me that note."

"What note? You two are crazy!" His face scrunched up, a mix of anger and apprehension.

"And I know you've been prowling around the Kingsways at night." She paused a moment, letting that register. "The police can probably do some kind of test to link the type of marker you used in the note to you or maybe you even left fingerprints on the paper."

His eyes dropped, but not before Clare saw the increased fear in them. "I don't know anything about no note," he insisted. "And I don't prowl around people's houses at night, either. So leave me alone!"

"Forget it, Clare. Let's take this hotshot to the police right now."

Now Jason looked as though he might cry. Clare felt a tad guilty about the lies they were throwing at him. But only a bit. He had, after all, wanted to frighten her a few days ago. "Did you vandalize the posters in the bookstore, too?" she asked.

That grabbed his attention. The surprise in his face suggested he hadn't but Clare had a hunch he knew who might have. "Or maybe it was someone you know?"

He quickly shook his head but remained silent. Clare was about to suggest to Gil that they leave when the boy spoke up. "Okay, okay. I wrote the note. How much of a crime can that be? What're the cops going to do? Lock me up?" he sneered.

"Maybe not," Gil said. "But they might do a check on any unsolved petty crimes in town. You know—small thefts, car break-ins. That kind of thing. Once they fingerprint you, hey, it's a whole new ball game."

After a moment's thought, Jason said, "I just wanted to give her a message," he said to Gil. Then his eyes swung round to Clare. "You don't know how much trouble you've caused since we first heard you were coming back here."

"How have I given your family trouble?" Clare asked.

"Soon as my mom found out, she was on the phone yelling and screaming at my dad. Then he came over to the house—something he hasn't done in almost a year—and they had this big fight. All because of you."

Clare glanced at Gil and raised her shoulders, speechless.

"Maybe you should be a little clearer, pal," Gil said. "Or maybe we can just continue this talk down at the sheriff's office."

"If I knew any more, I'd tell you. But I don't. Just that it had something to do with that book you wrote. That you wrote a bunch of lies. They were scared people would believe them."

More confused than ever, Clare turned a blank face to Gil. He looked as bewildered as she did. "So?" Gil asked her.

She shrugged. The boy appeared to be telling the truth although there was no sure way of finding out. "So you have no idea why your folks were so upset by my book?"

"I told you!"

"Okay, then, I suppose we should pay a visit to your father," Clare said. There was little reaction from the boy, other than a slight lifting of his shoulders as if to say, "See if I care."

Gil stepped away from Jason and said, "Be grateful we're not pressing charges."

Jason brushed past them, cockier now that he was out of Gil's reach. "Go ahead, jerks!" he said. He loped across the street and turned the corner.

"Nice fella," Gil muttered.

"Hmm," Clare agreed. "Gil, remember that Saturday night we went for dinner with Dave and Laura? Before the christening? You walked me back to the hotel and on the way I bumped into a woman who gave me a real dirty look."

"Yes, why?"

"I'm pretty certain she was Helen Wolochuk."

"I guess that makes sense, if she knew you were coming to town, as Jason said."

It made sense on one level, Clare thought, but it didn't clear up any of the mystery around Helen and Jason's hostile reaction to her.

By the time they got back to Gil's car. Jason was nowhere in sight. The curtains in the bungalow where he lived with his mother were still tightly drawn. But as the car pulled away from the curb, Clare glanced once more to the house and saw the center of the curtains part ever so slightly. Just enough for a pair of eyes to witness their leaving.

CHAPTER ELEVEN

CLARE FLIPPED the tab on her take-out coffee and blew gently across the opening.

"Thanks for the breakfast," she said, eyeing the bag of muffins on the seat between her and Gil. "I left in a rush."

"Rough night?" he asked, turning briefly as he shifted into Drive and steered his car away from the curb in front of the Kingsway home. "Did Emma keep everyone up?"

"Not really." *Not Emma so much as my own doubts about the sanity of today's mission.* But Clare had a feeling if she expressed those doubts, Gil would make a sharp U-turn and deliver her back to the Kingsways. "Maybe some anxiety about things."

His head pivoted back to her. "How so?"

Clare took a moment to edit some of last night's conversation with Dave and Laura about the incident with Jason. They'd both been shocked, though not at learning that Jason had confessed to writing the note.

"You two were lucky he didn't call the police," Laura had commented.

"She's right, Clare. The boy's still a minor. Intimidating him the way you did could have led to a serious charge," Dave had added.

The talk had gone downhill from there. By the time they'd finished their Chinese take-out and Emma was ready for bed, Clare had gratefully slipped off to her room to escape further discussion.

So she decided on a short version of the conversation instead.

As soon as she finished, Gil said, "They're right, I know. I've been kicking myself for being such a hothead. That isn't my normal behavior and I can't explain it. Just something about the tough-guy act the kid gave me. His complete lack of remorse."

"I know. I felt the same. But my experience with teenagers has taught me that sometimes cockiness is a cover for fear or insecurity. Given what we saw of Jason's mother yesterday, I can sort of understand his resentment against the world. Still, we should direct our inquiries at his parents now."

"Agreed." Gil's eyes connected with hers. He looked concerned. "So what exactly do we want to ask Stanley Wolochuk about?"

Clare sipped her coffee. She'd been thinking about that, too, in the wee hours of the morning. "Jason said his parents were upset about my book but I can't figure out why they would be."

"Me, neither. You don't mention a teacher at all, let alone name Wolochuk."

"Of course not. Why would I?"

There was a silence then, until Gil asked, "Having doubts about this trip?"

She cleared her throat, startled by his knack for mind reading. "Why do you ask?"

"That look in your face. It's a look I remember."

Clare averted her gaze to the road ahead. *Best not to go there,* she told herself. "I think it's normal to feel apprehensive about what we're doing. But I wonder if there's any point in going to see Mr. Wolochuk. Didn't you tell me that he and Rina were arguing about her chemistry mark that day?"

"Yeah. But I've a feeling there was something more to

it than that. She seemed to be a hell of a lot more upset than she ought to have been over some term paper.''

"Not if it meant she wouldn't get into the college of her choice.''

"Maybe. But I'd like to find out, if possible.''

"What if we don't learn anything at all from him?''

"We chalk it up to a day's outing,'' he said, and flashed a quick smile.

Clare glanced away, ostensibly to finish her coffee. She tried not to think about those other outings years ago, when Gil had borrowed his parents' car and they would drive for hours into the countryside, searching for a private place away from the prying eyes of a small town. She leaned against the headrest and stared out at the scenery, realizing it had been a long time since she'd seen Connecticut in its entire autumn splendor. Cutting herself off from the past had also included missing out on days like this.

An hour later, the sprawling suburbs of Hartford came into sight. When they found Stanley Wolochuk's house, they stared silently at the run-down bungalow.

"That makes his wife's house look like a mansion,'' Gil remarked.

"Hmm.'' Clare was almost hoping her former teacher wouldn't be at home.

"Ready, then?''

She took a deep breath. "Let's go,'' she said, opening the car door. They walked up the broken cement sidewalk to the front steps, which were in a similar state of disrepair.

"Definitely not a home maintenance kind of guy,'' Gil said.

Clare stifled a nervous giggle. She pushed on the door buzzer and, when nothing happened, rapped on the door itself. After a long moment, the door was wrenched open.

"I told you I wasn't interested—oh. Sorry, I thought you were someone else." Then, recognizing Clare, Stan Wolochuk said, "Good heavens! Clare Morgan." His eyes shot to Gil and he frowned. "You look familiar. A former student of mine, as well?"

"Nope, I avoided sciences. But I did go to Twin Falls High." He extended his right hand. "Gil Harper."

The frown deepened. He ignored Gil's hand. "Uh-huh," he muttered, looking from one to the other.

There was an uncomfortable moment when Clare thought Wolochuk was about to close the door in their faces. But eventually he asked, "What can I do for you?"

"We'd like to speak to you about your son, Jason," Clare said.

He thought for a minute before opening the door farther. Something in common with his estranged wife, Clare realized. Worry over a son. "Then I guess you'd better come inside." Unlike his ex-wife, however, he waited while they squeezed past him into a tiny entranceway and, after closing the door, he led them to the living room.

The room boasted less furniture than Helen's, but was tidier. It also, however, reeked of stale tobacco. Clare scanned the room but failed to see an ashtray. Except for the day's newspaper lying scattered on the sofa, there was little more in the room than the sofa, a small television sitting on a bookshelf, and a single armchair. Wolochuk gestured toward this. "Have a seat," he said to Clare.

She did, grateful not to have to sit next to him on the sofa. There was something strange and unnatural about meeting with her former teacher in these surroundings. She watched him clear away the papers for Gil and when they were all sitting, got right to the point. "Do you recall when I was talking to you at the book signing here that I mentioned paying a visit to one of Lisa Stuart's English classes?"

He looked puzzled. "Yes. Why?"

"You didn't mention then that your son, Jason, was in her class."

His mouth turned down. "It didn't occur to me. She likely has a few classes."

"A day or so later I found a note in the copy of my novel that I had passed around in the class." She dug it out of her purse and handed it to him.

He gave it a quick read and raised his face to Clare and Gil. "What's this got to do with Jason?" Then it hit him. "You're not suggesting he wrote this note?"

"We know he wrote it, Mr. Wolochuk," said Gil. "Because he told us he did. He also admitted to sneaking around the place where Clare has been staying in Twin Falls. At night," he added.

The paper trembled in Wolochuk's hand. "What's this all about? Why are you coming to me with this?"

"Jason said he wrote the note because he'd seen you and his mother having an argument about my book."

The note fluttered from Wolochuk's hand to the floor. He didn't say a word, but the redness in his face continued to deepen. The room was silent except for Wolochuk's heavy breathing.

Clare recalled that he'd said he had a heart condition and felt a surge of alarm. "Are you okay, Mr. Wolochuk?"

He waved a hand, dismissing her concern. "Of course I am. You think I'm going to have a heart attack over Jason? I've had more than this to get shook up about, trust me."

She caught Gil's eye. "Clare and I are making some inquiries about Rina Thomas's death, Mr. Wolochuk, and we were wondering if you could help us," Gil interjected.

Beads of sweat broke out on Wolochuk's forehead. He passed the back of his hand across his brow. His gaze shifted to the floor. "I don't understand why Jason would do this," he repeated.

"Mr. Wolochuk, we don't mean to upset you," Clare said. "But apparently Jason was affected by this argument you and your...uh, ex-wife had. That's the only reason I can come up with to justify why he lashed out at me and my book. Some posters in the bookstore in Twin Falls were also vandalized."

Stan Wolochuk was mute, shaking his head back and forth, as if trying to awaken from a bad dream.

"Do you remember the quarrel you had with Mrs. Wolochuk?" Clare prompted, trying to keep the impatience out of her voice.

He heaved a loud sigh. "My ex and I are always quarrelling. Usually about money. That is, the lack of it." He uttered a harsh, bitter sound.

"So are you saying there was no quarrel about the book?" Gil asked.

"I haven't finished reading the book," he said, shrugging. "As for my wife, I doubt she'd even buy a copy. I did only because I remembered Clare." He raised his head directly toward her.

She felt her face redden.

"Mr. Wolochuk," Gil said, breaking the silence. "We'd appreciate it if you would speak to your son about his actions. He obviously caused some distress to Clare and, since she plans on being in town a few more days, I'm sure she'd like to feel comfortable during her stay."

"Of course I'll speak to him. What he's done is inexcusable." Wolochuk stooped over to pick up the note and then got to his feet. "I'll call him right away."

Clare looked at Gil. Obviously, the visit was coming to an end.

"One other thing, Mr. Wolochuk, and then we'll be on our way." Gil paused while the note was passed back to

Clare. When he had Wolochuk's attention, he asked, "Clare and I have been going over our memories of the day Rina Thomas was killed."

Wolochuk stood still, his face giving nothing away.

"And uh, I was wondering what you and Rina argued about that day in your office."

Wolochuk frowned. "I don't recall seeing Rina that day."

"Oh, but you did, Mr. Wolochuk," Clare said. "I was finishing off a lab experiment, and while I was working, Rina came to see you in your office."

"Oh? Well, if you say so."

"Did you remember? She was very angry and you were both shouting at one another for a minute. Then she stormed out."

"What were we shouting about?" He looked at Clare, his face impassive.

"I don't know because the glass partitions blocked most of the sound. But you both seemed very angry."

"The little I recall about Rina Thomas is that she was not only remiss in doing her schoolwork, but she was also hot-tempered. If we argued about anything, it was probably over some assignment she had failed to submit." He moved toward the hallway. "I'll see you two out."

Clare regretted the visit, realizing it had unnecessarily upset the shell of a man who had once been her teacher. She followed him into the hall, noticing on her way a bicycle propped against the wall farther along.

"Do you still cycle?" she impulsively asked.

He spun around, puzzled. "Yes, why?"

"I remember you used to ride your bike to school every day, didn't you?"

His face softened. "Yes, I did. But then I rode it for exercise. Now, I do it to save myself some money."

She hesitated, wanting to say something kind to the

man, but thought she might sound patronizing. "Thanks Mr. Wolochuk, and sorry we had to trouble you about Jason."

He opened the front door and stood aside for her and Gil. "I apologize on behalf of my son, Clare. And I will ensure this doesn't happen again." He closed the door as they stepped onto the small porch.

"Well, we've definitely struck out with all of the Wolochuks," muttered Gil, unconsciously echoing her own thoughts.

Clare stared at the closed door a moment longer before joining Gil on the sidewalk. "He's obviously had a lot of bad luck," she said.

"That may be an understatement."

They didn't speak again until they were heading onto the highway to return to Twin Falls. "I haven't been in Hartford since I flew in here when my father died," Gil unexpectedly said.

"Oh." Clare thought about Gil having to deal with the death of his father on his own. The idea of it made him seem vulnerable, more like the Gil she'd had glimpses of years ago. "Did you see Laura and Dave then?"

"Nope, but Laura's parents came to Dad's funeral. Her father and mine both worked at town hall."

"Yes, Laura mentioned it."

Gil looked over at her. "Did she say how Dad got the job?"

"No. Didn't he just apply?"

"No, he didn't. It happened shortly after I left town that summer."

Clare held her breath. He was referring to the weeks immediately following Rina's murder. After Gil had been released from questioning, talk in town continued to escalate about the possibility of his guilt. Although he wasn't slated to leave for Yale until the end of August, his parents arranged for him to leave sooner.

"Dad had been let go from the mill the year before—remember?—and, other than doing some odd jobs for people, he was unemployed all that time. Then a couple of weeks after I had left, he got a phone call from the personnel department at town hall. Actually, from Laura's father—offering him a job in the public works department."

Clare was astonished. "Laura's father? But...Laura never mentioned that to me at all. You'd think she might have."

"Maybe she doesn't know. Anyway, Dad thought it strange because those jobs were hard to get. Getting a phone call out of the blue like that was nothing short of miraculous for my parents. It made a huge difference in their lives, especially later, when Mom's health deteriorated and their medical bills doubled."

Clare thought back to her conversation with Laura about Gil's father, recalling the surprise Laura herself had expressed over the job. "So did Laura's father say anything to you about it at your father's funeral?"

Gil shook his head. "Not at all. I don't think Mr. Dundas is the type of person to...you know...lord it over someone about a favor."

"I just wonder what motivated him? I mean, he and your parents scarcely knew one another. Or am I wrong about that?"

"No, you're absolutely right. That's what made it seem even more peculiar. But as my dad said, 'don't look a gift horse in the mouth.' He jumped at the offer."

"Of course." Clare gazed out the passenger window, thinking about how all of their lives took such different directions that summer. Not only hers and Gil's, but her mother's. Now Gil's father was part of the pattern, too.

"So what did you think about Stan Wolochuk?" she asked, breaking the spell of memories that had fallen over them.

"A sad man," Gil said. "Can it get any worse for him?"

"I hope not, for his sake. But I know what you mean. After we got into that shabby living room, I felt so awful. I realized he could ill afford to buy my book, but he had. And when I realized we were there to cause more grief for him about Jason, I just wanted to leave right away."

"I could see that. It was odd that he'd forgotten about the quarrel with Rina. Did you believe him?"

"I guess. It was a long time ago."

"Yeah, but we were talking about the day she was killed. You'd think the argument would have registered a lot more." Gil checked his rearview mirror and changed lanes. "Do you know if the police questioned him about it?"

"I doubt it. I mean, they probably didn't even know about it."

"You and I were the only ones who did," Gil said.

Clare paused. He knew because Rina had told him while they were talking on the football field. She wanted to ask him about that, but was afraid of spoiling the easy mood between them. "I guess," was all she said and devoted the next few minutes to staring out the passenger-side window at the passing countryside.

Then Gil broke the silence. "I've been thinking about what Jason said. I know Wolochuk denied his argument with his wife was about your book, but maybe what we should do is go through it together and look for anything that might have set them off."

"There isn't anything," Clare said, looking across at him. "He's not in my book. It's not about Rina Thomas," she said, wondering how many times she'd have to repeat that all too familiar sentence.

"But some of your own personal thoughts—insights, whatever you want to call them—are there. We've missed something." He locked eyes with her for a second before turning back to his driving. "I think we should go over what we both recall of that day. I know we've already tried that, but I think we should give it another shot. It's important." He paused. "Are you with me?" he said when she didn't answer.

He wanted her to say yes, she realized, so she did and offered to take notes while Gil started. That would put her in the position of commenting on what he said, rather than the other way around. She pulled a notepad from her purse and waited for him to begin.

"I hung around that day after baseball practice, hoping you'd soon come along, but then Rina came running out of the school. She was crying and ranting about Mr. Wolochuk. I tried to calm her and next thing she was in my arms. We hugged until she relaxed. I'd been keeping my eye on the back door but I must have missed you when you finally came out."

Clare focused on the notepad on her lap but was really seeing the scene all over again.

"I knew I couldn't leave Rina like that," Gil continued, "and I also remembered that you'd said you might be late and to go ahead if I had to wait too long. I made a judgment call and told Rina I'd walk her to her friend's house so she could call home for a ride. She'd missed the bus." After a minute, he added, "It was a decision I later regretted."

Clare tapped her pen against her lower lip and stared out the passenger window. She'd stopped writing when he'd mentioned his judgment call, thinking he wasn't the only person who regretted his decision. She didn't trust herself to speak, waiting for him to go on.

"While we walked toward the ravine, she started telling me about her Chemistry mark and how she wasn't going to get a scholarship. Her parents couldn't afford to help her out, and she was afraid if she had to work for a year, she might end up not going to college at all. There wasn't much I could do, except listen. When we got to the bridge—you remember the old wooden bridge we used as a shortcut across the river?—she suddenly said she wanted to stay there a bit. Do some thinking. That surprised me because she was a lot calmer, but…well, it was typical of Rina to change her mind for no apparent reason."

You should know. She played with the pen, wishing he'd hurry and finish.

"She seemed okay so I said goodbye and promised to see her the next day. When I paused halfway across the bridge to wave to her, she wasn't even looking my way."

The Twin Falls sign appeared on the side of the highway and Clare stared blankly at it, as if seeing it for the very first time. She'd given up all pretence of taking notes and waited for Gil to continue. When he failed to, she turned his way. His eyes were fixed on the windshield, but Clare suspected that, like her, he was looking at another scene entirely.

CHAPTER TWELVE

WHEN GIL FINISHED speaking, a silence as heavy as the past itself fell over the car. As they passed the town limits sign he sneaked a look at Clare. She was absorbed in the scenery outside her window. Either that or she was trapped in memories, as he was. It was her turn, but Gil hesitated to remind her. He was beginning to think none of this had been a good idea. Exploring ancient history was intended for hardier souls, he figured. Right now, he questioned whether he and Clare were up to the task.

He drove automatically to the Kingsway home and it wasn't until they were a block away that Clare finally spoke up, her voice trembling. "I know it's my turn, Gil, but I doubt I can get through it before we arrive at Dave and Laura's place. And if they see the car out front, I'm sure they'll want us to come in."

"Then what say we go to my place? We can take as long as we want and order in some food or go out later." When she hesitated, he added, "Unless you don't feel up for it. I could just drop you off and call you tomorrow."

She looked away and sighed, as if coming to a difficult decision. "No, we should finish what we've started."

A crazy idea occurred to him to offer her a place at his parents.' There were still two beds there. Rough accommodation compared to what she was getting at the Kingsways' but cheaper than a hotel. But as soon as the thought flashed in his mind, Gil dismissed it. Too problematic for both of us. "So what would you like to do?" he prompted.

She swung her head toward him. "Let's go to your place and take it from there."

He looked at her a few more seconds, trying to decipher the expression in her eyes but couldn't. At least she'd made the right choice. They had to finish what they'd begun. When he stopped at the intersection leading to the Kingsways', he turned in the opposite direction.

They were walking up the concrete strip of sidewalk to his front porch when Clare said, "I should phone Laura when we get inside and tell her I'm back. She'll want to know if I'm going to be there for dinner."

"Sure. You can use my cell phone." Gil unlocked the front door and stood aside for her to enter.

"Want anything to drink?" he asked. "Coffee? Juice? Soda?"

"Water would be great. Then we should get to work." She unbuttoned her trench coat.

"Here, I'll hang that up for you." As he helped her off with it, his knuckles brushed against the back of her neck. He froze, mesmerized by the memory of that slender neck. He wanted desperately to touch her there, to stroke her soft white skin and press his lips against those downy copper hairs. He remembered the first time he'd done just that, lifting aside the end of her long ponytail and, hesitantly at first, kissing the nape of her neck. She'd shivered. Spurred on by her low moan of pleasure, he'd moved from her neck to throat and down to the tiny hollow at the opened neck of her shirt.

"Something wrong?"

Gil shook himself out of his trance. "I thought your coat was caught on something." He whisked the coat off her shoulders and took it to the hall closet on his way to the kitchen. Her footsteps echoed behind him.

"Didn't we try to do this the other day?" she quipped when she came into the room.

Glass in hand, he turned from the counter. He realized what she meant when he saw her nod toward the writing supplies on the table. "Maybe we'll have better luck the second time around," he said.

He saw at once that she'd picked up on his double meaning. The silence in the room was thick enough to touch. Gil kept his eyes on hers, but what he was really seeing was the seventeen-year-old Clare, standing awkwardly in the shadowy corner of his bedroom. He remembered how quickly their clothes had come off then they'd stopped suddenly, aware of the significance of the next step. He'd guessed that she was having second thoughts and he waited, giving her a chance to back out if she wanted to. But then that tanalizing smile of hers lit up the dark room as she'd moved slowly toward him. He shivered, thinking of that first cool touch of her body against his.

"You okay?" Clare asked, looking up at him from the same chair as the other day, her notepad open in front of her.

Gil nodded and took the glass of water to the table. "Before I forget," he said, avoiding her gaze, "I'll get my cell phone and you can give Laura a call." He dashed into the hall for the phone, tucked in his jacket pocket, and brought it back to her. Thinking she might want some privacy, he left the kitchen to hover in the hall until she was finished.

"Laura was okay with the hotel," Clare said when he returned. "I think she realizes that one less person underfoot will be a good thing. I promised to pick up my things from there before dinner." She peered down at the watch on her wrist. "We've still got a couple more hours so that shouldn't be a problem. Is that okay with you?"

Gil hesitated. Should he offer his place or not? He thought of his reaction to the brief skin contact with her and decided against it. Staying alone in the same house together was just too damn risky. He couldn't trust himself to keep his distance. Her scent, the richness of that throaty laugh and intensity of her amber-flecked gaze would all be serious impediments to his peace of mind. Not to mention his determination to rectify all that had gone wrong between them so he could start anew with Clare Morgan.

"I guess I should begin," she was saying, her full lips breaking into an indulgent smile as if she'd known exactly where his mind had wandered.

"That day when Rina charged into Mr. Wolochuk's office I was working on my chemistry experiment. I couldn't hear what they were saying but she was obviously upset. Her face was red and she was shouting at him. That's what really held my attention. You know, as difficult as Rina could be with teachers, I'd never seen her behave like that. And he just took it! That surprised me, too. I mean, he looked angry and was red in the face, too. But he didn't kick her out or anything. I must admit, my curiosity got the better of me and I watched the whole thing. After a few minutes, she charged out, slamming the door behind her." Clare stopped to drink some water.

He saw that she was nervous and wondered why. "Then what?" he asked.

"I completed my write-up but when I was ready to leave, I saw that Mr. Wolochuk wasn't in his office. I didn't see him leave and didn't know where he went. I was…well, hoping to meet up with you so instead of waiting for him, I went into his office and put my assignment on his desk. His briefcase was still on the floor so I figured he was in the school somewhere."

Her eyes drifted back down to the notepad on the table.

Gil stifled his impatience. Finally she raised her eyes again, a thin smile playing on her lips. "I was putting my paper on his desk when I saw Rina's name at the top of another assignment. I'm ashamed to say that I pulled it out of the pile of papers he'd been marking so that I could see what grade she'd received. It was a failure and I figured that was what the shouting had been about." Her shoulders lifted as she took a deep breath.

She was getting to the part that made her nervous and Gil was guessing why. It was the basis of the accusation she'd thrown at him the last time they saw one another all those years ago. The night when they met in the park at John Calvin's statue and she told him she never wanted to see him again. He considered making it easier for her but decided it might be better for both of them to have the whole ugly mess out in the open.

She went on, this time directing her attention to a point beyond him. "When I got outside, I saw you and Rina hugging each other on the playing field. I was shocked and waited a few seconds, thinking you might look my way. But you didn't. Then you both started walking across the field toward the ravine and that's when I decided to take the long route home, through town."

He didn't say anything. She'd already heard his version of events and now knew he had been hugging Rina not in passion, but to comfort her.

Eventually she made eye contact again. "So that's it. I—I see now that I made a mistake then and uh…I want you to know I wouldn't have behaved the way I did if I'd known—"

"It's okay," he interrupted. "All water under the bridge. Isn't that how the saying goes?" After all these years, he didn't want her apology. What did it matter now, anyway? Hadn't both of them gone on with their lives? He had no idea of her current relationship status. His own disastrous attempts to find a person who could instill in him the same passion and zest that Clare once did had failed, but that was hardly her fault.

Her eyes flicked away from his, down to her lap. When she finally raised them, they seemed distant and detached. Gil had a sudden feeling that he'd missed an opportunity. He uttered a silent epithet.

"So what is there—in that whole story—that could have led the Wolochuks to argue about my book?" Clare asked.

"Maybe Jason was lying," he said. "We should consider that. Certainly Stan denied any quarrel. We could always go back to see his wife."

Clare grimaced. *My sentiments exactly,* Gil thought.

"We need to get hold of some official information," she said. "So far we've only got our memories of that day but they're not leading us anywhere."

She had a damn good point, Gil realized. They were like lab rats navigating a maze for the first time. *Official information.* Only the police had that. "Beth Moffatt," he said.

She frowned. "Who?"

"Remember my old friend we met when we went to see Carelli? The secretary, Beth?"

"And?"

"She has access to official records, doesn't she?"

Clare's eyes widened. "Yes, but…wouldn't that be illegal?"

"What?"

"Asking her to give them to you?"

"Definitely. However, I was thinking of asking her to photocopy them for us. You know, as part of the Freedom of Information Act. Only—" he paused, grinning "—I'd be taking a bit of a shortcut by not going through official channels."

She thought for a long moment. "Okay. That gives me an idea, too. Maybe I can get hold of my mother's personnel records and find out more about why she was let go from the bank."

"Why don't you call her right now?" He pushed the cell phone across the table. "I've got some labeling to do on the boxes I'm sending to Hartford tomorrow." Gil got to his feet and headed for the doorway.

As he reached it, she said, "Thanks Gil, for doing this with me. In spite of my earlier hesitation, I really think we're going to finally resolve some…some things." She dropped her gaze to the phone in her hand.

Gil nodded. *Resolve some things. About bloody time.*

CLARE STARED out the car window at the Kingsway home. She and Gil were picking up her suitcase and then he was taking her to the Falls View Hotel. Fortunately, they had a vacancy. There'd been a moment at Gil's house, when she'd been afraid that he was going to suggest she stay there. Afraid, she had to admit, because the idea wouldn't have been so inconceivable. The pleasure she'd felt in his company the last couple of days had to be a sign that they were managing to forget about the past at least some of the time. But, she reminded herself, establishing a kind of friendship with him was her goal, not attempting to revive a relationship that existed seventeen years ago.

"Should I come in, too?" Gil suddenly asked.

She turned her head. "Laura will think it odd if you don't."

He pursed his lips. "True. But what about you? Want some moral support with our account of the day? I'm sure they'll ask."

She hadn't considered that, but he was right. No way would Laura let her slip off to a hotel without learning

what had transpired from their meeting with Stan Wolochuk. "Yes," she said. "That's a good idea."

On the way up to the front door, Gil said, "Look, we'll
tell them what Wolochuk said but let's not mention our
plans about getting information from Beth."

"Okay." Her eyes connected to his. She smiled.
"Thanks again, Gil," and then, confused by the unexpected warmth in his gaze, Clare looked away and pressed
the doorbell.

Dave answered. "Hey! Welcome strangers. Come on
in."

Dave, moving slowly on his crutches, led them to the
living room where Laura was talking to a teenaged girl.
Her happy greeting produced a tinge of guilt in Clare
about concealing information from her friend. Over the
years, they'd been very frank with each other about the
events in their lives, corresponding through e-mail and
connecting on the telephone. Even though she hadn't seen
Laura since her wedding two years ago, the gap hadn't
affected the bond of their long friendship. And Clare knew
Laura would expect that openness to continue.

"Hi, you two! Come and meet Tia," Laura gestured to
the girl sitting beside her on the sofa. "This is Tia Ram-
say, who's going to be helping with Emma. Tia, our good
friends Clare Morgan and Gil Harper. They're also
Emma's godparents."

Clare smiled at the tall, slender young girl. "You look
familiar," she said.

"You came to speak to our English class," she said
shyly. "You were great. We all really enjoyed your talk."

Not quite all, Clare thought. Jason's face came to mind.

"So how was your day?" Laura asked.

Clare saw the eagerness for details in her face. She
glanced quickly at Tia.

"Tia, could you take Emma upstairs?" Laura swiftly

asked. "She's already eaten and I'll come up and change her for bed before we have our own dinner. If you put her in her carrier seat, you can amuse her for a few minutes with some of her toys. Okay?"

"Sure." Tia took Emma from Dave and headed upstairs.

"She seems competent," Clare said.

"She ought to be. She's got a younger brother and two sisters at home. Would anyone like a drink?"

"Not for me," Gil said. He sat down in the chair opposite the sofa.

"Me, neither," said Clare, not wanting to prolong the visit any longer than she had to. She was anxious to get to the hotel and phone the woman whose name her mother had provided.

"So tell us about your visit with old man Wolochuk. Is he as weird as his wife?"

Clare sat down next to Laura. "Not really. More sad than anything." She gave Laura and Dave a quick recap of her impressions about the former teacher.

"What did he say when you told him about Jason?"

Clare looked across at Dave. "He refused to believe his son was capable of being so sneaky. He also denied having an argument with his wife about the book. He said they fought all the time, mainly about money."

"Do you think Jason made it all up, then?"

Laura was quick to get to the same conclusion she and Gil had reached, Clare thought. "We were wondering the same thing, but then what was his motivation for the note?"

"If he's not lying, then his parents are," said Dave.

"We'll have to go back to see his wife," Gil added.

In the lull that followed, Clare said, "I'll go upstairs and get my suitcase." She'd packed before leaving that morning so that Laura could prepare the room for Tia.

"I'll get it," offered Laura. She was on her feet and out of the room before Clare could protest.

"Would you two like to come for dinner tomorrow? I know Laura would love to talk more about all of this," Dave said.

Clare glanced across at Gil, but his expression was unreadable. "Sure, that's fine with me," she said.

"Gil?"

He smiled. "That'd be nice, Dave."

Laura returned with Clare's luggage and they all rose to go. Clare waited until Gil went out the door, followed by Dave.

"Laura, Gil told me that your father was the person who got his dad the job at town hall."

Laura pulled her head back in surprise. "What? My father?"

"Wasn't he head of personnel there?"

"Well, yes, but I don't think he knew Mr. Harper back then."

"Gil said your father just phoned out of the blue with a job offer. Mr Harper didn't even apply for it."

Laura frowned. "That's strange, Clare. I've a good mind to call Dad in Florida and ask him about it."

Clare placed her hand on Laura's arm. "Don't bother him about it. I'm sure there's a reasonable explanation and besides, it doesn't have anything to do with our inquiries about Rina Thomas. Gil just happened to mention it when we were reminiscing on the trip back from Hartford."

"Reminiscing?" Laura grinned. "Is that what you were doing when you called from Gil's house?"

Clare bristled at the innuendo, but refused to let her feelings show. "It was all business, I assure you." She smiled.

"You can fool yourself, Clare baby, but you aren't

fooling me.'' She laughed aloud and hugged her. ''Did
Dave ask you guys for dinner tomorrow night?''

Clare nodded.

''Good. See you at seven?''

''Sure,'' Clare said and descended the porch steps to
where Gil was waiting.

''I guess you'll be driving over to the hotel in your
car,'' he said.

''Hmm.'' Hadn't she already told him that?

He hesitated a few more seconds. ''Listen, how about
dinner tonight?''

She wanted to plead fatigue but the softness of his gaze
washed away any doubts about spending more time that
day with Gil. ''All right. Where shall we meet?''

''I can pick you up at the hotel. Maybe we can go back
to the place where Dave and Laura took us.''

''Great,'' she said and headed for her car in the driveway before she could change her mind. As she reversed
out of the drive onto the street, she caught a glimpse in
her rear mirror of Gil still standing on the sidewalk. He
watched her until she rounded the corner and left him
behind.

HE FELT A SHARP intake of breath when she stepped out
of the elevator. She was wearing the same form-fitting
dress she'd worn the night they had dinner with Laura
and Dave. Her freshly shampooed hair glistened and her
eyes seemed to sparkle under the lights. Gil swallowed,
realizing that dinner was not going to be a simple meal
with an old friend.

''You look—'' he hesitated about using the word but
did so anyway, ''—ravishing.'' He saw at once from the
high color in her cheeks that the compliment pleased her.
She was carrying her trench coat over her arm and he

helped her into it. "I was able to get reservations at that restaurant—Serendipity?"

"Wonderful. The food was great." She started toward the door, then turned suddenly, jostling against him. "Sorry," she said. "Are we...uh, walking or driving?"

"It's a beautiful evening so I thought we could walk. If you don't mind?"

"Not at all. I'll get to work up an appetite."

Feeling as awkward as a teenager on his first big date, Gil led her out the door. He instinctively linked arms with her and was pleased when she didn't pull away. "By the way," he said as they made the short walk to the restaurant, "I called my friend Beth from the sheriff's office and asked her to photocopy that file for me."

She missed a step, sharply turning her head. "What did she say?"

"She was reluctant at first, but I managed to convince her that no one would find out. She's going into work early in the morning to do it, then will meet me during her lunch break to give me the file."

"That's amazing, considering she could get into a lot of trouble."

"She said that since it was what they call a cold case, it wouldn't matter too much as long as I destroyed the copy when I was finished with it."

"What reason did you give her for wanting the file?"

"I told her the truth—about hoping to set the record straight about my own involvement. For my parents' sake. She understood completely."

"And I called the woman my mother worked with— Fran Dutton is her name—but she wasn't home so I had to leave a message. Mom didn't think she'd be able to do much for us but said that Fran had been one of the few people to express sympathy about what happened."

"Is this Fran still working at the bank?"

"Yes. Mom thought she might be in some high-level position now so...I've got my fingers crossed."

"Me, too," he said. Secretly, he doubted that Clare would be able to find any evidence that her mother had been framed. But he also knew that taking on the task of exonerating her mother was as important to her as his mission was to him. And if neither of them had any success at all, well, at least they'd managed to resolve the bitterness between them, he hoped.

"What say we dispense with business talk for the rest of the evening?" he impulsively suggested. "I think we can both use a break from—"

"The past?"

She was smiling. A good sign. "Exactly," he said.

The smile broadened and as they entered the restaurant, Gil felt his step lighten. He was having dinner with a beautiful woman who was turning a lot of heads as she followed the host to their table. Right then, he wouldn't have wanted to be anywhere else in the world.

That unexpected thought stayed with him throughout the meal. He found himself watching her every move. More, he wanted to hear all about her. Warmed by his interest, she became animated as she told him about her struggle with her first novel and its subsequent sale.

"Your turn now," she declared when she finished a story about those early days.

He didn't know what to say or where to begin, sensing that telling her about those first few months at Yale—the bleakness and despair he went through after their breakup—would definitely dampen the ambience of the evening. So he focused on his postgrad days. "After I passed the bar exam, I got a job with the public defender for a few months."

"That must have been interesting."

"Oh, it was. I liked the work a lot, but had so many

loans to pay off that when I got the offer from the company I currently work for, I had little choice but to take the job.''

"So it's not really what you'd love to be doing?"

The question took him aback. She'd managed to get right to the nub of his dilemma back then. Pay off the debt or live with it a lot longer and be the kind of lawyer he'd once dreamed of being. "There are different challenges with corporate law. I enjoy them now," he said.

She tilted her head. The candlelight from their table flickered in her eyes. "Now?" she asked softly.

"I'm older and I admit, accustomed to the substantial material benefits of corporate law," he said.

"But it's not your first love," she prodded.

No, you were. Gil was rattled by her comment. He needed to take control of his emotions. The woman across from him was not the teenaged girl he'd once loved. His gaze tracked across her face. When had she become so impossibly lovely, he wondered? Of course he'd noticed her beauty that day in senior English class and later, had come to know the rest of her—her gentle but indomitable spirit, her zest and sense of fun. Traits that had set her apart from other girls at Twin Falls High, especially girls like Rina Thomas.

The waiter appeared with their meals and Gil gratefully concentrated on his. Occasionally his eyes met hers as they ate, but he forced himself to focus on the act of eating rather than reminiscing. When Clare rose from her chair and excused herself between dinner and coffee, he couldn't take his eyes off her as she meandered around the tables on her way to the ladies' room.

Had she always had that natural yet provocative sway? He wondered at what point in time the teenage Clare had metamorphosed into this sensual and mature woman. A rush of regret flowed through him that he hadn't been there to witness the transformation. That his seventeen-year-old self had never imagined a woman like her. That maybe—and he hated to admit it—he ought to have fought just a bit harder to keep her.

All water under the bridge now. Isn't that what he'd told her? Gil finished his wine and when coffee was delivered, asked for the bill. He recognized that the evening was heading in a risky direction and now was his last chance to keep a lid on emotions he hadn't felt for a long time. When Clare returned, he'd already finished his coffee and paid the bill.

Her eyes flickered in surprise, but she didn't say anything. The walk back to the hotel was silent, though Gil's mind raced frantically to find some appropriate good-night line. Confessing that he'd been overcome by fear of being in her presence a minute longer wasn't the best one, even if it was the truth.

"Shall we meet sometime tomorrow?" she asked when they were half a block from the hotel.

"Yes, of course. Any particular time?"

"It's up to you." She stopped walking and looked up at him.

"How about I call you about nine or so in the morning and we decide then?"

She nodded but still didn't speak. The faint splash of freckles across the bridge of her nose seemed embossed on her face in the halogen glow of the streetlight. The effect made her look like a young girl again, and Gil had a sudden flash back to the first time he'd kissed her years ago.

They'd been to a school basketball game and Gil had walked her home. It was their third date and she'd been unusually quiet. They'd stopped on the sidewalk outside her house, under the streetlight. It was January and she was bundled up against the cold. Her breath puffed tiny frozen clouds into the chilly night air and the tip of her nose was red. He'd wondered if he'd said something that night to trouble her and cautiously asked what was on her mind. Her face broke into a big smile and she'd whispered, *I was wondering when you were going to kiss me.*

"What are you thinking?"

Gil shook himself. The Clare in front of him was speaking. "Uh…"

Her eyes shone with amusement. "You had such a faraway expression on your face," she said. "Where were you?"

Gil blurted, "Thinking of our first kiss."

The smile disappeared. Her lips parted, as if she were about to speak but couldn't find the words. She was standing so close to him that Gil swore he could hear her breathing and he would have drawn back were it not for what he read in her eyes.

She was remembering it, too. He placed his hands on her shoulders and drew her closer. When she didn't resist, he slid one hand up behind her neck and the other, beneath her chin. Then in a motion so slow he thought he was dreaming, he tilted her face up to his and lowered his mouth onto hers.

He tasted the warm, salty sweetness of her lips and closed his eyes. The miracle was that she didn't pull back. He felt her hands move to the back of his head, pressing him against her. Her lips parted and the kiss deepened. He was sinking into her, unable to stop himself. The tumble of water from the falls up ahead was nothing compared to the rapid drumming of Gil's heart against his chest. The crisp night air was like a breeze across the Caribbean Sea, bringing with it the tantalizing scents of frangipani and Clare.

Her soft body sank into every hollow of his and Gil lost himself in the rhythm of hands and lips. The world beyond their two bodies was muted as Gil surrendered all thought to the past.

CHAPTER THIRTEEN

CLARE PEERED DOWN at her watch, although she knew no more than five minutes had passed since the last time she'd checked. She'd arranged to meet Gil in Mitzi's Café at twelve-thirty, after his rendezvous with Beth at a nearby coffee shop. He wasn't any more than ten minutes late, but still she fretted. And although she told herself her anxiety had nothing to do with their parting last night, she knew deep inside that the kiss had somehow transported her back into adolescence. She felt as nervous meeting him in the harsh light of day now as she had after the first—and last—time they'd made love, just two weeks before Rina Thomas was killed.

Clare sighed. It seemed that ever since her return to Twin Falls, time and events had been measured in terms of before or after Rina's murder. How ironic, Clare thought, that a girl whom everyone had considered an outsider should continue to exert so much influence long after her death.

"More coffee?"

Clare glanced up at the young woman waiting on tables. "No, thanks. And if my friend doesn't arrive in the next five minutes, I'll order lunch for myself."

"No hurry. It's a slow day." She carried the coffeepot to another customer.

Clare had chosen a booth midway down the length of the diner and was facing the door. Her heart skipped a beat when she saw a familiar figure enter the diner. Not

Gil, but Helen Wolochuk. Clare ducked her head, but not before she'd been spotted. When she heard movement at her side, she was forced to raise her head to Helen Wolochuk's red and angry face.

She sat down across from Clare and pointed an index finger at her. "Why are you and your boyfriend causing my family so much grief? What have we ever done to you?"

Inexplicably, Clare focused on the word *boyfriend*. She briefly considered setting her straight but something in the woman's face told her she wasn't there for small talk. "I'm sorry you feel that way, Mrs. Wolochuk, but—"

"It's Helen and you're not sorry at all. You went to see Stanley yesterday and filled his head with complaints about Jason."

"You knew we were going to see your husband."

"Then he phones to give Jason a tongue-lashing and had the poor boy in tears."

Clare doubted that. "Maybe it's a good thing that Jason was upset—"

"What do you know about upset?" she snarled, leaning forward. Her eyes blazed. "Someone like you. What kind of life do *you* enjoy?"

"Mrs. Wolochuk—Helen—I'm sorry that life has turned out the way it has for you but that's hardly my fault."

"No one's saying it's your fault. I know whose fault it is, believe me."

Just then the waitress arrived. "Would you ladies care to order now?"

Realizing that she'd mistaken Helen for her expected lunch partner, Clare sputtered, "Uh well, no thanks. She's—"

"I'm leaving." Helen reluctantly got to her feet, glaring at the waitress for interrupting. Then she turned her attention back to Clare. "You want to know who's to blame for my wrecked life? For all the crappy things that have happened to us?" She moved closer, standing next to Clare, and bent down. "Rina Thomas. That's who." Then she wheeled around and marched out the diner.

Stunned, Clare watched her leave. Vaguely aware of the waitress hovering nearby, she summoned a faint smile. "I think she's having a bad day," she said. The waitress gave a doubtful nod and moved off to another booth. Clare shakily picked up her water glass and sipped. She was debating leaving herself when Gil walked through the door. It was all she could do not to run to him.

As soon as he sat opposite her, beaming a smile that carried her instantly back to last night, Clare mentally pushed Helen Wolochuk aside. She'd spent most of the night trying to paint a picture of Gil in her mind's eye as he lowered his mouth to hers, but all she came up with was the sensation of his lips on her skin. The confident but light sweep of his fingertips at the nape of her neck and skimming up through her hair. A memory of seventeen-year-old Gil Harper had surged through her and for a moment, she'd convinced herself she'd actually gone back in time. That really she was curled up on his lap in the back seat of his father's car.

But the Gil of last night was new to her. His ardor was just as intense, but more restrained and he skillfully built her own desire for him to a point where she was about to invite him up to her room. Until someone strolling along the dark street came upon them and Clare froze. There'd been a flurry of whispers and even an apology but the magical moment had vanished.

"Sorry I'm late."

He still hadn't taken his eyes off her and Clare felt her face heat up under his almost raptured gaze. "That's okay," she said, reaching for her glass of water again. Then casually, she asked, "Did you get the file?"

He nodded. "It's in my car. I was thinking this isn't the best place to read through it. Shall we go back to my place now or do you want another coffee?"

"Let's go now. I'd like to get out of here before Helen comes back."

Gil frowned. "Helen?"

Clare told Gil about the confrontation with Helen Wolochuk minutes ago. "She sounds like she's going off the deep end. Maybe we should keep our distance from her."

"She's definitely wound up about all of this. Her reactions seem out of proportion to what happened, though. I mean, she's bound to be upset by what Jason did but she ought to be grateful we didn't simply report him to the police. We could have."

"Exactly. The other thing I don't get is that comment about Rina Thomas being the person responsible for all the Wolochuk troubles." He thought for a long moment. "The Wolochuks don't have anything to do with the Thomas case, as far as I can see."

"They must know something about the Thomas case. That's got to be what's bothering them. There's no other explanation for all the fuss they've been making—all three of them—about me and my book." Clare shivered. "They're involved somehow and they're afraid of public scrutiny about Rina's death."

Gil smiled. "I can see why you're the writer and I'm not. That's quite an imagination. But I think we need to read the file first, before we continue with all of this speculation."

Clare knew her blush stemmed not from the compliment, but from the expression in his eyes. *In spite of what he's saying, his thoughts are on last night, too.*

"Shall we go, then?" she quickly asked.

The file lay on the passenger seat of Gil's car and Clare had to pick it up before sitting down. She resisted peeking inside, though. She wanted to give it her full concentration, which would be difficult with Gil sitting inches away from her. She sneaked a few glances his way, focusing mainly on his hands as they rested on the steering wheel. Imagining those fingers stroking her face as he had last night occupied her thoughts on the short ride to Gil's place and when he helped her climb out of the car, she almost jumped at his touch.

"You okay?" he asked.

"Hmm? Maybe a bit stressed from…you know…Helen Wolochuk." She accepted the hand he held out to her and walked with him up the sidewalk.

Memories flooded back. She and Gil, hand in hand and burdened by backpacks, going to the Harper home to do their homework together. When she reached the front door, Clare was certain she was trembling all over.

But he seemed not to notice. As soon as they were inside, he said, "Make yourself at home. I just want to check the voice mail on my cell phone. I've got things set up in the kitchen," and proceeded into the living room.

She wandered along the hall, risking a glance into his old bedroom where they'd spent many an afternoon playing music, talking or kissing. Kissing. *Snap out of it, Clare.* She entered the kitchen and sat down.

"The place really looks empty with all those boxes gone," she commented.

"For sure. The truck came first thing this morning." He brought coffee mugs to the table. "Got your book with you?"

"Here in my bag." She dug into her canvas carryall and set her novel onto the table next to the file folder.

She watched him, fascinated by the methodical way he had organized the table.

"What?" he asked suddenly, glancing up and catching her stare.

She flushed. "Nothing. Just wondering when you became so...so..."

"Anal retentive?"

Her flush deepened. "I was going to say orderly."

He grinned. "You're being polite. I think my tendency to organize increased after I left home to go to college. It was a way for me to have control over something in my life. That—" he paused a second "—that...uh, seemed important after what happened."

He didn't have to spell it out. Clare knew at once he was referring to the night he spent in custody. She stared at the papers in front of her, unable to meet his gaze. Then, as soon as it had happened, the moment had passed. Gil sat down and opened up the file folder.

"How shall we do this? Split it in half, then tell each other what we've read? Or shall we both read everything?"

"I think the last idea," she said. "In case one of us misses something."

"Good point." He deftly thumbed through the papers and handed her a sheaf.

What struck her immediately was the paucity of information in the file. "There's not a lot to go through," she said.

He looked up from the paper in his hand. "I agree. I would've thought a murder investigation file would be a lot thicker than this."

"Maybe there's another file. Or a book. Don't police put together what they call a Murder Book?"

Gil shrugged. "Yeah, but I don't know what they do here in Twin Falls." He began to read.

Clare picked up the top sheet of her portion. It was a form completed by the officer who responded to the first emergency call at the scene. "Did you know that Rina's death was reported by an anonymous caller?"

Gil's head shot up. "No, I didn't. Is there a time given?"

She skimmed through the report again. "Yes, here it is. 5:10 p.m. The call was made by an unknown person from an unknown location. When the officer got to the scene, some man walking his dog in the ravine had also spotted Rina and called police. His name is here—if you think it's important."

Gil shook his head. "Nah, but who was the officer who responded?"

Clare read the bottom of the report. "Kyle Davis. Isn't he the current sheriff?"

"Yes. Maybe worth a visit to see him."

"Except how will we explain where we got this information."

Gil raised an eyebrow. "Got me there. We'll think on it." He resumed reading.

Clare went on to the next sheet of paper—a transcript of a statement from Rina's parents. She skimmed over it. They'd expected her home late that day because she'd told them she had to see a teacher about a mark. They thought she was referring to her chemistry teacher, Mr. Wolochuk. Rina was supposed to call for a ride home if she missed the school bus.

Clare recalled Gil's assertion that he'd been walking Rina to her friend's house on the other side of the river. She'd missed her bus and needed to call home. Clare shivered. For the first time, she had a mental picture of Rina confronting her attacker. What if she hadn't missed her bus? Clare took a deep breath and continued.

The next witness statement was her own. She rushed

through it, already knowing what it contained. Then she stopped, her eyes caught on a couple of sentences. She went back, read them again. "Gil?"

"Hmm?" He raised his head and looked across at her.

Clare noted a slightly stunned expression in his face. As if he'd just been aroused from a bad dream. "Last night I decided to skim through my book again, to look for anything I might have missed in my recollection of the day Rina—or Marianne, in the book—died. I did find something that puzzled me and now, in this witness statement I gave, there's a reference that corroborates what I'd overlooked."

His forehead crinkled. "Oh?"

"It says here that after I saw you and Rina walking toward the ravine path, I ran around the corner of the school and saw someone on a bicycle riding onto the playing field."

The lines in his brow deepened. "Yeah?"

"The person seemed to be heading toward the ravine, too. But he—or she—was quite a ways behind you and Rina."

"Do you remember anything about this person?"

"Not really. I'd even forgotten about seeing him until now. I think he was too far away."

"Sure it was a he?"

"No."

"Put that sheet of paper aside," he said. "We'll keep separate anything that looks especially important."

Clare set the paper down on the table and went on to the next report. It was the statement taken from Gil that night. She glanced quickly at Gil, but he was staring into space, deep in thought.

The time on the report form was 9:00 p.m. She suddenly remembered that they'd had an English test the next day. Instead of studying, Gil had been sitting in an interrogation room in the sheriff's office. Later, he was in a cell. Tears prickled the corners of her eyes. He'd been seventeen years old. Alone and, Clare imagined, frightened. To top it off, he was there because of what she'd said in her own statement to police two hours earlier.

She forced her way through the rest of the report, noting that it corresponded in every detail with what he'd told her the other day. Except for one thing. She raised her head. "Gil?"

"Hmm? Something else?" He looked across at her.

"It's…uh…your statement. You saw the same person I did."

"What? The person on the bike?"

She nodded. "Here's what you said. You were standing on the bridge and had turned back to wave goodbye to Rina. It was about 4:35, because you'd both left the field at 4:20 p.m. Rina was sitting on a tree stump and had her back turned to you. She was looking down the path leading to the school. You thought you saw someone on a bicycle riding up that same path, but couldn't tell who it was. The person was too far away." He didn't move for a long moment. Clare wondered if he'd heard everything, but then she realized he was synthesizing it. Putting it into context with his present memory.

"So we both forgot this person on the bike. Maybe we were thinking he—or she—was simply another student on the way home." He massaged his forehead. "This is important, Clare."

"He could have been the last person to see Rina alive."

"The very last," Gil emphasized.

Clare dropped the paper onto the first one. She was almost afraid to continue. The final witness statement in her pile was from Stanley Wolochuk. "Here's Stanley's statement. He says that Rina burst into his office about four o'clock, very upset about her chemistry grade. They *discussed it…*'' Clare glanced up and muttered, ''He's definitely sanitized what really happened. Anyway, he says she left about four-fifteen.''

''That'd be right,'' Gil said. ''She bumped into me on the field less than five minutes later.''

''But he makes the whole scene sound so normal, when it wasn't at all. And there are no other witness statements,'' she added, ''except for the one given by the man walking his dog. You'd think there'd be more.''

Gil picked up his coffee and drank slowly.

''The police should have questioned other people, like students.'' Clare went on. ''Rina could have made plans to see someone else that day. Someone else might have seen her leaving with you. And why was there no attempt to locate the unknown bike rider?''

''They did talk to Rina's girlfriend. I've got that report here. She just said that Rina often came to wait there if she missed her bus.''

''Did that happen a lot?''

Gil searched for the paper and scanned it. ''Looks like it did. She said Rina came over at least once a week— almost every Thursday—to wait for her father to pick her up.''

''What was Rina doing in town every Thursday? I mean, she didn't belong to any clubs, did she?''

''I don't think so.''

''And she obviously wasn't working on her chemistry.''

''Not likely,'' he murmured. His eyes never left her face.

Clare had a feeling he guessed where she was heading. Finally, he said, ''She wasn't with me, either, Clare.''

Heat rose up into her face. She lowered her eyes to the papers in her hands. ''I wasn't implying that,'' she whispered.

"Just so you know," he said.

She heard him shuffling through papers, but kept her
eyes down. *There's no hope,* she thought, *of ever having
a normal relationship with him. Every other word or sentence is fraught with some unintended meaning or reference to that day. We simply can't put it behind us.* The
realization stung as she remembered her exhilaration after
his kiss last night. She furtively dabbed at her eyes and
got back to reading.

But the heading on the next piece of paper caught her
breath. The autopsy report. She was tempted to shuffle it
back into the pile, but knew she couldn't. Time of death,
she noted, was between four-thirty and five o'clock, based
on status of the body and witness reports. No wonder Gil
had been a suspect, since he'd said goodbye to her at
about 4:35.

Clare read on. Cause of death was a blunt trauma injury
to the head. Part of a bloody tree branch had been found
a few feet away. No fingerprints taken from it. She
skimmed across a lot of medical terminology until she
came across a phrase that shocked her. *Victim was carrying a six-week-old fetus at time of death.*

HE HAD NO WARNING and had scarcely registered the
sharp intake of breath when two stapled papers were
slapped down on the table in front of him. Clare was on
her feet. Gil's head jerked up.

"You'd better read that," she snapped.

Her face was bright red and her eyes looked teary. *What
the hell,* he thought. He placed his index finger on the
papers and slid them closer. *The autopsy report.* Hands
trembling, he picked it up and skimmed through it. Much
he'd already heard from the police. Even the last part, at
the very bottom. He looked up but she'd already left the

kitchen. Gil jumped to his feet and swore. He should have mentioned it himself.

"Clare?" He went into the hall and thought he heard her crying somewhere. Not in the living room, nor the bathroom. Inexplicably, she'd chosen his old bedroom. He found her sitting cross-legged on his bed, hands over her face.

"I wasn't the father," he said from the bedroom doorway.

She ignored him. Gil perched on the edge of the narrow bed. "That's why the police kept me in custody for a night," he said. "They wanted to hold on to me until they got the autopsy results. Then, when they learned Rina had been pregnant, they asked me to take a blood test. When that came up negative, they checked my alibi. If I hadn't bumped into a guy on the baseball team shortly after I left Rina, I might have stayed in jail longer. Even still they kept hounding me for days afterward." The old emotions rushed back. He tightened his jaw, reining in the frustration and anger that surfaced every time he thought about what happened.

She was sitting upright now, eyes big in her tearstained face. "Why didn't you tell me? Not now, but back then. The night we met in the park. It would have made all the difference."

Because you would have jumped to the same conclusion you just did, seconds ago. Only then it would have been worse. Then you would have really believed it. After a moment's silence, he had to speak. Some perverse inner voice wanted her to know exactly what he'd endured that night in custody.

"It wasn't like television, you know, shows like *Law and Order*. The police didn't let me make any phone calls for almost an hour. I still remember the sound of my mother's voice—the fear and panic in it—when I told her where I was. And there was no good cop, bad cop kind of thing. They both believed that I had killed Rina.''

Gil closed his eyes for a minute, replaying the sneers and cold voices of the two police officers. Intimidating him with their calculated and brutal description of how Rina had been killed and what she'd looked like in death.

He took a deep breath. ''I was only seventeen.''

She didn't speak for a long time. ''Do you blame me for what happened to you?'' Her voice was shaky.

There it is, he thought. *Out in the open.* Good question. Did he? At first, definitely. But by the time he was back home the next evening, he only wanted to hold on to her. To have her wrap her arms around him and tell him everything would be all right. *Except it didn't happen.* He saw the misery in her eyes and knew he couldn't say any of that.

She got up from the bed and for a wild second he thought she was going to embrace him now, the way he'd wanted her to years ago. But she kept walking to the door and was out of the room before he clued in to the fact that she was leaving.

He dashed after her and caught her pulling on her coat in the hallway. ''Where are you going?''

''I think I should leave, don't you? This has been draining for both of us. Maybe we should take a break.''

''This isn't a good time to leave, Clare. Not in the middle of it.''

''We can get back to the file tomorrow.''

''I don't mean the bloody file. I mean you and me— finally talking about what we did to each other. How we felt and why.''

''I thought it was you talking about what I did to you.''

That stopped him. ''Where did you get that idea?''

''It always boils down to that, doesn't it Gil? How I betrayed you to the police.''

''No it doesn't. I mean, maybe in the beginning, when I first saw you the weekend of the christening. I admit to having negative thoughts. Cleaning out my parents' house and finding all that hate mail—it was painful. But I knew you had to tell the police. You didn't have a choice.''

She finished buttoning her coat. When she looked back up at him, her eyes were dark with anger. ''I'm finally glad to hear you say that, Gil. But unlike me, you *did* have a choice. You didn't have to hug Rina or walk her to her friend's house.''

''That's a preposterous thing to say, Clare. After what she'd just told me, I couldn't very well say, *sorry you're pregnant but I have to go now, my girlfriend's waiting for me.*''

''But you could have told me later, that night in the park. You could have told me why you were with her.''

''I promised her I wouldn't tell anyone.''

''She was dead, Gil. How could the truth hurt her?''

''You know how. People were talking about her, anyway—blaming her for her own murder. It was disgusting.''

''But no one seemed to know that she was pregnant, or I'd have heard from Laura. Why is that?''

''I don't know. Obviously no one else knew or no one leaked it. I don't know why,'' he repeated. Her silence drove him on. ''Besides, you wouldn't have believed me anyway. I tried to explain part of what had happened but you refused to listen. You'd made up your mind and that was it.''

Tears welled up in her eyes. ''I was still in shock. We'd just made love for the first time two weeks before and suddenly I see you hugging Rina. What was I supposed to think?''

''That's not what I meant about making up your mind. We could have sorted out all that other stuff eventually.

What held me back that night was something else. The look in your eyes when you saw me. You *believed* that I had killed Rina, in spite of my release.'' He waited for her to deny it, but she said nothing. Her eyes were locked on his and totally unreadable. ''It was all over your face, Clare,'' he said.

She turned to go out the door and he didn't stop her.

CHAPTER FOURTEEN

SHE WAS GRATEFUL for the walk. Although Gil's house was on the edge of town, it was a mere half hour on foot back to her hotel. Their working together had been such a bad idea, she kept telling herself on the way. How many times in the past week had she left Gil's house either on the verge of tears or brimming with irritation?

You should have listened to those first doubts, when he suggested investigating Rina's death. You should have recognized the impossibility of taking on that task without uncovering all those buried emotions. Most of all, you should have acknowledged a basic fact of life. You can't go back.

Clare was mentally played out by the time she reached her hotel. She headed straight for a hot shower and afterward, noticed the red voice-mail light blinking on her phone. As she retrieved the message, her heart rate increased.

Was it Gil, calling to apologize? For what? the voice of reason argued. Speaking the truth? Telling you something about yourself you really didn't want to hear?

Clare sagged onto the edge of the bed as Fran Dutton's message played. She'd be happy to talk to Clare about her mother and was she available for a drink about five-thirty. Clare looked at the clock radio next to the bed. Five o'clock. She quickly dialed Fran's number and accepted the invitation. Then she called Laura, asking if she could be a bit late.

"No problem," Laura said. "Gil just called to say he couldn't make it. Something came up, he said. Know anything about that?"

A little. "Uh, I'm not sure. He didn't say anything when I left a while ago."

There was a brief silence, then Laura said, "I'll feed Emma first and we can eat whenever you show up. It's a casserole, so it can wait a bit. But I can hardly wait to hear all your news."

Clare hung up. There wasn't much information from the afternoon with Gil that she wanted to share with Laura. She rushed to finish dressing and headed for the hotel parking lot.

Fran Dutton lived in the new subdivision of Twin Falls, on the opposite side of the river. Driving over the bridge crossing Main Street, Clare took a quick glance left to the falls and to her right, where the greater part of Twin Falls sprawled south of the river. From the bridge, she could barely make out the wooden bridge spanning the river downstream and wondered if it was still in use. It had seemed rickety years ago, when she and other Twin Falls High students took it as a shortcut home. She wondered why the town council hadn't replaced it when they'd constructed the high school on that side of the river. Hadn't they figured out that teenagers would be reluctant to take the long way home?

The subdivision where Fran lived was typical of many in urban America. Concentric circles of streets merged unexpectedly into one another and appeared to change names with utter disregard for those hapless souls who might have to navigate them. Clare noticed that four or five architectural styles of houses were repeated frequently and erratically within the subdivision, upping the challenge of locating an address. She was about eight minutes late when she coasted into the driveway of what she prayed was Fran Dutton's house.

The woman who greeted her at the door was at least fifteen years younger than Clare's mother. She seemed a bit harried and was wearing a tracksuit that had seen better days. "I apologize for the mess," she said, leading Clare into a small foyer. "We're in the middle of painting, so be careful where you step." She gestured to tarpaulins spread over the hall floor ahead. Paint containers and other paraphernalia littered the way.

"I hope I didn't inconvenience you." Clare said.

Fran waved a hand. "No trouble, believe me. I read that you were in town recently and had been thinking about your mother. So when I got your message, I packed up my husband and sent him and the kids off to dinner and a movie. They were all happy to get out of the house." She directed Clare to a pretty solarium off the living room. "We moved in here about six months ago."

Clare took a wicker chair padded with plump, chintz cushions. There was a tray of crackers and cheese on a coffee table, along with an opened bottle of white wine and two glasses. Touched by the generosity of the gesture, Clare regretted not having brought a gift of some kind. "I hope you didn't go to any trouble," she said.

"I'm happy to take a break, Clare. Besides, I was pretty excited about meeting a real author—not to mention Anne Morgan's daughter."

"I know you and Mom haven't kept in touch, but she remembers you with as much fondness, believe me."

Fran smiled. "When I started at the bank, your mother took me under her wing. She was a wonderful role model."

Fran poured the wine and handed Clare a glass. "Help yourself to the nibbles," she said, slicing a piece of Brie cheese and plopping it onto a cracker.

Clare followed suit and for a few seconds, conversation turned to the new house and questions about their former home in the town's center.

"After I got my promotion at the bank," Fran said, "we made the big decision to move. Two of my kids are already teenagers and another is going to be next year. Teenagers take up a lot of space!" She laughed.

"Mom said you worked in her section at the bank."

"Yep. I was on the verge of thirty and recently married. My husband—Peter—got a transfer here from Hartford. He's now the manager of the Wal-Mart in the new mall. We were a bit worried about living in such a small town— I'm sure you can relate to that—but now we love it. We've been here eighteen years, and compared to most of the people in this subdivision who commute to Hartford, we're old-timers."

"Mom said she'd call you to explain the reason for my visit."

Fran set down her glass of wine and straightened in her chair. The transformation to serious, take-charge businesswoman was instant and Clare had a sudden glimpse of the woman who was now vice president of First National.

"I've spent many an hour these past seventeen years trying to figure out what happened to your mother." Fran shook her head, obviously still bothered by the incident. "The whole business was so strange, right from the beginning. We didn't even know any funds had gone missing until the day Mr. Carelli called your mom into his office. I still remember how shaken she looked when she came out. The money had apparently vanished from an old trust fund that the bank was managing. It had been set up years before your mother started at the bank and belonged to some octogenarian living in Florida. The fund sent small payments to this guy's nursing home once a month and he'd recently died. One of his beneficiaries questioned the amount left in the fund and that got the ball rolling.''

''What made Mr. Carelli point to Mom?''

Fran pursed her lips. ''Anne was in charge of daily debits and credits, but she also had access to an assortment of trust funds and other odd accounts the bank operated. Still, that shouldn't have automatically made her a suspect. I mean, you'd have thought Mr. Carelli might have targeted someone like me first—a relatively inexperienced newcomer. But he never considered the loss might have been accidental. As far as he was concerned, embezzlement was the issue right from the start.''

''From what Mom told me, it doesn't sound like Mr. Carelli had any proof that the embezzler was her. He just kind of put two and two together.''

''Yeah, right. And got five.'' Fran grimaced. ''He was one weird dude, as my son would say. One of those very patronizing, old-school bosses who really didn't think women belonged in the executive echelon of the workplace. He was also moody. A big man with a blustery personality. It was easy to imagine how your mother might have been intimidated by him.'' She paused, adding, ''I tried to persuade her to go to the police to clear her name. But she seemed to think doing that would involve hiring a lawyer—which she couldn't afford—and might end up ruining her reputation anyway.''

Guilty by assumption. Clare saw Gil's face in her mind's eye that night in the park years ago. Was there a parallel here, she asked herself?

Then she thought of her mother and the no-win predicament she'd been forced into through no fault of her own. She wondered what she might have done herself, under the circumstances. Taking care of a daughter and protecting her from vicious gossip had been the priority, rather than proving innocence. A lump formed in her throat and for a minute, she couldn't speak. She stared at the wine-glass on the table in front of her, the dancing sparkles of light reflected in it.

Fran reached over and patted her arm. "Your mother did the only thing she could do, in that situation. It wasn't fair, but she told me the day she left that you had been through enough what with the murder—of that high school student and a breaking up with a boyfriend. She couldn't bear to add more stress to your life."

Tears blurred Clare's field of vision. She saw a tissue thrust at her and grasped it, dabbing her eyes and blowing her nose. When she looked across at Fran, the older woman gave her a gentle smile.

"She never said a word about any of this," Clare explained. "Not even when I was an adult."

"That's the kind of person your mother is," Fran said. "I'm just sorry we haven't kept in touch. My life is hectic these days, but I know that's no excuse. I'm eager to do something for Anne now that I have the opportunity."

"I appreciate that," Clare said, regaining her composure. "But what can you do? It's so long ago now and it sounds like there was little evidence at the time, anyway."

"It's a long shot, true. But at least I can try. My current office happens to be the one Mr. Carelli used back then. I bet the old files are still hanging around somewhere. Nothing seems to get tossed out at the bank."

"Are there any other people at the bank who were there at the time?"

"A few. I'll nose around and see what I can learn."

"This is so kind of you," Clare blurted.

"Hey, I'm doing this for Anne and my own guilty conscience." At Clare's puzzled frown, she added, "For not speaking up at the time. I was afraid to jeopardize my new job."

Clare smiled and, happening to notice the time, said, "I really have to go." She stood up.

"Is there a deadline for this?" Fran accompanied Clare through the living room back to the front hall.

"Kind of."

"Then I'll start first thing in the morning. You'll still be at the hotel, right?"

"Yes." Impulsively, Clare hugged her. "Thanks again, Fran. I can see why Mom has never forgotten you!"

"Likewise, believe me. I'll give you a ring as soon as possible."

On the drive to the Kingsways', Clare decided her conversation with Fran would be a good story for Laura. One that would veer completely away from Gil Harper. When she related it after dinner later, Clare knew her instincts had been on target.

Laura was shocked but, at the same time, eager for details. "This is incredible," she gasped. "Your poor mother, to have to go through that all alone. Why didn't she tell anyone?"

Clare shrugged. She could understand, but doubted that Laura's limited perception of human weakness would be able to. As much as she cared for her longtime friend, she knew all too well that Laura measured everyone else's efforts, or lack thereof, by her own personal benchmark. "She probably was afraid that people would believe she was guilty. You know the saying—where there's smoke…?"

"That's ridiculous! She was innocent. She should have proclaimed it loud and clear."

"Well, let's hope that woman—what was her name?— can find something out," Dave said.

"Fran Dutton. Yes, I hope so, too." Clare set her empty teacup down on the table. "Let me help you clear up, Laura, and then I ought to be going."

"No, no. I'll do it later. You know, Tia's only been here a day and already I've blessed her presence a hundred times."

Clare smiled at the hyperbole. "She's working out, then?"

"So far so great. It was wonderful to be able to hand Emma over to her at four o'clock and go do some shopping on my own. Even making dinner was a pleasure."

"That's reassuring," quipped Dave. "Maybe the quality will continue to rise, too."

Laura gave him a playful poke on the shoulder. "I've asked her to stay on every second weekend and she's agreeable as long as her mother says it's okay. So now," she said, her voice assuming a conspiratorial tone, "what's the latest with you and Gil?"

Clare's heart sank. She figured Dave had caught something in her face for he swiftly interjected, "Laura, give it a rest." He reached for his crutches and struggled to his feet. "Clare, I'm heading to bed now. I've got an early doctor's appointment. You be careful, okay? With all this investigating, you never know what ugly secrets you'll overturn."

"I will, Dave. Good night."

As soon as he left the room, Laura asked, "Well?"

"Well, what?"

"Don't give me that, Morgan. We go back too far. Why didn't he come for dinner with you?"

Clare hesitated then said, "To be honest Laura, we, uh, had an argument and I really can't explain what it was all about. I'm sorry, but I do have to go, Laura." She turned away from the disappointment in her friend's face and moved into the hall for her coat. "By the way, did you get an answer back from your dad? About Gil's father and that job?"

"No, they were out. But I left a message so when I do

hear from him, I'll let you know." She trailed behind Clare to the door. "You know, this whole business with your mother, Gil's father and even Rina, probably goes a lot deeper than we think. Don't you agree?"

Reflecting on what she and Gil had learned that day, Clare gave a firm nod. "I think we've just scratched the surface, Laura. And after what I heard from Fran, I can't help but think my mother was a scapegoat for someone."

"But why, Clare? It doesn't make sense."

Those words were still on Clare's mind fifteen minutes later when she was climbing out of her car in the parking lot behind the hotel. The lot was on a side street running off the continuation of Riverside Drive that fronted the hotel and was eerily empty at nine o'clock. Clare walked briskly, pulling up the collar of her trench coat against the wind gusting down from the cliffs on the far side of the river. She had just rounded the corner when she heard rapid footsteps behind her. Before she could turn around, someone ran into her, pushing her to the ground.

Her hands flew out in defense, breaking her fall. She was aware of her purse flying off her shoulder and as she raised her head, thought she would see someone running away with it. But the figure dashing across the street toward the intersection wasn't carrying a purse. And as soon as he emerged into the spillover of light from the hotel entrance, Clare recognized her attacker. Jason Wolochuk.

GIL MIGHT HAVE MISSED the call entirely, had he not bothered to check his messages. He'd purposely kept his cell phone turned off, in case Clare decided to apologize. *As if.* After she'd stormed out of the house, he'd headed right for the beer store. Then, beer in hand, he'd gone through the entire police file. The exercise failed to improve his state of mind, which had taken a dive after the argument with Clare.

She'd been right on target when she'd suggested the police had done a shoddy job of investigating Rina's murder. The case had basically gone nowhere fast and that puzzled him. He suspected that if Rina's parents had been in a different social class things might have been handled differently. In the beginning, there had been quite a few telephone inquiries from both parents and a letter from Mr. Thomas to the sheriff. But even their small efforts to keep the case alive had fizzled out.

The one person who appeared to have persisted longest was the first officer on the scene, Kyle Davis. The discovery of a cryptic memo from the sheriff at the time—a George Watson—to bring a close to the case because of budget cutbacks convinced Gil something had gone awry with the police investigation. He decided a visit to the current sheriff was high on his agenda for the next day. Along with a call to Clare, of course.

There was no way he'd allow today's scene to drive a wedge between what they'd finally reestablished. He'd expected a torrent of memories and all the pain that came with them when they examined the file. And he'd thought Clare had been aware of what they were getting into, as well, but he'd misjudged her reaction to Rina's secret. Or to his keeping that secret from her.

That's what had really gotten to her, he guessed. Another example of his deception. The fact that it was the *only* example in the history of their former relationship seemed to have escaped her. The one time he'd ever lied to Clare Morgan had been when she'd asked him point-blank why he'd gone off with Rina Thomas that day.

So when he heard her voice on his cell phone he was expecting some other message. What she began to say chilled him. He was on his way out to the car before the recording finished, zipping through every stop sign but the ones that mattered and thankful he hadn't had any more than that one beer, hours ago. Gil made it to the hotel in record time, and was sprinting from the parking lot to the entrance when he saw a police cruiser pull away from the curb. He didn't bother with the elevator, remembering she was on the third floor, and was knocking at her door seconds later.

"I just got your message," he said, placing a hand on the door frame. The move wasn't nearly as casual as it looked. He had to restrain himself from pulling her into his arms. She looked frightened. "Are you all right?"

"I'm fine, Gil. Really. I should have told you not to worry." She stepped back, allowing him inside. "It's just that I made the call right after I spoke to the police and…I guess was still feeling a bit shaken."

"What did he do?"

"Jason? He sneaked up behind me and pushed me to the ground." She uttered a laugh that fell far short of amusement.

Gil closed the door behind him and followed her into the room. The bed had been turned down and Clare's coat had been flung across it. The telephone was sitting on the bed next to the coat. She'd reached for it right after ditching her coat, he guessed.

"Did he hurt you?"

"A skinned knee, that's all. More pride wounded than my body, fortunately."

He said a silent amen to that. "Sit down," he said, tilting his head to a corner chair. "Can I get you anything? A drink?"

"That would be nice, actually. I could use something to calm my nerves." She pointed to the minibar. "I haven't cracked into that yet, but be my guest."

Gil used the opportunity to do something to calm himself, as well. He bent down in front of the small fridge and picked out two tiny bottles of bourbon. "This okay?" he asked, holding aloft the bottles.

"Fine."

He grabbed the two clean glasses standing on top of the fridge and carried the lot to the seating corner where Clare was curled up in an armchair. Then he poured the drinks, handed one to her and swallowed the first mouthful of his own. When she had taken a sip of hers, he said, "Tell me what happened."

"There's not a lot to tell. I was walking from the parking lot around to the front of the hotel when I heard someone running behind me. Next thing I knew I was falling to the ground. I managed to lift my head in time to see him before he got away."

"Definitely Jason?"

She frowned. "Oh, yes. I mean, he was wearing that same nylon windbreaker he had on when we last talked to him."

"Hooded sweatshirt, too?"

She thought for a minute. "I'm pretty sure he had a hood up, yes. It had to be Jason, Gil. Who else could it have been?"

"I was thinking his mother."

She looked shocked. "Oh, no. I can't see her doing something like that, as strange as she is. I mean, Jason has been responsible for everything else. It must have been him."

"Just a thought," he said, dropping it right away. The last thing he wanted to do was to upset her even more. "I saw a police cruiser leaving as I came in."

"I called them as soon as I got back to my room. Guess who took the call? Vince Carelli," she said.

"Really? Sounds like a low priority for the deputy sheriff," he said, adding, "if you know what I mean."

"I thought so, too. He said when he heard my name

on the dispatch he thought he ought to come. Given what we'd reported the other day.''

"Does that mean he's going to take all of this a bit more seriously now?''

"I got that impression. He seemed very concerned. Although I almost gave us away.''

Gil leaned forward. "How so?''

"I told him that you and I had gone to see Stan Wolochuk about Jason and he wanted to know why. Then I had to explain how we'd caught Jason spying and how he'd admitted sending the notes. Vince wanted to know why we hadn't called him to report that and I babbled on about not wanting to upset the family further. That they'd obviously had a lot of troubles since Rina Thomas was killed and that they didn't deserve any more.''

Gil closed his eyes, picturing Vince Carelli knocking on his door in the morning. He quaffed the rest of his drink. "How much more did you tell him?'' he asked, trying to keep his voice neutral.

"Nothing more. I mean, he asked me how I knew about all their troubles and I told him what Helen Wolochuk had said.'' Her brow wrinkled. "Did I say too much?''

A bit, he wanted to say. But he managed a shrug. "I guess we'll find out if Vince comes demanding the file we've got.''

"I didn't say anything about that!''

"Did you mention that we were looking into Rina's death?''

She shook her head. "I was tempted to, but it didn't seem like a good idea.''

Relief breezed through him. He stared at her, noticing the way she was slumped in the chair. "You look tired,'' he said. "I think you should get some rest. Maybe take a hot bath.''

Her sigh echoed in the room. "Yes. I want to forget about everything and just go to sleep."

He stood up and offered a helping hand. When he pulled her gently out of the chair, she was inches away from him. Gil stroked back a tendril of hair that had fallen across her eyes. He bent his head and lightly kissed her in the center of her forehead. It was an effort not to continue.

"Good night, Clare," he said tenderly, drawing his head back. "I'll call you first thing in the morning."

She nodded silently and as he walked to the door, he felt her eyes on him. She stopped him just as he was about to leave.

"Thanks for coming, Gil. You were the first person I thought of, after the police."

Gil paused a beat, then said, a bit huskily, "Thanks for that," and left the room. When he got to his car, he sat and thought for a long time. His first impulse had been to drive over to the Wolochuk house and grab Jason. But he talked himself out of that. No way did he want to spend another night in the Twin Falls jail.

Halfway home, another impulsive idea occurred. He made a sharp right turn at a key intersection and drove by the Wolochuk house after all, to see what was happening there. A police cruiser was sitting out front and lights blazed inside. Gil waited a few minutes before continuing on home. At least Carelli had followed through on something.

By the time he pulled up into the drive at his place, Gil had come to the reluctant conclusion that he and Clare should drop the whole inquiry business. It was proving to be too damn risky, both physically and emotionally.

CHAPTER FIFTEEN

THE KIND OF HANGOVER that awoke Clare next morning had nothing to do with the half inch of bourbon she'd imbibed the night before. Her body ached all over, a result of her tumble. But her pounding head was definitely connected to a tortured sleep, fraught with recollection of Jason Wolochuk's fury, etched indelibly in her mind. And of course, visions of Gil recurred with alarming frequency throughout the night.

She dragged herself out of bed and into the bathroom, then changed into the pair of cords Laura had lent her and her last clean top. The hotel laundry service was available but she decided to take her laundry over to Laura's. She wanted to find out if Laura had heard back from her father in Florida.

The last thing she did before leaving her hotel room was to check her voice mail in her New York apartment. She hadn't done so for a few days and was expecting a message from her editor regarding her new book proposal. The good news was that her publisher was on board with the proposal. The bad news, that her editor was hoping to schedule a meeting at the end of the week.

Clare hung up. She'd been in Twin Falls twelve days and, other than several tense moments with Gil Harper, had little to show for her efforts in resolving the conundrum of her mother's abrupt departure from the town. Not to mention learning anything more about Rina Thomas's

death that could pinpoint a killer. The impending meeting
in New York set an instant deadline for her and Gil.

Gil. Contemplating his name slowed her to a near stop.
She wandered listlessly to the bathroom to finish getting
ready and stared zombielike at the reflection in the mirror.
Leaving Twin Falls could be a permanent goodbye to Gil.
She wasn't going to kid herself that they would reconnect
once back in the city. There was simply too much ambiv-
alence attached to each contact with him here, in Twin
Falls.

Clare massaged skin cream into her face, then set to
work to conceal the dark circles beneath her eyes. She
could remember the days when a daub of lipstick was
sufficient and had a sudden, painful awareness of the years
rushing by. Oh, yes, she'd accomplished much. The brief
but satisfying career in teaching. The realization of a
dream in writing and publishing two novels.

But what about her personal life? What had she gained
from the very few relationships with other men that she'd
had since leaving Twin Falls? Something had always intervened, preventing her from having a long-term commitment. That something, she knew now, had been the
memory of Gil Harper. She'd sought to replace that memory with other men, but had never succeeded. Now time
was literally running out for her and the possibility for a
second chance with Gil was more remote than ever.

So, she silently declared to her mirror image, make the
most of the next couple of days. *No expectations mean
no disappointments.* That would be her mantra for the rest
of her time in Twin Falls. Clare turned off the bathroom
light, picked up her coat, purse and plastic bag of laundry
and headed out the door. First stop of the day, she decided, would be Laura's washing machine.

Fortunately, Laura had no laundry plans herself. "Don't
be silly, of course I don't mind," she said and grabbed

the bag from Clare. "The machines are in the basement. Come on, I'll help you get started." Her gaze narrowed in on Clare's face. "You don't look so great. Has something happened?"

"I'll tell you all about it over laundry," Clare said with a wan smile. "Where's Emma?"

"I just finished bathing her and she's cooing away in her infant seat in the den with Dave."

"How's he doing?"

"Fine. The doctor said his cast won't be off for a while, though, and he's got to start going to physiotherapy. He's getting antsy about work, so I've set up the laptop for him and he's arranging with his boss to do some work here at home."

"Great." She followed Laura down the basement stairs.

"Kind of gloomy down here," Laura said. "I wanted a laundry room on the second floor, but we'll have to save some money for renovations. Another reason why I need to get back to working. So tell me, what happened?" She perched on top of the dryer.

As Clare began to sort her laundry, she recounted what had occurred after leaving the Kingsway home the night before.

Laura kept shaking her head in disbelief while Clare was speaking. "This is too much," she said, shocked. "Thank heavens you called the police. Do you know what happened after?"

"Not yet. It was Vince Carelli who came to see me— remember Gil and I had already spoken to him about the note? He said he'd go talk to Jason."

"He should do more than talk. You should lay a charge, Clare. The boy should be held accountable for his behavior."

Clare had considered that, but hoped she wouldn't have to. "He's only seventeen and has enough problems at

home and at school.'' She caught the expression in
Laura's face and hastily added, ''But if he does one more
thing, then I'll certainly make an official complaint.''

''What more do you want him to do? Really hurt you?
Come on, Clare.''

''There won't be a next time. I'm positive about that.''

''Well, I hope you go see Carelli and find out exactly
what he plans to do.''

''I'm going to the sheriff's office after I leave here.
Hey, did your father ever get back to you, about Mr. Harper?''

''Yes, he called late last night.'' Laura thought for a
minute. ''This is confidential, right? I mean, there's nothing that can happen to Dad because he's retired and all,
but he and Mom have to live in this town. And I don't
want a bunch of rumors to circulate about my father's…well…his professional ethics.''

''Good grief, Laura. This is just information that Gil
was curious about. It's got nothing to do with the Rina
Thomas thing and of course we'd never reveal any of it
to anyone.''

''All right, relax,'' Laura said, raising her palms in a
gesture of defense. ''Here's what he told me. Sometime
in late July, that summer after Rina was killed, Dad got
a phone call from the mayor. I think his name was Mac-
something.'' She screwed up her face. ''MacRoberts!
Anyway, he's long gone. Retired to Arizona or someplace
shortly after his term of office ended that same year.''

Clare sprinkled detergent into the washing machine and
turned the dial to the correct setting. She didn't pull out
the knob to activate the machine, but waited for Laura to
continue.

''Dad said he was completely flummoxed by what the
mayor asked him to do. That was his word, Clare. *Flummoxed.* Isn't it funny? That's how Dad talks,'' she said in
a digression that set Clare's teeth on edge. ''The mayor

said a good friend of his was in desperate need of a job and, although he knew it was highly irregular, would there be an opening somewhere in Twin Falls administration for Desmond Harper.''

"Mr. Harper was a good friend of the mayor's?"

"That what MacRoberts said."

"How could they have been friends? I mean, the Harpers were in a completely different..." Clare searched for the appropriate phrase.

"Social class. Let's face it, they were. Even my parents didn't hobnob with the mayor and his buddies."

"What was your father's reaction? Other than incredulity."

"He gave the mayor a lot of reasons why it was a bad idea, all of which were perfectly valid. But MacRoberts refused to listen to any of them and insisted if Dad couldn't come up with a suitable job, then he'd do it himself."

"That is so peculiar." Clare shook her head. "Gil said that his dad had no idea at all why he was offered the job. I'm sure that if he had been friends with the mayor—which I don't believe for a second—he wouldn't have made such a point of claiming ignorance about the job offer to his wife or to Gil."

"True enough. Anyway, Dad said he finally gave into pressure because he valued his own job so he made the phone call to Mr. Harper. And that was the end of it."

After a moment, Clare said, "I'm sure Gil will be as astonished by this as we are."

"Hmm. And speaking of Gil—"

"Were we?"

"Don't play Miss Innocent, Clare." Laura's expression sobered. "Have you told Gil yet about what happened to you last night?"

Clare peered down at the washing machine. No way

out now, she thought. "Yes. Actually, I called him right after I called the police. He...uh, he came over to the hotel."

"And?"

"And what?"

"You can be so exasperating sometimes, Clare Morgan. What happened when he came over? Was he beside himself with anxiety? Anger? What?"

"He was upset, of course."

"You could have called me. I'd have come over."

Clare smiled. "I know, Laura. But...it's hard to explain. I just wanted Gil. I've no idea why. His name was the first thing that came into my head the instant I hung up the phone with the sheriff's office."

Laura stared at her, a smug Cheshire-cat smile on her face. "What does that tell you, sweetie? And please, no protesting ingenue routine."

"I honestly don't know, Laura. I simply wanted him to be there."

"To comfort you."

Clare's gaze flicked away. "Yes."

There was a minute's silence until Laura said, "Then I hope you're going to give that more thought before you go rushing back to New York."

Clare sighed and started the machine. "Speaking of New York..."

THE WOMAN behind the counter was giving Clare a strange look. A blend of curiosity and worry. "Uh, so you'd like to speak to Vince? Or the sheriff?"

"Vince, if possible. I haven't called for an appointment or anything," Clare said, questioning at the same time if one had to do that with the police.

"I think he's free. Just a sec and I'll buzz him." She picked up a receiver and paused. "Remember me? You were in here the other day with Gil Harper. I'm Beth Silverstein. Used to be Moffatt.''

Of course. She'd been so busy focusing on seeing Carelli that Clare had forgotten Beth was the person who had photocopied the police file on Rina Thomas. For a split second, she wondered how much of the file Beth had skimmed as she was copying it.

''You…uh, will be careful not to…uh…say anything to Vince, won't you? About the file?''

That was it. ''Don't worry, please. And thank you so much for your help.''

Beth spoke into the receiver and replaced it. ''Vince said to go on in.''

Clare waved her fingers and headed along the carpeted hall to Vince's office. On her way, she caught a glimpse of a man sitting behind a desk in an office marked Sheriff Kyle Davis. She sneaked a quick peek, recalling he'd been the officer who'd investigated Rina's murder, but saw little more than a sturdy frame in a khaki uniform.

Vince Carelli was reading some papers on his desk when Clare tapped at his door. He leaped to his feet when he saw her. ''Miss Morgan, this is a bit of a surprise. I planned to call you myself sometime later today. How are you feeling?'' His face wrinkled in concern.

''Not too bad. A bit sore.'' Clare took the chair he motioned to as he sat down again. ''I came to find out what happened at the Wolochuks'. I assume you went to see them after you left me.''

He nodded. ''I did, I did. And as you might have also assumed, young Jason denied even being in the area.''

''I saw him!''

''I explained that and he still refused to admit it. Short of coming up with any other witness, there's little I can do. However—'' he leaned his elbows on the desk ''—I did unofficially warn him off. Put the fear of God into him, as my father would have said.''

Clare summoned a wan smile at the look of pleasure in Carelli's face. His comment, though, gave her pause. And an opening. ''Your father—wasn't he once president of First National Bank?''

''Yes. You knew him?''

''No, but my mother once worked for him. In the bank.'' She watched his face, but he wasn't making any connection. ''Her name was Anne Morgan. She worked there for about ten years.''

''Really? Small world, isn't it? Especially in Twin Falls, as I'm sure you know all too well. Now, is there anything else I can do for you? As I said, Jason's not going to bother you again. If he does make any kind of contact at all, let me know at once. Okay?''

She wondered if he knew the circumstances of her mother's leaving the bank, but decided at once that wasn't likely. He was at least a year younger than she was and from what she'd learned about old Mr. Carelli from Fran, she doubted the man would have confided in his sixteen-year-old son.

She thanked him for his trouble and rose to leave. Partway to the door, he stopped her. ''One other thing. I spoke to Mrs. Wolochuk about that remark of hers. You know, you told me she'd said that Rina Thomas was the source of all their troubles.''

Blood rushed into Clare's head. She met his gaze, keeping her face blank. ''Oh, yes?''

''She flatly denied making any such claim. Said you'd got it all wrong. That she'd meant since the girl's death, the family had had nothing but trouble. It was just a misunderstanding on your part,'' he said. ''Thought you'd like to know. You seemed concerned about it last night.''

Clare nodded dumbly. She wasn't certain why he was

making a point of the comment. Had Helen or Stanley told Carelli that she and Gil were inquiring about the Rina Thomas case? She hoped not. She mumbled a faint thank-you and left the office, wishing she'd simply phoned for the information.

Beth was on the phone as she walked past the counter and out the door. On the sidewalk, Clare paused to deliberate her next move. One person who might have more information about her mother's leaving town was Jeff Withers, though Clare resisted the notion of seeing him again. While she was conducting an inner debate about what to do, a voice from behind made her jump. She spun around and smiled.

"Lost in thought or just plain lost?" Gil asked.

"The former for sure. Maybe the latter, too. I've just been to see Vince Carelli to find out what happened with Jason last night."

"And?"

"As might be expected, Jason denies being anywhere near the hotel."

"He's lying."

"I know that, and I think Vince does, too. He warned Jason off and told me that if he bothers me again I'm to call right away."

"Helpful," he muttered.

"That's what I thought." She held his gaze a moment longer. He was wearing the same black cords, gray sweater and black leather jacket he'd worn the day of her book signing and looked, she thought with an inner sigh, damn good.

"So where are you headed now?" he asked.

"I was just deciding that."

"I'm going to see Kyle Davis, the Sheriff. I want to ask him why he suddenly gave up on the investigation. Want to come with me?"

Clare thought about the chances of bumping into Vince Carelli. "Maybe that's not a good idea," she said. "Vince will think it's odd that I'm seeing the sheriff."

"Point taken. How about meeting afterward to fill each other in on things? And, uh, I want to talk to you about something."

She was slow to reply, focusing on the last part of what he'd said. "Where?"

"There's a coffee shop a few doors down from here, on the north side of the street. I'll meet you there in about fifteen minutes. I'm not expecting this talk with Davis to take too long."

Clare agreed and watched him walk into the Sheriff's office before heading to the coffee shop. On her way, spotting a pay telephone, she decided to call Jeff Withers at the *Spectator*.

Mr. Withers, the receptionist informed her, was on holiday leave. No, she didn't know when he'd be back. Was there someone else who could help?

Clare hung up and browsed through the telephone book. Surely there weren't too many Witherses in Twin Falls. Unless Jeff had an unlisted number, she might be able to pay him a visit later. In fact, there was only one and she quickly made the call. The telephone rang until the voice mail picked up. Clare left a brief message, asking him to call her at the hotel. She continued on to the coffee shop to wait for Gil.

He arrived shortly afterward, his manner suggesting the talk with Kyle Davis had been unproductive. Clare waited for him to order a cappuccino—declining one for herself—before asking, "How did it go?"

"I'm not sure, to be honest. He remembered who I was and was courteous enough to ask how I'd made out after leaving Twin Falls. I appreciated his interest, considering the reception I got from the other cops who interviewed me at the time. Of course, I didn't want to let on that we were making inquiries into the case. Just said that I was in town to close up my parents' house and wondered if any other developments had arisen. The usual bull.'' Gil waved a dismissive hand.

''What did he say?''

''What could he say? He hedged around the fact that the case had been buried, making some excuse about cold leads or whatever. Police jargon. But here's the thing. Last night I found a memo in the file Beth copied for us from the former sheriff, more or less telling Davis to close the case. He wrote some bull about cutbacks and not spending any more department money on a case that wasn't going to get solved.''

''Really? Isn't that a bit unorthodox?''

Gil shrugged. ''I'm sure it happens all the time, but the fact that it happened at the end of what was mainly poor police work is suspicious. Anyway, I couldn't mention the memo without revealing how I knew about it. Although I did think, just as I was leaving, that I ought to have used that reporter as a possible leak. Didn't he tell you he had a source of information?''

''Yes. I called the newspaper a few minutes ago and found out Withers is on holiday leave.''

''Taking time off to write his book?''

''Maybe.'' Clare thought. ''We should go around to his house tomorrow and see if he's there. I called, but got the answering service. Maybe he's just not picking up.''

''Uh-huh. That's an option.'' He sipped the last of his cappuccino, then leaned forward, resting his elbows on the table.

Clare had a feeling he was about to get to the *something* he had to discuss with her. She moistened her dry lips and asked, ''What is it?''

''I've been thinking. After what happened to you last

night—and our general lack of success—maybe we ought to call it quits.''

Clare didn't speak, listening to the drumming of blood at her temple. He was merely articulating the conclusion she'd already reached, but the fact that he was beating her to it rankled just a bit.

''You may have a point. But I went to see the woman who once worked with my mother yesterday afternoon. Her name is Fran Dutton and I liked her a lot. She's vice president of the bank and get this, she's using Mr. Carelli's old office. Apparently he left a lot of stuff behind when he retired, and she's promised to dig through it to look for any evidence of what really happened to Mom. I plan to stick around at least a couple more days until she can get back to me.''

''Okay, that's reasonable. So, have you set a target date or something?''

Clare frowned.

''For going back to the city?'' he clarified.

''I have to be there Friday afternoon for a meeting,'' she said.

Something indecipherable flickered in his face but he didn't avert his eyes. They stayed straight on Clare's face, as if searching for some hidden message. Finally, he said, ''I guess that's a target date, then.''

She waited for him to go on, but he didn't. Was he thinking the same thing that had occurred to her? That the chances of seeing each other again later, in New York, were slim?

He cleared his throat and suddenly asked, ''How about dinner tonight at my place? I'll cook for you.''

The invitation took her completely aback. Her immediate reaction was a definite no. Best to leave things as they are. But something in his expression held her in check. There was a hint of pleading in his eyes. "Okay," she whispered, wondering what she'd just gotten herself into.

Gil's smile brushed away any doubts about spending another evening with him. Perhaps this was her last chance, Clare reasoned, to make a connection with him that would permit future get-togethers as Emma grew up.

He glanced at his watch and asked, "What's a good time for you? Five? Six?"

She had few plans for the day. In fact, she'd expected Gil to come up with something. Dinner, she reckoned, was a long way off. "Whatever's good for you. I could come earlier and help."

"That's a great idea."

"Can I bring anything?"

"Your appetite. What plans do you have for the afternoon?"

"I think I'll drop in on Laura—maybe offer to look after Emma. There's only so much Dave can do when he's alone with her so Laura doesn't like to leave them for long periods. And Tia won't be home from school until four."

"You're more comfortable with baby-sitting now?"

She smiled at his question. "I'm definitely a slow learner. Tia's far more adept at handling Emma than I am, but I've become good at jiggling her in my arms when she fusses. And she loves it when I make towers out of her plastic rings and then knock then over."

Gil's deep laugh rang throughout the coffee shop. Personally, Clare didn't think she'd conjured up quite such an amusing picture.

"I can't envision you sitting on the floor playing with Emma and her toys," he said.

"It's a more believable image than you changing a nasty diaper."

He pulled a face. "Tell me about it. All right then, we'll make it five." He stood up and unexpectedly leaned down to kiss Clare on the cheek before he headed for the door. *Okay,* she thought, *a connection's been made.*

It wasn't until he left that she remembered Laura's revelation about her father and Mr. Harper's job at Town Hall. Would Gil be upset by the information, or merely puzzled by it, as she and Laura had been? Whatever, she knew she had to tell him.

On the way to her car, she thought that although Jeff Withers was on holiday, he might be at home and she felt too restless to wait for him to return her call. She made a quick stop at the telephone kiosk again to jot down Withers's address. It wasn't on her way to Laura's, but in a town the size of Twin Falls, it wasn't exactly out of the way, either.

Ten minutes later, Clare's Jetta was idling in front of a three-story duplex at the edge of the commercial section of the downtown area. It was a mixed neighborhood of small, family-type businesses, a couple of low-rise apartment buildings and a string of houses that had been converted into apartments. The duplex, a salt-box-shaped brick building, boasted a tiny front lawn and, from Clare's vantage, a gravel drive that led to a large parking area behind.

There was no sign of life around the duplex. Clare noticed half a dozen mailboxes tiered next to the front door of the side where Jeff Withers lived and dug into her purse for a pen and paper. She scrawled her name and hotel phone number, folded the paper and went up to the front porch. Withers's apartment was on the third floor and she pressed the buzzer. Again. She searched in the rows of mailboxes for his and tucked the note inside. As she turned to leave, a young man in his twenties came out of the building.

"Can I help you?" he asked, checking her out with a pleasant smile.

"I'm looking for Jeff Withers. I rang his buzzer but he doesn't appear to be home. Have you seen him today?"

The man frowned. "No, come to think of it I haven't seen him since the weekend. Have you tried his workplace? The *Spectator*?"

"I did, but the woman I spoke to said he was on holiday leave."

"Jeff? I doubt it. We were talking about holidays just last week—commiserating about the fact that our work schedules were too tight to even think of a vacation. And when I bumped into him in the parking lot out back on the weekend, he didn't mention anything about going on a holiday. In fact, he looked more harried than ever from his job."

"If you see him, please tell him Clare left two messages. Phone and note. If you could remember, I'd appreciate it."

"Clare," he repeated. "I don't think I'll have a problem remembering." He kept his gaze on her a moment longer, then headed for the sidewalk.

Clare stood back on the porch and stared up at the third floor. The curtains on all the windows were drawn, as if Withers had indeed gone away. She thought about what the tenant had said on the roundabout route she took to Laura and Dave's house.

No doubt Withers had taken leave to get a start at his book, as she and Gil had thought. But he could easily have found out that Clare was still in Twin Falls and yet, hadn't attempted to contact her again. Such restraint didn't match the aggressive reporting style Withers had shown. If he was working on the book, she decided, surely he would have to follow the same line of inquiry that she and Gil had by a visit to the sheriff's office.

Clare made a sharp U-turn back to the center of town.

CHAPTER SIXTEEN

"I'M SURE they think I'm a crank," Clare said. "One of those people who are always imagining others are out to get them." She was watching Gil mince vegetables for the ragout he was making.

He glanced up for a split second and grinned. "Don't worry. You've got a ways to go before you're in the same league as...well, as someone like Helen Wolochuk."

"Thanks for the vote of confidence," she said, returning a smile.

"Ready for a refill?" he asked.

"No, thanks, not if you want me to stay conscious for the ragout."

"Definitely, especially after I've been slaving away over a hot stove all afternoon." He checked his watch. "At least, part of it." Grabbing his glass of wine from the counter, he carried it to the table where Clare was sitting and straddled the chair across from her. "What made you decide to go see the sheriff about Withers? I mean, what is there about the holiday story that doesn't ring true for you?"

"I can't put my finger on it. Just a feeling I had after I talked to the tenant in his building. And the other thing was, I wondered why Withers hasn't been trying to see me again about my book."

"Maybe he figured you'd gone back to the city."

"Yes, but don't you think he'd check around to find

out? And that if he knew I was still here, he'd take advantage of my presence to ask more questions?''

Gil shrugged. ''Got me. Still, I can see why the sheriff wasn't thrilled with your request to check out Withers's apartment with nothing more to go on than your hunch, which I imagine he—''

''Totally dismissed. The funny thing was that Vince Carelli was more interested in my report about Withers than the sheriff. I had to explain why I was concerned by pretending I'd offered to help Jeff with his book.''

''You did? God, what made you do that?''

''Because as you just said, I had no reason to go looking for Withers. At least, not a reason I could tell the police. I didn't want to bring up the whole thing about my mother and what Withers said.''

''No, I can see that.''

Clare recalled the embarrassing scene at the sheriff's office. What a crazy impulse that had turned out to be. ''But you're right about Kyle Davis and his memory. He didn't recognize me by sight, but remembered my name as soon as I introduced myself. He had this funny little frown on his face, too. I guess because I was there almost on the heels of your own visit with him this morning.''

''Did you see him first, or Carelli?''

''Him. We were talking in the corridor outside his office when Vince came along. Needless to say, as soon as Vince filled him in on the stuff with Jason—the note and the pushing incident—I gained a bit more credibility with Sheriff Davis.'' She ran the tip of her finger along the edge of her wineglass, her thoughts back to the afternoon. ''There was one odd thing I picked up, before I left.''

''What was that?'' Gil tilted his glass to finish his wine.

''I got the feeling there's something between Vince and Davis. The way Davis squinted at Vince when he filled him in on the reports I've made the last couple of days. As if he were thinking Vince had screwed up somehow.''

''Yeah? Hmm. Interesting, but I hate to say it, Clare, that's another hunch, just like the one about Jeff Withers.'' He craned round to the stove behind him. ''I think, from that heady fragrance, our dinner is almost ready. Want to bring the salad into the dining room?''

''Of course.'' Clare picked up the salad bowl from the kitchen table. ''We could eat in here.''

''Nah. We've spent too much time in the kitchen the last couple of days. Time for a change of scenery.'' He led the way to the tiny dining area off the living room. A small round table was set with a linen cloth, plates, silverware and candles.

''Nice!'' she exclaimed. ''I'm amazed you could put this together, considering the move.''

''As you know, most of the stuff has been shipped off,'' he said. ''I had to dig into one of the boxes I plan to take back to the city with me.''

''So you're going to keep some things?''

''The dishes and silverware were wedding gifts to my parents and my mother was always so proud of them, I couldn't bring myself to give them away. The tablecloth, napkins and candles all came from the dollar store on my way home.''

His slightly mischievous grin, as if he'd been caught in the act of something, made her laugh. The Gil Harper she'd been chatting with for the past hour while they prepared dinner had reminded Clare more of the adolescent Gil she'd dated.

''I think it's nice of you to keep something of your parents','' she said. ''I wouldn't have suspected that you'd have such a sentimental side.'' She placed the salad bowl on the table and took the chair that Gil had pulled out for her.

"I'm actually a very sentimental person in many ways," he said, lingering behind her chair. "Though I doubt that trait was much in evidence when I was a teenager. Here, I'll take the plates back into the kitchen and serve the ragout and rice from there."

Clare sipped her wine while he came back and forth with plates of steaming food. "It smells delicious," she said, bending over her plate. "You can cook for me anytime."

"I'm hoping there will be another time," he said as he took his seat. Then raising his glass to hers, he added, "To that other time."

Clare knew the heat rising in her face wasn't from her dinner. She'd made the remark innocently, the way people do when they murmur polite nothings at the table. And she suspected Gil had guessed that, from the twinkle in his eyes as he'd given his playful toast.

She lowered her eyes to her dinner and began to eat. "This is wonderful," she said. "Where did you learn to cook?"

"Fending for myself at university. I never liked those instant macaroni meals a lot of students live on. Of course, I could ill afford to flavor my cooking with imported wine back then."

"Do you...uh, have a special person to cook for at home? In the city?" she impulsively asked.

"Are you asking me if I'm in a relationship with someone?" He paused to smile. "If so, the answer is no, not at the moment. And you?"

She shook her head.

"Well, we've cleared the air about that. Now, ready for seconds or are you saving yourself for dessert?" He grinned.

"Is the dessert worth sacrificing a second helping of ragout?"

"Hmmm. Depends on how you feel about chocolate mousse cake. Though I have to add that I didn't make it."

Clare groaned. "My problem is I want it all."

Gil stood up and reached for her empty plate. "You always had difficulty making decisions. Especially choosing ice cream. I remember all too well standing at the counter in Ernie's variety waiting for you to choose a flavour." He winked and carried their plates off to the kitchen.

Clare knew she was blushing again. The memory he'd conjured was still in her mind's eye when he returned with dessert and coffee. Clare decided it was time to steer the conversation away from the past and told him what she'd learned from Laura that morning.

He carefully set his fork onto his plate. "That's bizarre. My parents didn't know Laura's mother and father, except to say hello to them at church or on the street. As for the mayor—I don't think Dad even voted for him, much less counted him as a friend." He shook his head in disbelief.

"If it's any consolation, it was a riddle to Laura and me, too. Her father implied that if he hadn't done as requested, Mayor MacRoberts would personally have called your father with the offer. And Mr. Dundas also said that he felt his own job was at stake."

"I'm certainly glad Dad didn't have to know any of this. How would you feel finding out your job had nothing to do with your skills or abilities but because some person wanted someone else to do a favor?" He peered down at his dessert, momentarily forgotten.

Clare couldn't answer his rhetorical question but felt she had to say something. "Don't you think it odd that my mother and your father had these puzzling events at roughly the same time that summer? Is there a connection?"

His head shot up. "Like what? There is no common link is there, other than the timing?"

"It seems too coincidental."

"I'm not making a connection at all, Clare. Your mother lost a job and my father gained one. But they were two very different jobs for different employers."

She had to agree on that point, but couldn't shake the nagging sensation in the back of her mind that they were both missing something. But what?

"Very strange," he was muttering. "I found nothing at all in my father's papers that hinted at any of this. I only recall what he told me himself, at the time. He didn't understand any of it, but he wasn't going to let that stop him from accepting a job."

"I wonder if we could track MacRoberts down and ask him about the job thing with your dad."

Gil shot her a look as if she'd just reported being abducted by aliens. "Even if we managed to do that," he said slowly, implying that was unlikely, "I doubt he'd come right out and tell us. Why would he?"

They'd reached a dead end, Clare realized. She pushed the last bite of dessert around her plate before giving up on it. "That was an incredible meal, Gil. Thank you very much. It was nice not to have to eat in a restaurant or to impose on Dave and Laura again." She gazed out the window to the dark street. "I should go soon, but let me help you with the dishes first."

He protested, but she resolutely carried plates into the kitchen and began rinsing. "Unfortunately, the dishwasher went with some of the other appliances to Hartford," Gil said as he joined her at the counter. "How about if you dry and I wash?"

"Suits me. Got any towels?" She peered around her.

"Hmm. I've kind of been letting them drip in the rack." He cocked his head at her and smiled. "Guess you're off the hook this time. But tell you what, to make my job more pleasant, how about sitting right there—" he pointed with his finger "—and talking to me while I work."

She didn't mind at all, wanting to prolong the evening as much as possible. "Do you realize," she began as he stacked dishes into the sink, "that this is the first time we've spent more than a few hours together doing something...well, I'm not sure what the word is that I'm looking for—"

"Ordinary?"

That was it, she thought. She watched his hands moving with deft assurance at his task and for a bright, painful second remembered those same hands and fingers exploring the unseen and untouched parts of her body. The furtive groping under blankets at his parents' house while they watched television in the basement and the exhilarating discovery of her sexuality. Though Gil had been her first sexual partner her passion had not been restricted to his physical touch. She had once loved him.

He turned abruptly from the dishwashing. "What's the sigh about?"

"Just thinking about what you said. Doing something ordinary for a change, instead of dwelling on all that happened years ago."

"Yeah," he replied. "I'm glad we had this opportunity to be together again in the present, if you know what I mean."

"I do know and I'm glad, too, Gil. I wouldn't have wanted to go back to my life in New York thinking that we...well, that we couldn't be friends."

He placed a wineglass in the dish rack, then dried his hands on a paper towel from a roll above the sink. "*Can* we be friends, do you think?" he asked. He turned around from the counter, standing inches away from where she was sitting.

"I hope so," she said softly. She could swear her pounding heart echoed in the small kitchen.

"Me, too." His voice was low and husky. "Maybe we could even…you know…get together—as friends—when we get back home."

She smiled, not wanting to disillusion him. But part of her wondered if it would ever be possible to be *just friends* with Gil Harper. They hadn't managed to do that as teenagers, she realized, recalling how quickly their dating had turned serious.

"So tell me," he murmured, "what's missing in your life?"

The question startled her. Searching for an answer, she was slow to respond when he was suddenly leaning over her, pulling her gently to her feet. His hands settled on her shoulders and he drew her closer. "If you could add anything to your life right now," he whispered, his breath sweet with a hint of chocolate puffing lightly on her brow, "what would it be?"

When she tilted her head, the tip of her nose nudged against the edge of his chin. He didn't wait for an answer—not that she had one to give. His mouth came down on hers, his tongue running along the outline of her lips. Clare swayed into him, raising her arms up behind his neck, and held on as if letting go would be irrevocable. She felt his heart hammering against her own and when she opened her mouth to him, heard from far away a slight gasp.

His hands—that touch rushing up from deep recesses of memory—forked through her hair then trailed along the nape of her neck, up and down to her jaw, circling from one side to the other and back, a feathery sweep of cheek, lips, eyes and ears. "Oh, Clare," he groaned, his mouth at her lobe. "I remember this—your smooth skin, the hollow at the base of your throat, your soft hair."

His mouth moved from her ear down her neck to kiss that hollowed place and Clare shuddered, pressing closer. The hardness she felt against her groin ignited some long-buried spark and she heard someone moan—was it her?—as she closed her eyes, yielding completely to the sensation of Gil touching her and wanting her. When his hands slipped beneath her sweater and unclasped her bra, she gasped.

"You're so beautiful," he moaned, lowering his face into the niche between her shoulder and neck. Her nipples hardened under his fingertips.

Clare raised her arms up behind his neck, holding him tightly against her. She wanted his mouth on hers again, to soar back through time and make it all turn out so very different.

But he pulled away, letting her sweater drop around her. Visibly trembling and breathing hard he sagged against the counter, his arms draping loosely over her shoulders. "I'm not sure this is such a good idea," he said, his voice hoarse. "Maybe we should focus our energy on laying to rest the ghosts of our past and then... well...see what happens after."

Clare felt the tremors subside. She fought to regain a steady intake of breath, calming herself, and focused on the pulse drumming at the base of Gil's throat, inches away. His neck was still flushed and as she stared at the tuft of dark hairs below that hollow, she remembered the first time she'd teasingly unbuttoned his shirt and skimmed her fingers through the nascent chest hair of his teenage body.

She closed her eyes, feeling a stab of regret so acute she knew he'd see it if she didn't hide it. Her most vivid sexual memories were linked with a seventeen-year-old youth. Now, she wanted to experience the man he'd become. But deep inside, she wondered if it was too late.

"You're right," she whispered. She cleared her throat and quipped, "Besides, there's only that narrow bed in your room left, isn't there?"

His laugh was husky and uncertain. "We didn't seem to mind it when we were seventeen."

"But we were much narrower ourselves."

He gave her a smile that made her ache. "I'm glad that part of you hasn't changed, Clare. The quick comeback. That resilience."

If he only knew how slack that resilience is at this very moment. She slipped free of his arms and moved a safer distance from him. "I should go," she said, meaning it this time.

He didn't argue, but cast a look that she thought was almost mournful. "Shall we meet in the morning? Maybe discuss where we go from here?" he asked.

She frowned, thinking at first that he was referring to what had just happened.

He must have had the same thought for he swiftly clarified, "What our next step is going to be."

"Sure," she said, disappointment breezing through her. "Laura has to take Dave to a doctor's appointment and Tia will be at school. I offered to baby-sit Emma about ten."

"Maybe I could drop by there. I try to go for a run first thing every morning since I don't have a bike here."

Clare nodded dully and proceeded to the hall to get her coat from the closet. Something he'd said nagged at her and as she pulled on her coat, the murky thought surfaced.

"Remember when we went to see Stan Wolochuk? He had his bicycle in the hallway? We talked about how he used to ride it to school every day."

Gil seemed mystified for a second, but then he said, "Yeah. Why?"

Clare stopped, one arm still outside her coat. "That day. The day Rina was killed. When I finished my work and went to hand it in, Wolochuk wasn't in his office. Remember?" Her brain seemed to be operating in slow-motion as the sequence of events rolled in her mind.

"Go on." His eyes narrowed as he tried to follow her line of thought.

Clare paused, visualizing the scene again. "The parking lot was half-empty when I left—most of the students and teachers had gone for the day. The bike rack was empty, too. In fact," she stopped to catch her breath, "there were no bikes in it at all. Not even Stan Wolochuk's."

Gil's impassive shrug deflated some of the excitement coursing through her, but Clare didn't drop her thought. "He always rode that bike, Gil. Every single day."

"So he left before you did."

"But his briefcase was still in his office. And he hadn't locked up. I didn't know where he went, but I assumed he was still on school property."

"What are you suggesting?"

"What if he was the person I saw riding the bike across the field? The person you saw riding the bike on the ravine path, after you left Rina?"

He wiped a hand across his face. "I don't know, Clare. What reason would Wolochuk have had for riding after Rina?"

"To tell her something? Maybe to do with the argument they had."

He chewed on his lower lip, considering her explanation, nodding his head for such a long moment Clare wanted to reach out and shake him. "Then maybe we ought to pay Stanley another visit after you finish baby-sitting tomorrow morning. What do you think?"

"He has to be involved somehow, Gil. That's the only way that Jason's actions make any sense. The whole family seems to be afraid of me for some reason." Clare eased her arm into her coat and buttoned it up.

"Or afraid of your book."

The book. Of course. The poster vandalism and note were all about the book, rather than Clare herself. Except for the pushing. And perhaps that had occurred because she obviously wasn't taking any of the messages to heart. She hadn't left Twin Falls.

"This could be a real lead," she enthused.

He smiled. "Spoken like a true investigator."

She smiled back, her spirits reviving at the warmth in his face. "Thanks for dinner, Gil. It was wonderful."

"It was," he murmured. "It was good to do something ordinary for a change."

Clare felt a catch in her throat. As if being in Gil's presence could ever be ordinary. She opened the door and stepped out into the crisp autumn night.

"Want me to follow you back to the hotel?" he suddenly asked.

Startled, she turned around. "Why?"

"After last night…"

"I'm sure Vince Carelli has frightened Jason off for good." At least, I hope so, she silently added. She was tempted to take Gil's offer but after the kiss in the kitchen, would she be able to wave goodbye in the hotel parking lot? "I'll be fine. Honest. And if you like, I can call you as soon as I'm in my room."

"Okay. Do that."

They stood a minute longer on the porch, their eyes unwilling to let go. "I'm glad tonight happened," Clare whispered.

"Me, too, Clare. Me, too."

She went down the sidewalk toward the Jetta parked at

the curb. Gil stood in the doorway watching until she drove away. He was still there as she made a right at the first intersection. His parting words had been husky with emotion and she sensed that, had she wavered for an instant before climbing into the car, he might have dashed toward her. And she'd have gone back inside with him.

The deserted loneliness of the hotel parking lot scarcely registered with Clare as she strode toward the hotel entrance. Once, just as she reached the corner, she craned back, almost expecting to see Jason looming out of the shadows. But the cheery lights of the reception area reassured her. The night clerk was in the inner office, his back to her, as she quickly crossed the lobby. The hotel was quiet midweek. Except for the occasional traveling salesman or other businessmen, few people came to Twin Falls that time of year.

The elevator was already on the ground floor and Clare stepped inside, knowing that in a few seconds she'd be talking to Gil on the phone. Her heart rate picked up at the thought. As soon as it reached the third floor, she jumped off and briskly headed for her room at the end of the hall. She walked past the fire exit, recessed in a dark stairwell just feet away, and was about to insert her card key into its slot when a hand grasped hold of her shoulder.

CHAPTER SEVENTEEN

"I HAVE TO talk to you."

She knew that voice. Clare's hand, frozen over the key slot, dropped slowly to her side. The thumping against her ribs eased enough for her to catch her breath.

"Mr. Wolochuk," she said, turning around. "What are you doing here?"

"I have to talk to you," he repeated. "Please."

She didn't want Stan Wolochuk in her room. "Not here," she said. "We can go down to the lobby and talk." She met his gaze without flinching, her calm belying the quaking in her legs.

"It's not private enough. Please, Clare. I mean no harm. It's important."

Something in his drawn, pale face told her he meant what he said. He was Mr. Wolochuk after all, her old chemistry teacher. She dropped the card into the slot and turned the door handle. He followed her inside, flicking on the light switch next to the door.

The room was cool, because Clare had turned the heat off when she'd left that morning, and it smelled faintly of room freshener. Clare moved hastily to switch on all of the table lamps.

"I've never been inside a room here at the Falls View," he said.

Clare frowned. Had he been drinking? "What did you want to talk to me about, Mr. Wolochuk?"

He sagged into one of the chairs in the seating corner

of the room, next to the window, forking his fingers through limp strands of hair that hadn't seen a drop of shampoo in several days. "My life is unraveling," he moaned. "And it wasn't much of a life to start with," he added. "Not much to unravel."

She didn't think he was expecting a reply, and remained silent.

"First, I got a phone call from that sheriff—Davis—just before noon. He told me what Jason did last night—" He paused, waiting for her to speak. When she didn't, he said, "At least, what you *accused* Jason of doing."

"I saw him. He pushed me to the ground and ran away."

He shook his head, as if denying her claim. "I can't see him doing that. Anyway, the sheriff was concerned but he seemed satisfied when I told him I'd speak to Jason. I even offered to have Jason move in with me until you left Twin Falls."

"You came all the way here to tell me that?"

Another shake of head. "No. Later, in the afternoon, I had a personal visit. This time from the deputy sheriff. Carelli, I think his name is. Used to go to Twin Falls High."

That got her attention. Carelli was starting to take her complaints about Jason seriously. "What did he say?"

Wolochuk straightened in his chair. "*Say? What a joke.* The man threatened me. Said if my no-good troublemaker of a son didn't leave you alone, he'd have to make a few phone calls. Maybe have Social Services check out my disability payments, or Helen's welfare supplement."

Clare sat on the edge of the bed, shocked by what she was hearing. No wonder the man was upset. "I'm sorry about that. I don't know why Vince Carelli would do something like that."

"Because he's a cop, and they can do whatever they want."

She flinched at the bitterness in his voice. "I still don't understand why this has anything to do with me."

"But it does, doesn't it? You kept complaining about Jason and finally, the sheriff and his henchman Carelli got fed up."

She stood up, about to ask him to leave, when the telephone rang. They both jumped. "Don't answer that!" he cried as she leaned toward the phone. "I won't be interrupted," he shouted. "I want my say."

For the first time, actual fear pumped through her. The telephone rang until the voice mail came on. In the silence that followed, Clare stared at the flashing red light on the phone. It was Gil, she thought. Calling to find out why she hadn't telephoned him as promised.

The break in tension moved Wolochuk into action. He leaped to his feet and began to pace the room. "It was your book that started all of this," he said.

Clare eased back onto the bed, recalling Gil's assertion earlier in the evening.

"Everyone in town was talking about it and there were a few articles in the newspaper when it first came out, but the talk died down a bit after. Until you decided to come here for the book signing."

"You were in Hartford," Clare said. "What did it matter?"

"But Helen was here. In the days before you arrived, she kept calling me at all hours. She wouldn't leave me alone. Screaming over the phone that it was all going to come out in the open again. That it was all my fault and what was I going to do about it. That's what Jason overheard. Why he got so worked up himself."

Now she was confused. "What was going to come out in the open?"

"The murder. Rina Thomas's murder. What else?" He stopped pacing to look at her.

"What did you have to do with Rina Thomas's murder?" The pulse at her temples accelerated.

"When you and Harper came to see me, you asked me about an argument I had with Rina," he reminded her.

Clare tensed, hoping her face didn't reveal what she was thinking. "And you denied it," she said.

"Of course I did. What did you expect?" His voice rose. "Rina came to see me about her marks. She'd been pestering me for days. But there was nothing more I could do. I'd done enough for her. I told her that was it—no more."

Clare waited for him to continue. She eyed the flashing message light on the telephone and wondered what he'd do if she picked up the receiver. Best to wait. He was already on edge.

He slumped into the chair again, his anger deflated. "I couldn't handle any more of her. She was too much. I wanted out."

Clare could scarcely breathe. What was he saying?

"That's when the other Rina emerged. She was no typical seventeen-year-old kid, believe me." He gave a visible shudder. "She said if I wanted it to be over, then it would be. But if I didn't give her the grade she needed for college, then she'd tell everyone about us."

Clare stiffened, her eyes riveted on Wolochuk, his head lowered as he talked. She waited impatiently for him to go on, fearing a prompt would either shut him up or send him into another tirade.

"I still feel so ashamed. How could I have gotten myself into that situation? That's what I've been torturing myself with all these years. I can't remember where or how it started, but once I'd had Rina in my arms, I couldn't get enough of her. She was like a drug. My addiction."

He looked across the room at Clare. His thin smile begged for understanding. But Clare had only one thought in her mind. *Stan Wolochuk was the father of Rina's baby.*

WHEN THE VOICE MESSAGE came on, Gil hung up. His internal debate lasted no more than a few seconds. She'd promised to call and hadn't. So he called her and there was no answer. The fact that she might have been in the bathroom made him pause only briefly. He picked up the phone again and called back, this time connecting to the reception desk. The clerk seemed surprised at Gil's impatience but assured him he had no idea if Miss Morgan was in her room. He hadn't seen her come into the hotel that evening, but he'd been working in the office. Mr. Harper should call her room again.

Frustrated, Gil restrained himself from slamming the receiver down. Far easier and quicker, he decided, to damn well drive over there. Which is what he did, in an eerie replay of last night's race. He drove slower tonight, telling himself that there was no emergency. She was in the shower. Something like that.

The lobby was empty with no sign of a clerk. In the office? He jabbed at the elevator button and jumped on the instant the doors opened. The only thing that slowed him down as he reached Clare's room was the deep baritone of a man's voice.

Gil hesitated. If he left now, he might save himself from a humiliating situation. Or, he thought, he could trust his instincts about Clare and go on in. He chose the latter, rapping twice on the door and turning the handle. Surprisingly, the door was unlocked.

He figured he was gaping, standing in the doorway and witnessing the frozen tableau of Clare, perched rigidly on

the edge of the bed, and Stan Wolochuk, hunched in a
corner chair. No one spoke for at least thirty seconds and
then Gil muttered, ''What the hell?''

''Did you call him?'' Wolochuk glared at Clare.

''I called here—what's going on?'' He saw the red
flashing light, then put it altogether. ''What have you done
to Clare?'' Gil took a long stride toward the corner chair.

Behind him, he heard Clare clearing her throat. ''Nothing, Gil. Mr. Wolochuk—Stan—came to talk about Rina
Thomas.''

Gil spun around. *Stan? Rina Thomas?* Her pinched face
calmed him down. She wasn't hurt, but she sure as hell
was frightened. He clenched his fists, fighting the urge to
grab Wolochuk by the collar.

''He—he's been telling me that he and Rina had an
affair.''

Gil tugged at his earlobe. ''Say again?''

Her eyes met his and he thought he detected a warning.
He looked at Wolochuk, still huddled in the chair but his
head raised almost defiantly. *Daring me to express my
disgust,* Gil wondered? ''Oh, yeah?'' he said, his voice as
even as he could make it.

''And he was also the father of Rina's child.''

The lights in the room seemed to spin for a second. Gil
closed, then opened his eyes. Of course. It made perfect
sense. The identity of the father was the one thing Rina
had refused to reveal to him.

''Did you follow her that day? After I left her at the
footbridge?'' Gil suddenly asked.

Wolochuk's face was wary.

''Clare said she saw someone riding a bicycle across
the field when she left the building,'' Gil continued.

Wolochuk's expression altered ever so slightly. He had
to have been the rider, Gil thought. He pushed the point,
gradually closing in on where Wolochuk was sitting.

"Clare saw someone on a bike following Rina and me as we walked toward the ravine path." He paused, studying the man's face as he inched toward the chair. "And when she ran through the parking lot seconds later, she noticed that your bike wasn't in the rack." He stopped about a foot away from Wolochuk. "*Was* that you on the bicycle?"

Wolochuk almost cowered in his chair. "No, no, no. It wasn't me."

"Then who was it?" Gil held the man's frightened eyes. "If it wasn't you, who was it, Mr. Wolochuk?"

He jumped to his feet. "You can say whatever you want, but you can't intimidate me. I've gone beyond that." Wolochuk's voice dropped to a whisper. "Hell is no longer a scary place when you've been living in it for seventeen years." He started to move toward the door, but Gil held up a hand.

"Where do you think you're going?" Gil demanded.

"Home. You can't keep me here. I've done nothing to you." He turned toward Clare. "I'm sorry about Jason. And I'm sorry if I frightened you tonight. I—I was overwrought. I'm not myself anymore." He brushed past Gil, but stopped at the door to say, "I didn't kill her, if that's what you're thinking. And that wasn't me on the bike. I—I don't know who it was. I took my car that day." He opened the door.

"Clare?" Gil asked. "Do you want me to stop him? Do you want to call the police?" He saw at once that she didn't. In fact, her eyes filled with alarm.

She shook her head and whispered, "No, let him go, Gil."

Gil watched helplessly as Stan Wolochuk walked out the door. Then he turned around to Clare, still on the bed.

"Sure you don't want me to call the sheriff?"

"No, not now. I have a feeling we'll be talking to the

police soon enough. I couldn't stand the thought of any more questioning tonight.''

Gil closed the door behind Wolochuk and went over to Clare. He took hold of her hand. "You're freezing," he said. "Where's the thermostat, anyway? Maybe you should have a hot bath before getting into bed.''

"Bed?" She struggled with a smile. "I don't think I'll be able to sleep a wink tonight. Not after that unexpected visit. My head is spinning.''

"How did he get in here, anyway?" Gil sat beside her. "Tell me what happened from the start.''

He held her hand while she talked, telling him about Wolochuk coming up behind her in the hall. Her voice rose a notch then. Gil brushed the loose strands of hair away from her forehead, trying to calm her. Or trying to calm himself, he figured. Listening to her account of Wolochuk's ranting, Gil broke into a cold sweat thinking about how the evening might have gone. The man was definitely unhinged. Worse, and the realization sickened him, he could be Rina's killer.

But Clare didn't believe that, when he expressed his doubts about Wolochuk's denial. "Of course he's going to deny it," Gil said. "The man's not going to confess to murder. Why would he?''

"I know that, but it was just the look in his face. Not guilt, but something else." She thought for a minute. "I don't believe he did it, but he knows something he's not telling us.''

"I think tomorrow we definitely go to the sheriff.''

"After I'm finished baby-sitting," she said.

"God, Clare. You can't go on as if nothing's happened here tonight.''

"He admitted to the affair and fathering Rina's child. I can't explain why I feel the way I do. But there was something in his eyes. Something deep and sad, as if he'd been paying for his act all these years.''

"Well, I think you're more trusting than I am. He had one hell of a motive.''

Her eyes, huge in her pale face, locked with his. "Will you stay with me tonight, Gil. Please?''

"You didn't need to ask,'' he replied. "I decided I was going to right after Wolochuk walked out the door.''

THE MUTED SOUNDS of voices in the hall roused Clare from a sleep deeper than she'd had in the past week. She felt disoriented and had to blink a few times before registering the hotel room. But it was the unfamiliar sensation of extra weight on the bed that caused her to turn over. Gil was lying next to her, fast asleep.

The first thing she noticed was that he slept on his side with one arm raised up over his head, as if to ward off a blow. The second, that he had a disconcertingly satisfied expression in his face. Clare's mind raced back to last night. They'd sat and talked for almost an hour, after delving into the minibar for a nightcap. Then Gil had run a hot bath for her.

His low-key approach to caring for her was exactly what she needed. She let him lead her along as if she were a child, grateful that someone was there to divert her thoughts from Stan Wolochuk's disturbing revelations. And when she'd emerged from the bathroom after a long soak, clad in robe and nightie, she found Gil sitting in one of the chairs. The bed had been turned down and all the lights in the room, except for the lamp at her side, had been extinguished.

"You can't spend the night in a chair,'' she said, knowing her comment suggested only one other option.

He gave an awkward shrug. "May be better, though.''

"It's a king-size bed, Gil. I think we can handle the

situation.'' That had elicited a smile from a face that
looked drawn and tired.

Now, awakening beside him, Clare realized this was
another first. Seventeen years ago there had been one pas-
sionate yet inexperienced episode of lovemaking in Gil's
narrow bed. There had also been plenty of experimental
foreplay, but she'd never actually spent a night with him.

His eyes suddenly fluttered open. "Am I dreaming?"
His voice was languid with sleep.

"No," she said, resisting a giggle. "But if anything
happened last night, I assure you it was only in your
dreams."

He mocked disappointment, then rolled onto his back
and rubbed at his face. "What time is it?"

Clare craned round to the clock radio next to her.
"Nine. I better get moving." But she lingered, basking
not merely in the warmth of the bed, but in the heart-
pumping novelty of lying next to Gil Harper. It was a
feeling eons away from ten days ago, when she could
scarcely bear to be in the same room with him.

He turned her way again, propping himself on an elbow, and extended his other hand to brush away some
hair clinging to her cheek. "I can't tell you how many
times I've imagined this scene," he whispered. "Waking
up next to you. Gazing at your lovely face, flushed with
sleep, and your hair spilling across a snowy-white pillow."

Clare caught her breath at the longing in his eyes. She
was afraid to speak, of jeopardizing a moment that she
sensed was going to be a turning point. But her smile said
what her heart feared to.

He pulled her toward him, gently tucking her into the
crook of his arm and shifting onto his back, holding her
close. Her cheek pressed against his cotton T-shirt and
although she was on his right side, she felt the echoing

beat of his heart against his chest. If she could have, she'd have spent the entire day without moving from that spot.

The rising voices in the hall indicated the maids were making their rounds and Laura was expecting her. "I should get up," she whispered.

His chest heaved in a loud sigh. "I know. The cold light of day and all that." He shifted, propping himself above her. "Something happened last night, Clare. No—" he grinned at the look in her wide eyes "—not that. Unfortunately. Maybe I shouldn't say that just yet, but...I'm hoping that we've crossed a line. That from now on maybe we can—"

"Be friends?"

He sobered and shook his head. "I think I want more than that now. Don't you?"

She nodded. Not afraid of speaking this time, but of crying.

CLARE DUCKED HER HEAD to kiss Emma's brow. She was hoping to avoid Laura's penetrating scrutiny as she asked Clare about her dinner with Gil last night. Laura's internal radar, Clare mused, was acute enough to detect even a hint of new information regarding the ongoing saga of Gil Harper.

"Dinner was great. He's a wonderful cook, which was a complete surprise." She continued to focus her attention on Emma, squirming happily in her arms.

"And after dinner?"

Dave groaned. "Laura, we're running late."

"Okay, okay," Laura grumbled. "But you're not off the hook yet, Clare Morgan." She gave Clare a quick hug. "Just teasing. Honestly though, it's all over your face, honey."

Before Clare could feign a protest, Dave and Laura were on their way out the door. "All right, Emma, it's just you and me,'' she murmured. Laura had suggested Clare take Emma for a walk in her carriage after her bottle and promised to bring back food for a late lunch.

The fact that her baby-sitting job was going to extend beyond noon was a problem because Clare had arranged to meet Gil at Mitzi's Café prior to seeing the sheriff about Stan Wolochuk. She called Gil's cell before heading out the door with Emma, but had to leave a message suggesting he come over to the Kingsways' instead.

Half an hour later, as she wheeled a sleeping Emma up the drive, Clare was hoping to see Gil waiting for her. No such luck. She unlocked the door and carefully carried Emma inside, anticipating settling her in her crib to continue her nap. But as soon as Clare placed her onto the mattress, the baby awoke, crying.

Strike two, Clare thought. She carried Emma back downstairs and quickly heated up a bottle for her in the microwave. As she sprinkled some of the formula onto her wrist, testing its temperature, she thought how much more adept at caring for Emma she was now, compared to ten days ago.

"See? I can do this," she said, smiling down at Emma who was sucking hungrily on the bottle. While she fed Emma, Clare daydreamed about Gil and the possibility of another night with him. She daydreamed too, about what it would be like to be sitting in their kitchen, feeding their baby.

Don't get carried away, Clare, an inner voice warned. There's a lot to resolve yet. But she realized, with a strong sense of well-being, there was now all the time in the world to do it. If all worked out, she might have another chance at realizing her adolescent fantasy of marriage and family. Now, more than ever before, she wanted that to happen. The thought of returning to her old life in New York was suddenly unbearable.

Surveying the kitchen while Emma finished up her bottle, Clare noticed the message indicator flashing on the telephone perched on the small desk in the corner. Was it Gil, returning her call?

As soon as Emma's rosebud mouth slipped free of the nipple, Clare slowly righted the baby over her shoulder and patted her on the back. Then she rose from the chair and, with Emma still over her shoulder, picked up the phone.

"Hey Clare." Gil's voice resonated in the kitchen. "Just got your message. Don't worry about changing our plans because something's come up here, too. I had a call from the real-estate agent and the people who've bought the house want to renegotiate the closing date. It means a trip to Hartford and I'm leaving right now. I'll give you a call at the hotel when I'm back. I'm...uh, hoping we can do dinner tonight." There was a slight pause. "Oh, about the visit to the sheriff? Will you hold off on that? I want to go with you and we may have to do it tomorrow. I hope things are going well with you and Emma—talk to you later. Bye."

Clare hung up. She was disappointed, but not terribly. Tonight, however, looked promising. Buoyed by the thought, she carried Emma upstairs for her nap.

SHE DIDN'T GET BACK to the hotel until midafternoon. Laura and Dave had returned with fresh bagels and assorted cheeses and Clare knew she'd have to fend off Laura's questions. But she was surprised at her friend's uncustomary reticence.

"Dave warned me off," she'd muttered, handing Clare plates to set on the table. "But I expect to get the complete lowdown before you leave Twin Falls."

Laughing, Clare had promised. She was grateful for Dave's presence, however, knowing how tempted she was to tell Laura about the encounter with Stan Wolochuk. She and Gil had agreed to withhold that news until after they'd contacted the sheriff.

On the way back to the hotel, she was considering a nap before getting ready for Gil's arrival later in the afternoon. Then she noticed the message light on the phone and quickly picked up, thinking he'd returned earlier. The woman's voice on the other end dispelled that notion, though Clare was happy to hear from Fran Dutton. She had information Clare would be interested in, the message indicated, and please come to the bank if possible, or call her at home later in the evening.

Clare put her coat back on and headed for the door. The bank was a mere four or five blocks away, so she decided to walk. It was a blustery day, with storm clouds building up on the horizon, and the weather quickened her pace. Less than half an hour later, she was at the receptionist's desk asking to speak to Mrs. Dutton. There was another five-minute wait while Fran finished conferring with a client, then Clare was sitting opposite her, on the other side of old Mr. Carelli's oak desk.

"Sorry it's taken me so long," Fran began, "but I had to root around in the basement, if you can believe it."

"I appreciate this a lot, Fran, and I don't think a couple of days is long at all. What were you able to find out?"

Fran removed a black leather agenda book from a desk drawer. "This was in a box of files removed from the office after Mr. Carelli retired. Apparently the stuff was supposed to be sent to him, but he had a stroke shortly after he left here and I guess the family never got around to asking for it. The box ended up in the basement."

Clare listened politely, but couldn't take her eyes off the agenda book. She was itching to get at it.

"I know you'll want to take this with you," Fran said, "but I'll have to get it back, okay? In case—and I think it's very unlikely—the family suddenly remembers to ask for the stuff.'' She pulled a slightly guilty face. ''I hope you don't mind, but my curiosity got the better of me and I've already skimmed through most of it. You'll notice the Post-its where I've marked pages that seemed—to put it mildly—interesting.'' She passed the book across the desk to Clare and added, ''Do you want to look at it here, in my office? Then if you have any questions, I might be able to help. There are a few bank-type abbreviations and procedures you may want to know about.''

''That would be great,'' Clare said, knowing she wouldn't have been able to wait until she got back to the hotel anyway. She picked up the book, turning to the first marked page, dated June 30, a week after Rina Thomas was killed. The former bank president's handwriting was a narrow, spidery scrawl that took Clare a few seconds to adjust to. The entry summarized various meetings scheduled that day, including one for Sheriff George Watson. *Loan payment—$10,500.*

Clare raised her eyes to Fran. ''I don't understand why this page is marked.''

''You will. Just go to the other pages I've marked. They're in sequence.''

The next marked page had an entry for July 10. Fran had highlighted a notation that read: *See A.Morgan re trust fund.* Clare's mouth went dry. She quickly flipped to the next tabbed entry for July 14. *Trust fund—$10,500.* Her fingers fumbled at the next page dated July 16. *A. Morgan—resignation.* Clare glanced up at Fran.

''Making the connection?'' Fran asked softly.

''I'm not sure, but the missing money in the trust fund was $10,500. Right?''

Fran nodded. ''And I've checked the loan payments. Sheriff Watson paid off an outstanding loan for his car

June 30. The amount happened to be the same as the money missing from the trust.''

''Yes, but couldn't that be a coincidence?''

''You have to read the rest, Clare. I'll give you a run-down of what I think happened if you like, and you can take the book with you to go over it more carefully later.''

''Okay. Great.'' She set the book on the table and listened to Fran.

''Basically, it looks as though someone else in town paid off an outstanding loan that July, too. Mayor Sam MacRoberts. His payment came later, at the end of the month. At the same time, there was a debit from a special discretionary fund that had been earmarked for bank renovations in the bank's budget that year. The amounts were the same and curiously, the renovations never happened.''

Unsure what to make of the details, Clare asked, ''What's your opinion on all this?''

Fran leaned forward, resting her arms on the desk. ''I think old man Carelli was doing favors for people. Ensuring their loans were paid off.''

''In return for?''

She shrugged. ''I don't know. But bank presidents don't stick their necks out like this for nothing, Clare.'' They stared at one another a long moment until Fran said, ''Look, I hate to rush you but I have another appointment. I'm going to do some more digging in that box of files—you've got my curiosity in high gear now. I'll give you a call tonight or in the morning.''

''The morning would be fine,'' Clare said, rising to leave. She tucked the agenda into her purse and thanked Fran again.

She made the walk back to the hotel in a daze, thinking about the implications of what she'd just read. The first thing she noticed when she closed the hotel-room door behind her was that there were no new phone messages.

Gil had obviously not returned from Hartford. It was almost five and the gloomy day was sinking into an early dusk. Clare decided to curl up with the agenda book Fran had given her. She turned on the bedside lamp and was reaching for her purse when a sudden sharp rap at her door made her jump.

Gil. Heart racing, she ran to the door and flung it open. But the person standing in front of her was the last person on earth she wanted to see.

Helen Wolochuk.

CHAPTER EIGHTEEN

CLARE TRIED to close the door, but Helen shoved her foot inside and pushed hard. She stumbled backward as the woman brushed past her. Obviously distraught, she stood in the middle of the room and glared at Clare.

"What do you want?" Clare asked, trying to keep her voice level.

"I've come to tell you to stay away from us."

If only I could, Clare wanted to say. "I think you've got that the wrong way around, Mrs. Wolochuk."

"Helen," she mumbled, scanning the room.

"*I* am the person being hounded by members of your family, Helen. First Jason, then Stanley," Clare said.

Helen's eyes narrowed in suspicion. "Stanley? Was he here? When?"

"Last night. Look," Clare fought to keep the frustration out of her voice, "I think you'd better go. Maybe you should call your husband and ask him why he came to see me last night."

"I can imagine why he came. Can't you?" She cast Clare a cunning look.

"I don't know what you mean."

"Stanley always had an eye for the girls," she said. "That's what got us into this mess. I tried to tell you that the other day."

"Are you talking about Stanley and Rina Thomas?" Clare tensed. Was she making the right inference here, or had Helen slipped into some other reality?

The woman sagged into the same chair her ex-husband had been huddled in last night. "We tried to have a child for years and finally, after all the tests and disappointments, I got pregnant." Her face softened as she looked back to another time. But when she spoke again, her voice was brittle. "My happiness was short-lived. Stanley confessed he'd been having an affair with one of his students. A teenage girl! I couldn't believe it."

Clare moved slowly to the bed and sat down. She waited for Helen to go on, sensing that to ask questions or make comments would only prolong her visit.

"Of course he had all the usual excuses. *She'd* made the first advances. She was *mature* for her age." Her eyes shifted from Clare to the tightly clenched hands in her lap. "But the only reason he confessed was because she was trying to blackmail him, to get him to give her more marks. And then he confessed—crying, if you can believe it—that she was pregnant."

Her head jerked up. "Can you imagine how I felt?" Her voice rose. "I was his wife! I was pregnant with our first child—one we'd been trying to have for years. And he has the gall to say his eighteen-year-old mistress was pregnant, too."

Clare looked away from the pain in her eyes. This vignette of the Wolochuk household back then wasn't a pleasant one. "What happened?" she finally had to ask, though a premonition was taking shape in her mind.

"Stan called me from school that day—the day after he'd admitted everything. He said Rina had been there and was threatening to go to the principal. Stan would lose his job. He might even have been charged and sent to jail. I tried to calm him down. We needed to make some kind of plan." She paused to catch her breath, her chest heaving up and down. "I drove over to the school to see if I could find her. Someone had to talk sense into her!'' She looked across at Clare.

But Clare's thoughts were focused on the driving part, as she recalled Stanley's denial that he'd had his bike that day.

''I told Stan to meet me in the parking lot. When he came out, we could see Rina and some boy talking out on the playing field. Stan and I had a big fight then about what to do. I wanted to have it out with her right there but she was with that boy. We didn't know what to do, just watched them for a few more seconds. Then they started to walk toward the ravine shortcut and I couldn't stand there doing nothing. I grabbed Stan's bicycle and followed them.''

Clare sat perfectly still. The scene played out again in her head, but this time the bike rider had a face. Dry-mouthed, she quietly cleared her throat and murmured, ''And then?''

''I couldn't ride very fast. As I got closer, I could see that the boy was leaving and I knew I had a chance to talk to her alone. She even seemed to be waiting for me, sitting on that tree stump and watching me. But when I got closer, I could see that she wasn't expecting the person to be me.'' Helen fell silent for a long moment. ''She had a funny look on her face. Kind of scared and sassy at the same time. Do you know what I mean?''

Clare nodded, thinking what Rina's state of mind must have been like that day.

''But when I begged her to leave us alone, she changed. Just like that.'' Helen snapped her fingers, her face tight with anger. ''She didn't care that I was pregnant, too. *At least you're married,* was what she said. Huh! What kind of marriage did I have to look forward to then? That's what I wanted to know.'' She paused, catching her breath.

''We were shouting at each other and then she just

stood up and said she was going. Too bad for us, she said. She had her own problems and she didn't care if Stan gave her the marks or not. Maybe she'd tell anyway.'' Helen rose from the chair, as if to leave. She swayed slightly and put out a hand to the floor lamp to steady herself.

"I can't take this anymore,'' she said, her voice low and hoarse. She walked slowly toward the door, still ajar from her entrance. Then she stopped and turned to face Clare. "That's when I slapped her. I hated that gloating look in her face. She slapped me back, of course. And so I pushed her. Hard. She fell backward over the stump and didn't move.''

Clare swallowed the mouthful of acid that rose from her stomach. She kept her eyes on Helen, but the woman was lost in another world. Finally, she glanced at Clare one last time and said, "I killed her.'' Without another word, she walked out the door.

GIL CHECKED the dashboard clock. Just after five and he'd been on the road a mere ten minutes. He wouldn't make it to Twin Falls until at least six. A bit later than anticipated, but given what he'd found out, he doubted Clare would be annoyed. Of course, if he'd simply left Hartford after his meeting, he'd have been there by now. But as he was heading for the highway, he had suddenly decided to go see Stan Wolochuk.

The man had practically leaped out of his skin when he opened his front door. "What do you want?'' he asked.

"Some unfinished business from last night, Wolochuk. Can I come in or shall I just go to the police right now?''

That got the door opened fast enough. Gil winced at the state of the house. Wolochuk's personal life was definitely in a tailspin. He followed the man into the living room, stepping gingerly around the debris of someone who'd given up every pretence of order.

"So what's the business?" Wolochuk asked, slumping onto the couch.

"Last night Clare told you she saw someone riding a bike across the field that day. You said you'd taken your car to work that day. But you were lying, weren't you?"

Wolochuk's shrug made Gil's blood pressure soar. He wanted to shake the man, but he had a feeling that would only shut him up. "I can understand why you were upset that day. Your whole life was falling apart, wasn't it? Everything you'd worked for."

Stan's eyes, watery and red-rimmed, settled on Gil. "Rina wouldn't listen to reason. I offered her money so she could go to Hartford for an abortion. If she wanted to keep the baby, I would send her child support. As long as she didn't tell anyone. But I don't even think it was about her grades by then. She wanted me to pay for what I'd done."

"Did your wife know?"

Stan looked away and nodded. "She guessed something was up. I was late getting home every Thursday—that was the day Rina and I met at her friend's place. Things came to a head the day before Rina died. Helen fell apart, as I thought she might. She's never been a stable person and the pregnancy had been difficult from the beginning. I tried to explain to her how it was with Rina. That she had this power over me, like an addiction. But Helen wouldn't listen. She just kept screaming, how could I do this to her?"

"And that day?" Gil prompted.

"After Rina left my office I called Helen to tell her Rina was going to the principal in the morning. Helen told me she was coming to the school and to meet her in the parking lot. She was determined to confront Rina.

When I met her, we could see Rina out on the field." He paused. "She was with you, I guess, though I couldn't tell at the time. When you two started toward the ravine, Helen said she was going to follow you. I tried to talk her out of it but she grabbed my bike and before I could stop her was riding across the field after you."

Gil had a sudden flashback to the wooden footbridge, where he'd turned to wave goodbye to Rina, who had been looking down the path. He could still see the unknown bike rider slowly heading toward Rina. Now he knew who that rider was.

"Did Helen kill Rina Thomas?" he asked, fighting to keep his voice calm.

Wolochuk nodded. "Yes," he said, his deep sigh echoing in the quiet room.

Gil wasn't certain the man even heard him leave the house. He headed quickly for his car, his mind teeming. By the time he was driving toward the highway, he still hadn't sorted out what to do next, but getting to Clare right away figured high on his list.

Gil glanced at the clock once more and increased his speed. He hoped Clare had heeded his suggestion about waiting for him to return to Twin Falls before contacting the sheriff. He had a feeling Davis wasn't going to be happy about their amateur detective work, even if it meant Rina's murder was solved, and he didn't want Clare to endure any interrogation by herself.

Not that she couldn't handle a bit of intimidation, but he felt a need to protect her. She hadn't fallen apart at Wolochuk's forcing his way into her room or ranting about Rina, although her tight, pale face had signaled her distress. The Clare he'd dated long ago had been spunky, too, beneath her shy exterior. She was a perfect example, he realized, of how appearances can deceive.

That sparked another thought. He could understand how

she had misinterpreted the scene on the playing field that day. And in the same way he, too, had misjudged her reaction that night in the park. It hadn't been doubt about his innocence in Rina's murder that he'd seen in Clare's face. Instead, his failure to be frank about what Rina had told him as they embraced on the field had led Clare to assume he still cared for Rina. That was the disbelief he'd seen. Disbelief in his love for her.

Gil sighed. What a bloody waste of years, not to mention the loss of exquisite happiness during those years. *If only…* Those two words had plagued him since that night he walked away from Clare. Part of him had sensed right then that she'd been on the verge of forgiving him. The tears in the corners of her eyes and the huskiness in her voice had been signs he chose to ignore because his hurt was too big, all encompassing. So his life had gone in a direction he never could have imagined those months when Clare Morgan was all he got up for every morning—before Rina was killed and before he and Clare broke up.

Now, if luck was finally on his side, he and Clare might have a second chance. Not at reliving their adolescent dreams, of course. Those drifted away that night in the park. But this time Gil figured the experience gained by the intervening seventeen years was bound to make their union richer and much more valued. There was no way he would ever in his life be able to take Clare Morgan for granted again.

When he caught sight of the Twin Falls Welcome sign, Gil slowed down and dug into his jacket pocket for his cell phone. It was a few minutes past six but already dark. The stormy weather that had been brewing all day looked ready to burst. At the first stop sign, Gil punched in Clare's number. Five rings later the voice mail clicked on.

Disappointed, he said he was on his way and to please wait, that he had something important to tell her.

The storm hit two blocks from the hotel. Lightning bolts tore at the sky and rain tumbled from black clouds. Gil eyed the illegal parking slot at the hotel entrance and, after a nanosecond's debate, angled his car into it. He hopped out and dashed into the lobby. The place was empty except for the night clerk on duty behind the counter and a woman who seemed to be waiting for someone, sitting on one of the lobby chairs.

He considered going straight up to Clare's room but hated to waste the time if she really was out somewhere. And he prayed, if the latter was true, that she had her car.

"Can you tell me if Clare Morgan is in?" he asked the clerk.

The twenty-something kid peered up from the music magazine he was skimming and frowned. "You're the second person in the last ten minutes to—"

"Is she or isn't she?" Gil barked.

The kid's frown deepened. He gave Gil a wary look.

Curbing his impatience, Gil softened his tone. "We arranged to meet more than an hour ago and she's not answering her phone."

"Like I told that lady—" he tilted his head to a point behind Gil, "—Miss Morgan left here about twenty minutes ago, but said to tell anyone who called that she'd be right back."

"That was it? No other messages?"

"Yeah, she left a note for a Gil Harper. Is that you?"

"Yes, it is," Gil said curtly, wishing the guy had got to the point right away. He drummed his fingers on the countertop while the youth turned around to retrieve a folded piece of paper from a cubbyhole.

He snatched the note from the clerk's hand and flipped it open.

Dear Gil,

I've just figured something out, something important that I'd forgotten. There were two bike riders that day. I'm off to the sheriff's office. See you soon, I hope, with good news.

C.

Two bike riders? How did that fit in with what he'd learned from Stan Wolochuk? He forced himself to take a deep breath. There was no cause for worry, he told himself, just puzzlement. "Okay. So, uh, she hasn't come back then?"

"Like the I told the lady, I've been standing here the whole time."

"What lady is that?"

"The one behind you. Over there in the chair."

Gil slowly pivoted around, half expecting to see Helen Wolochuk, but the only person behind him was the woman he'd spotted on entering the lobby. He walked slowly toward her. "Are you looking for Clare Morgan?" he asked.

She smiled, rising to her feet. "I certainly am. And you would be—"

"Gil Harper. I'm a friend of hers."

"Well, I know Clare wasn't expecting me, but I found something I thought she might want to hear tonight, rather than wait till tomorrow."

"And you are—?"

"Oh, sorry." She extended her right hand. "Fran Dutton."

CLARE CALLED the sheriff's office as soon as Helen left, asking to speak to Vince Carelli. He'd called in sick that day, Beth informed her. Would Clare like to speak to the sheriff?

Clare thought quickly. An idea was forming in the back of her mind, one she wasn't certain about just yet. She really needed to speak to Vince, because he was part of the memory trigger that occurred after Helen Wolochuk confessed to Rina's murder.

"I don't suppose you could give me his phone number?"

There was the slightest hesitation, followed by a long sigh. "Oh, I couldn't do that, Clare. Sorry."

Knowing Beth had already done more than enough for her and Gil, Clare didn't press the point. Besides, she had a telephone book at hand and how many Carellis could there be in Twin Falls anyway? Not many, as it turned out, and only one V. Carelli. She grabbed her jacket and purse and headed downstairs.

When Clare saw the clerk at the reception desk, she remembered her dinner date with Gil and hastily scrawled a note to leave at the desk for him. Then she dashed toward the parking lot and, armed with Vince Carelli's home address, got into her rental car. She peered up at the darkening sky through the windshield and hesitated, her fingers wrapped around the car keys in the ignition. What was she expecting to accomplish by this visit to Vince Carelli?

Helen Wolochuk had vividly recreated the scene that day, admitting she'd been the bike rider in pursuit of Rina and Gil. Clare pictured it all in her mind as Helen rambled on, first seeing the unknown rider, then the empty bicycle rack in the parking lot as she'd run through it. She'd been crying and had almost collided with a boy on a bike entering the parking lot from the street. *Vince Carelli.*

She couldn't understand why she'd forgotten running into Vince that day, except that in light of everything else that happened, it hadn't seemed important. She had a vague memory of Vince asking her about Rina and re-

membered pointing wordlessly toward the field and the
ravine beyond. Vince had thanked her and ridden on while
Clare went home.

A rumble of thunder rolled somewhere in the distance.
Clare peered up at the sky, noticing for the first time the
building storm. She started the car. If Vince had continued
after Rina that day, he might have seen Helen Wolochuk,
too. She didn't recall seeing a statement from Vince in
Rina's case file, but perhaps he hadn't gone all the way
to the ravine. At any rate, it wouldn't hurt to have some
corroboration about seeing Helen, just in case the woman
changed her story. No doubt she'd realize the blunder
she'd made in confessing.

Having made a decision, Clare shifted into Drive and
headed for Vince Carelli's house. The worst that could
happen, she reasoned, would be that he'd send her on to
the sheriff. The rain hit just as she pulled up at the curb
in front of Carelli's address and she ran to the front door,
knocking sharply. Clare was thinking she ought to have
given the matter more thought but as she was about to
turn away, the door flew open.

"Clare? What is it?" Vince asked. He was in jeans and
a flannel shirt and didn't look as though he'd risen from
his sickbed.

Clare's gaze flicked from his stubbled face to the beer
bottle he clutched in one hand. "I...uh, sorry to disturb
you at home, Vince, but—"

"You'd better come in out of the rain." He motioned
inside with the hand holding the beer bottle.

She stepped into the dark entrance hall. When he closed
the door behind him, the house fell into darkness.

"You said to call if anything came up about the Wolochuks and—"

"Don't tell me someone in that family's gone off the
deep end again."

"I've just had a visit from Helen and she basically admitted killing Rina Thomas," she blurted.

He didn't move for a long moment. When he did, he tilted his head to one side and seemed to squint at her. "Yeah? So, why aren't you talking to the sheriff right now, instead of me?"

"Because she said she'd ridden Stanley's bike after Rina that day and I saw her following Rina and Gil toward the ravine, though at the time I didn't know who the person was. Then after Helen left today, I remembered meeting you when I was coming out of the school parking lot so I thought that…well…you might have seen something, too. Between the two of us, we might be able to put together what really happened." She stopped, breathless, her heart pounding against her ribs.

"But you said Helen confessed."

"She did, but won't witnesses be needed anyway? What if she denies saying anything to me? I mean, I can't prove that she did. We can talk about it before heading off to see Sheriff Davis."

"Come on into the living room, " he said, turning to his left into a small room off the hall.

Clare hesitated in the doorway. All the drapes were drawn in the room and she could barely see.

"I woke up with a migraine this morning, that's why I'm not at work." He switched on a table lamp next to an easy chair. "Have a seat. Sorry about the mess," he said, gesturing to newspapers scattered about the room along with an assortment of empty junk food bags.

Clare sidestepped an empty beer bottle on the floor. *Kind of an unorthodox treatment for a migraine,* she thought, as she sat gingerly on the edge of the couch.

He lowered his large frame into the easy chair across from her. "So Helen Wolochuk just showed up at your door and confessed to the Rina Thomas murder?"

She shook her head. "Not quite like that. Maybe I should give you some background. You see—Gil Harper and I have been doing a little investigating into the Rina Thomas case."

"Oh? Why is that?"

"It's a long story and it's kind of connected to the vandalism of my book posters. Apparently Helen Wolochuk started hearing all kinds of gossip about Rina's murder after the word came out that I was coming back to town to promote my book."

"Heard some of it myself," he said.

"I think she was afraid that some people would read the book and believe there was more fact in it than fiction. Some of the details in the book are close enough to the real case that, well, people might put two and two together. And there was a bike rider in my book."

"So although the book is fiction, there might be some details that someone—say, in the know—could believe to be fact and therefore, be worried about."

"Yeah, I think that's what I meant." She laughed. "Maybe you should try writing, Vince. You seem to have a way with words."

He smiled. "Thanks for the compliment, but I doubt I'd have the discipline. Okay, so the Wolochuks were worried someone would point the finger at them and had a big fight. Jason overheard them and, without really having all the facts, pegged you as the bad person upsetting his parents and making his life miserable."

"Yes. Gil and I went to see them about Jason and in the course of our visit, some information came out about the murder."

"Such as?"

"The thing about the bike rider."

"And how did you connect the bike rider to Helen Wolochuk?"

Clare told him about Stanley's visit the night before. "He denied being the person on the bike but I didn't really believe him until Helen confessed."

Carelli's thoughtful gaze locked on hers. The only sound was the muted fall of rain on the roof of the house. "Did she say how she killed her?" he finally asked.

"I think she thought the fall to the ground had broken Rina's neck but that was the one thing that jarred in her confession."

"How so?"

She hesitated, knowing she was about to get Beth into trouble, but it would all have to come out anyway. "According to the autopsy report, Rina was killed by a blunt trauma to the head and police found a bloodied tree branch in the vicinity."

"And how do you know what the autopsy said, Clare?"

"Because I...well, uh...I read it. But I can't tell you how I got hold of the report. At least, not yet."

He shook his head, obviously unhappy with her. "I think maybe we should go down to the station and continue this talk with Davis."

Clare sighed. There was no way out, she thought. She checked her watch, noting that it was past six and Gil must already have arrived at the hotel. She considered asking to go to the station later, but one look at Carelli's face ruled out pleading. He looked royally ticked off.

There was a crash of thunder outside. "I should go," she said, rising to her feet. "I'm supposed to meet Gil back at the hotel."

Carelli shook his head. "You'll have to forget about that, Clare. We need to go to the station and talk to Davis, get the ball rolling on an arrest warrant for Helen Wolochuk."

"I hope it won't take too long," she said.

"I can't guarantee how long it'll take. Depends if the

sheriff is as bugged about this as I am. I'm not even going to ask how you got the file, 'cause I've got a hunch about that already.'' He gripped the arms of the easy chair and stood up.

Clare closed her eyes. God, she had really blown it. She wondered if he and the sheriff would believe her if she insisted that Beth had had no choice but to copy the file. That she and Gil had threatened her or something?

When she opened her eyes again, Vince was staring at her, his face flushed.

''Give me a second to…uh…get ready,'' he mumbled. He weaved slightly as he moved toward her.

Clare stepped back as he drew nearer. His foot came down on the empty beer bottle and he stumbled, his arms flailing as he lost his balance. Clare reached out for him, dropping her purse onto the floor where it tumbled open. Vince clutched onto her, righting himself. Catching a deadly whiff of stale beer and body odor, Clare pulled away from him.

''Sorry,'' he mumbled. He stood perfectly still, shaking his head back and forth as if to clear it of its alcoholic haze. ''Guess I should've been eating as well as drinking today,'' he muttered. ''Let me get that for you.'' He stooped to retrieve Clare's purse and the items that had fallen out.

Too late, Clare's gaze shifted from Vince to the carpet and the agenda book, with its gold-embossed R. Carelli on the cover.

''What's this?'' he asked, picking the book off the floor and holding it up in front of Clare. ''How the hell did you get hold of my Dad's book?''

She didn't have a chance to respond. As if the gods were as accusing as Vince, an earsplitting clap of thunder sounded above and the house fell into complete darkness.

CHAPTER NINETEEN

"WE'LL TAKE MY CAR," Gil said, ushering Fran out the
hotel door. He wasn't certain what Clare was up to but
figured it couldn't be good. Especially when the desk
clerk revealed that there'd been a visitor to Miss Morgan's
room shortly before she left. A strange-looking woman.
Helen Wolochuk? Gil was more mystified than ever.

On the way to the sheriff's office Fran told Gil about
the agenda book and its contents. He listened half-
heartedly, imagining Clare sitting on the hot seat in Sheriff Davis's office at that very moment. Even when he registered Fran's assertion that the former bank president had
been moving money around in the bank in a very curious
fashion, Gil still was unable to figure out how that fit into
the Rina Thomas puzzle.

"I found a letter," Fran explained. "I was going to
wait and go through Mr. Carelli's box of files tomorrow
but I was too curious, especially after what I read in his
agenda book." She peered down at her watch. "Everyone
at home will be wondering where I am."

"Hmm?" Preoccupied, Gil turned from the windshield.
"Do you want to go home?"

"Heavens, no. My kids are big enough to fend for
themselves. Besides, I want to find out what's going on.
Clare told me about her mother, but I think there's something bigger here than an embezzlement case." Her pale
blue eyes locked with Gil's.

Damn right about that, he thought. He managed a faint

smile. "I think so, too, Fran. So, what was it you found in this box?"

"A letter from the former Sheriff—George Watson—thanking Mr. Carelli for taking care of his car loan and advising him that the business concerning the Rina Thomas file had also been taken care of."

The car swerved as Gil lost momentary control of it. "What? You have that letter with you?"

"In my purse."

"I'm not sure how it fits into the picture but Sheriff Davis will want to see it."

He did. Gil forced himself to stay calm while he and Fran rushed through the reason for their visit to a confused Kyle Davis who had no idea that Clare Morgan was supposed to be there.

"She left a note for me," Gil explained, "saying that she'd remembered there were two bike riders the day Rina was killed and for some reason she considered that important. I'm not sure why. I assumed she was heading here when she left the hotel—to talk to you about the case."

"The Thomas case?"

Gil glanced at Fran and said, "I guess Ms. Dutton and I should fill you in."

Davis nodded. "I guess you'd better. Take a seat."

Gil barely perched on the edge of a chair in Davis's office while he rapidly summarized the events of the last twenty-four hours. Then Fran pulled out the letter which both Gil and Sheriff Davis studied carefully.

"I'm not sure what to make of this," said Davis. "Why would Mr. Carelli at the bank have anything to do with the Rina Thomas case file? I worked that investigation and it was brought to a close not long after you were cleared of any possible charges, Gil."

Gil saw Fran turn his way, a look of surprise in her

face. "Any idea why the investigation came to a halt then?"

"Sheriff Watson called me in a couple of weeks or so after the murder and said if I had no new leads, to close down the case. He said I could reopen it if anything new turned up, but nothing ever did. I was ticked off, as you can imagine, but he was the boss." He glanced at the letter once more, his face lost in thought. "There is one thing, but...nah, it's too crazy."

"What is it?"

Davis pursed his lips as if reluctant to continue. Finally he said, "Just that in those first few days I questioned a bunch of kids who'd been around the school that day. Clare was one of them. She told me that after she saw you and Rina in the field, she left the property via the parking lot and met Vince Carelli, who was looking for Rina."

"The Vince Carelli who's now your deputy?"

Davis shot Gil a look as if to say, *who else?*

"Clare's never mentioned seeing Carelli to me."

Davis shrugged. "Maybe she forgot or thought it wasn't important. There were at least three or four other kids hanging around the front of the school at the same time, and I interviewed them, too." He paused, narrowing his eyes at Gil. "But none of them had seen either you or Rina."

"Why was Vince looking for Rina? What did he say?"

"Whoa! Hold on, Harper. I'm thinking." Davis rubbed his face. "He said something about wanting to talk to Rina about a school assignment. He said he never found her and he went on home. End of story. The interview's on file, anyway."

"I don't remember seeing that statement in Rina's file. Maybe that's the business Sheriff Watson was referring to in that letter to old man Carelli. Maybe he took the interview out of the file.''

"What the hell are you talking about?'' Davis leaned forward, his expression suggesting Gil was speaking some foreign language.

Gil bit down on his lower lip, silently apologizing to Beth. ''I...uh...I've got a copy of the file and there's nothing in it about your interview with Carelli. And please don't ask how I got hold of the file because—''

Davis briefly closed his eyes. "At this point, I don't want to know, Harper.''

"I was expecting Clare to be here, because of the note. But now I'm wondering if she might have gone somewhere else—to clarify the mystery of the two bike riders.''

"I'm not following,'' Davis said.

"Where's Carelli?'' Gil asked, ignoring Davis.

"He called in sick today.'' Davis frowned. "What connection are you making here, Harper?''

"Look. Vince Carelli was looking for Rina that day, too. What if he followed Rina and me to the footbridge?''

Davis's frown deepened. "After Helen Wolochuk?''

"Yes! He might have seen Helen kill Rina.''

"That doesn't explain why his old man would get Sheriff Watson to take Vince's statement out of the file. Unless, as you suggest, Carelli was lying and did go after Rina.'' He paused, then pressed his intercom phone and said, ''Beth, will you give Vince a call for me? Let me know as soon as he's on the line.''

The room filled with silence. Seconds later, Beth's voice rang out. "He's not answering, sir. Shall I try again?''

Gil's stomach lurched. He stood up. "We've got to go looking for Clare. I think she's with Carelli.''

"At his place?'' Fran asked, getting to her feet, as well.

Sheriff Davis looked her way. "Ma'am, I'm afraid you're going home. I'll have a car take you back to the hotel for your own vehicle. Harper," he said, "you and I are going for a drive. But no way am I putting out a bulletin on Carelli without carefully checking into this."

Gil spun on his heel and led the way out the door. They were almost out of the building when the power went out.

CLARE WAITED for her eyes to adjust to the sudden dark. She saw Carelli's shape looming over her. His voice, almost at her ear, hissed, "You have something that doesn't belong to you. That's enough to take you in for questioning."

"Then shouldn't we be going to the police station?" she asked. She hoped her voice didn't sound as anxious as she was feeling. Something in his manner—not to mention his physical state—was triggering major alarm bells.

"Because first I need to talk to you, Clare. To find out why you've got my dad's old agenda book. Maybe to find out what's inside it. So we're going to have a little chat. Okay? Starting with how you got hold of it."

"I can't tell you that," Clare said. She could feel her heart thudding against her chest.

He inched closer. "Yeah? Well, you will eventually. Right now I'm more interested in what is in the book."

"Nothing really," she stammered. He seemed more angry than curious about why she had the agenda book, and she sensed that revealing that his father was corrupt wouldn't improve his mood. "Just some stuff about my mother and something that happened at the bank. That's why I had it. I…uh …wanted to find out for myself why my mother lost her job there."

"Uh-huh. And what did you learn?" His sour breath fanned across her face.

Clare looked away. "That your father accused my

mother of stealing some money,'' she said in a low voice, not wanting to sound confrontational.

"No kidding. So dishonesty must run in the family, eh?'' He snorted, weaving slightly.

She thought about what she'd read in the agenda but bit back the reply she might have made about his father. "Your father forced her to resign.''

"So my old man was mean to your mother. Is that what you're saying? Is there supposed to be a link here to Rina Thomas's murder, or am I missing something?''

Angrily, Clare blurted, "The amount of money she was supposed to have taken is the same amount as a loan your father forgave. To the former sheriff.'' Her voice fell as she added, "It was the same amount that was taken from a trust fund that my mother was responsible for.''

"I'm not making the connection to Rina yet. You have to spell it out for me.'' He pressed against her.

A waft of alcohol fanned across her face. She took a step back and cleared her throat, trying to hide her revulsion. "I don't know. As I told you, I only wanted to clear my mother's name.''

"Then why the interest in the murder? You and Harper have been asking questions, contacting the Wolochuks and that reporter, Withers. You got a copy of the case file somehow, so I guess you know all the details. Where has this detective work led you, Clare?''

She refused to answer, guessing he was trying to assess what and how much she knew. The problem was, she couldn't figure out exactly why he cared so much. Other than the strange business of his father wiping out a loan for Sheriff Watson, what did Vince personally have to do with any of it? Unless…

"I should go,'' she said, inching away from him.

He lunged out, grabbing her by the forearm. "Aren't you going to ask me if I went after Rina that day?''

She flinched, repelled by his breath. "Did you?"

"The bike rider," he said, ignoring her question. "See, that's what started the whole thing. I bought myself a copy of your book to check it out and there it was. The girl in your book told about seeing a friend on a bike, after she left school." He chuckled. "Kinda funny, isn't it? That it was right there in your book all along but for some reason you and Harper missed it."

Clare tried to swallow past the knot in her throat. Her mind raced ahead of him, guessing what he was about to say.

"See, you saw someone on a bike that day following Rina and Gil into the ravine and today you found out that person was Helen Wolochuk. That could have been the end of the story—for me, anyway. Even your remembering you saw me on a bike, too, was no big deal. But when I saw that agenda book, I knew you'd put the rest of it together sooner or later."

A thought was emerging from the haze in her mind. "Your father's favor to the sheriff. What was it in exchange for?"

"You're getting it, Clare. I knew you would. It was in exchange for the sheriff's removal of two statements from Rina's file. Still haven't got it?" He cupped Clare's chin and turned her head his way. "The two statements he destroyed were a section of yours and all of mine. 'Cause if someone were to investigate the fact that *two* bike riders headed into the ravine that day... Well, you can figure out where that might lead. To questions I wouldn't want to answer."

"*You* killed Rina?"

The surprise in her voice brought a smirk. "Congratulations, Clare. Rina was stringing me along the way she was Wolochuk. I'd been helping her for weeks, writing essays, doing her homework. I'd taken Wolochuk's course in the first semester. It was a senior course but science was my thing. And I had a major hard-on for Rina, which she used to full advantage. Teasing me on, leading me to think we'd come out as a couple as soon as the year finished. I didn't even know about the whole freakin' thing with Wolochuk until I found her near the bridge that day.

"Someone on a bike had come flying past me on the curve just before the clearing at the bridge. I didn't see who the rider was. Then I saw Rina, sitting on the ground, crying. She told me everything—about her and Stanley and being pregnant. I tried to comfort her. Told her that we could run off together—I'd help her with the baby even." He stopped and the only sound, other than his labored breathing, was the rain outside.

Clare realized how foolish she'd been to discount seeing Vince Carelli that day as important. But he was a year younger, in another class. She'd assumed he was only curious about Rina, never imagining he'd been connected to her in any real way.

Assumptions. She had to admit the irony. Her mistake boiled down to simply what the eye saw and what the mind chose to believe. It was exactly what Gil had been trying to tell her that night, seventeen years ago. *It wasn't what you think,* he'd cried, when he'd tried to explain why he'd been embracing Rina.

"She laughed at me." Carelli went on, his voice oddly detached, as if he were recounting someone else's story. "Said she'd been using me to help her with school. That I was a creep and she wanted nothing to do with me. I freaked out. I don't even remember picking up that tree branch. When I realized she was dead, I panicked and rode straight home. My mother called my dad at work and he came right home."

"So that was the favor for the sheriff. And what about the mayor?"

290 PAST, PRESENT AND A FUTURE

"Dad felt guilty. First, over the thing with your mother. He had to have someone to blame for the money going missing from the trust fund and she was the obvious choice. Later, he felt bad about how things had turned out for Gil and his parents. All the innuendo that was going around town about Gil really being the killer. So he went to the Mayor who had some gambling debt, only this time he got the money from somewhere else."

My mother conveniently gone. Bitterness rose in Clare's throat. "The job for Mr. Harper," she said.

"Yeah. After that, once the statements were gone from the file and the sheriff closed down the case, I had nothing to worry about. Even the book wasn't a threat. When I heard you were asking questions about the case, I knew eventually you'd figure things out. That you'd remember everything. That's why I stayed home today. To think things out—decide what to do." A flicker of regret crossed his face.

"I know what I'll have to do now, though. I'm sorry for this Clare, but you see, the booze has loosened my tongue just a tad too much. I think you 'n' me are going to have to take a drive somewhere."

Blood rushed into her ears, drowning out the slash of rain against the windows. Clare gulped a single, decisive breath and made her move, raising her knee up and smashing it into Carelli's crotch. He grunted and doubled over, releasing his hold on her. Clare sprinted for the front door.

He'd locked it. Her hands were clammy, working clumsily at the lock. She heard him staggering after her, his harsh gasps echoing in the hallway, and she began to hyperventilate. She worked faster, adrenaline firing through her. Unbolted the door and pulled it toward her.

Suddenly he was there—right behind her—his hand slamming against the door, trying to push it closed while she struggled to keep it open enough for her to slip through. His other hand shot out, grasping her by the shoulder as he tried to pry her away from the door. Clare turned her head toward him and bit down hard on his hand. He screamed, wrenching his hand away, and she squeezed through the gap.

THE STORM RAGED outside the cruiser but Gil, his eyes focused on the steady sweep of the wipers, saw only Clare's face. "She's in trouble. I know it! Can't you go any faster?" he asked Davis who was hunched over the steering wheel.

The sheriff glanced sharply at him. "Relax, Harper. You're already in enough trouble. Don't add to my aggravation."

Still, he increased the speed. *Unnerved by the wild look in my eyes,* Gil wondered? The trip to Carelli's house seemed to take forever as they drove through rain-slicked streets eerily dark due to the power outage. Then suddenly it was there—Carelli's house, squat and foreboding, backlit by sporadic flashes of lightning.

As soon as Davis killed the engine he held up a warning hand to Gil. "Let me handle this. You stay in the car." He opened his door and stepped out into the blinding rain.

Yeah, right. Gil yanked open the passenger door and leaped out. He heard Davis shouting but ignored him, dashing toward the front door. It opened just as he reached the porch and Clare was falling into his arms, sobbing. The rain beat down on them while Gil pressed her to him, silently vowing never to let her go again.

He lowered his head to hers as if to shield her from the drenching rain, though his efforts had little effect. He doubted she was even aware that both of them were getting soaked. Sheriff Davis had cautiously entered the front door as soon as Clare has burst out onto the porch and beneath the roll of thunder Gil thought he heard shouting from inside the house. He had no idea what was happening there. All he wanted to do was to get Clare away as quickly as possible. So he guided her toward the still-opened passenger door of the cruiser and helped her inside.

When he was behind the wheel, he took his first real look at her and grinned. "Do I look as bedraggled as you do?"

Her smile was a bit wobbly. She swiped a long strand of hair stuck against her cheek and tried to speak and gasp for air at the same time.

"Put your head between your knees for a sec, Clare, and take slow deep breaths."

As she struggled to regain control of herself, it was all he could do not to dash back into the house and help Davis deal with Carelli.

Finally, after several moments, Gil ventured the question he'd been afraid to ask.

"Did Carelli hurt you?"

When Clare shook her head, he felt relief oozing through him. "Thank God," he said hoarsely. "I was so damn scared, Clare. On the way over here I was still trying to figure out his connection with everything but all I could really focus on was that the guy might have killed Rina and could have…would have…"

"He did kill Rina," she said.

If Gil wasn't looking at her he'd have had trouble identifying that voice. He had trouble even accepting that the sodden creature across from him—so oddly frail, with eyes still dilated in fear was the Clare Morgan he'd once loved so passionately. And loved still, he realized.

He knew there were hours of questions and answers ahead of them—at the police station, at the Kingsway home and probably much later, with friends back in New

York. He didn't want to hear or talk about Rina Thomas and that whole tragic business anymore. From now on, all thoughts, actions and words were going to be centered on Clare Morgan.

"I love you, Clare," he whispered. He reached out to clasp her long cold fingers in his. "I've always loved you. Ever since that day in English class when the teacher caught you daydreaming. I'll never forget that moment— it was like seeing you for the very first time. And in a way, I guess I was. At least, seeing the sensuous, beautiful young woman you were going to become. If I'd been mature and confident enough to deal with everything that happened, these past seventeen years would have been spent with you instead of apart from you. No, don't speak yet," he said, squeezing her hand gently. "I need to get all of this out and then I'm going to start living out my longtime fantasy of holding you in my arms all night. I...I," he paused to clear his throat, overcome by the sudden bloom of color in her face and the moistness in her eyes. "I've always loved you. All these years, I've been torturing myself for all the things I could have said and never did. For not looking back the night we broke up in the park. For refusing to return your phone calls after you moved to New Jersey. So much wasted time." He stopped to catch his breath, his pulse drumming against his chest and rushing into his ears.

"I love you, Gil," she whispered. "I never stopped— not once—dreaming about you saying those things. Though I tried my best to make it seem otherwise," she admitted with a shaky laugh.

He pulled her toward him and kissed away a single drop of rain clinging to her forehead. "As soon as the other car gets here, I'm going to take you back to your hotel. And then we'll have a nice hot shower and spend—"

''The rest of our lives together?'' she asked, drawing her head back enough to meet his eyes.

''I dearly hope so,'' he said and lowered his mouth to hers.

''WHAT HAPPENED THEN?'' Laura asked, her eyes wide with disbelief.

They were sitting in the Kingsways' kitchen with Dave, and Laura. Baby Emma cooed contentedly in her infant seat.

''Carelli made a pathetic attempt to suggest Clare had an obsession about the Thomas case but by the time he was handcuffed and sitting in the back of the cruiser, he was already changing his story. Crying that the whole thing had been a tragic accident,'' Gil said.

''You must have been so scared,'' Laura said, looking across the kitchen table at Clare.

Clare could only nod, still shaken by the memory of Vince Carelli lunging toward her in the dark house. Gil drew her closer.

Dave shook his head. ''The whole story is bizarre. It sounds like Vince almost got away with it, too. If he hadn't been a bit—''

''Drunk?'' Laura interjected. ''God, Clare. I can't believe you went over there. You're usually so cautious.''

''Not a good judgement call,'' Clare admitted. ''But others I've made in the last twenty-four hours have been right on.'' She grinned at Gil.

He bent to kiss her gently on the forehead. ''Speaking of those decisions…'' he murmured, letting his voice trail off into a meaningful silence.

On cue, Clare turned to Laura and Dave. ''We should be leaving soon. We've a long drive ahead of us.''

''Not so soon,'' Laura protested.

But it was a weak objection, Clare noted. She smiled

fondly at her friend. "We've been up most of the night, Laura, and have spent all morning at the police station. I have to be back in the city tomorrow and…frankly—" she paused, feeling a wave of exhaustion sweep over her "—I want to leave Twin Falls as soon as possible." Gil draped an arm across her shoulders and gently squeezed.

"I know, hon," Laura murmured. "I…we just want you guys to know that our home is yours whenever you're in Twin Falls."

Clare smiled, fighting the prickling of tears. "We do know that. And I'm afraid you'll be hosting us in the very near future, when Vince goes to trial."

"But you haven't explained why the Wolochuks got all fired up about Clare being back in Twin Falls," Laura protested.

"Both the Wolochuks believed that Helen had accidentally killed Rina. That was the real secret they've harbored all these years and what really got them scared when my book came out and all the publicity it generated."

"So Jason figured the book had something to do with his parents' fear but didn't exactly know why?" Dave asked.

Gil nodded. "Yes. But without knowing all the facts, Stan misinterpreted what he'd read in the book about the bike rider. He assumed Clare was referring to Helen."

"That's the part I find confusing," Laura said. "I haven't finished the book yet. One more time, please."

"Okay," Clare said, stifling a sigh. She'd recounted the story several times since Vince was arrested. "In the book my heroine—Kenzie—last saw her best friend, Marianne, heading alone into the woods the day she died. Then on her way off school property, she met a boy in her class who said he was looking for Marianne. She pointed in the direction Marianne had gone and the boy took off. So you see, I blended both bike riders into one person for the sake of my plot. Probably—'' she paused, recalling what she'd concluded since last night "—because I'd done the same thing in my memory.''

"Hey, but what about that reporter? Withers?'' Dave asked.

Clare smiled. "He turned up in Hartford. Apparently he'd had a big fight with his girlfriend on the weekend and took off after her. So he really was on leave.''

Laura frowned. "But didn't you say he had a source of information about the case? I mean, how did he know about your mother?''

"This is even weirder,'' Clare said, almost laughing. "It turns out Withers's aunt was working as a teller in the bank when my mother was accused of embezzlement. She told him about it after he interviewed me. So that was his big source. His talk about writing a book was all a bluff to get me to admit something he could use in a follow-up article.''

No one spoke for a long time. Then Gil dropped his arm from Clare's shoulder and pushed his chair back. "We do have to go, folks. Thanks again for the lunch.'' He extended a hand to Clare and gently pulled her from her chair.

She was so tired she felt as though she could sit in the Kingsway kitchen all day. But when her eyes met Gil's, she knew that everything was going to be all right, just as he'd promised last night.

"What about your rental car? Want some help with that?''

"All taken care of,'' Gil said, "but thanks anyway, Dave. Beth—the sheriff's secretary—has arranged for it to be driven to the rental outlet in Hartford.''

"Okay,'' Laura said, heaving a dramatic sigh. "But I'm counting on you two to keep your word and make regular visits to Twin Falls to see Emma. Together,'' she stressed.

"Together," Clare echoed, smiling at Gil. She insisted on carrying Emma to the front door where she bestowed a farewell kiss on the baby's brow before handing her back to Laura.

"I look forward to coming back now," Clare assured Laura. Then she kissed Laura and Dave goodbye and followed Gil out the door.

As they walked along the sidewalk to Gil's car parked at the curb, Gil slung his arm around her. "Don't you feel like we've been here longer than a couple of weeks?" he asked.

Clare stopped to face him. "Know what it feels like? It almost feels like we never left. Like we're seventeen again and starting all over."

Gil drew her to him, holding tight. "Yeah," he said huskily. "But even better." He tilted her face to his and kissed her. It was a long, sweet kiss that sealed every word and promise they'd made to each other in the wee hours of the morning, back in her hotel room.

"Shall we go?" he asked, pulling away.

Clare nodded and climbed into the car and Gil closed the door behind her. She glanced one last time at the Kingsway house. Dave and Laura, arm in arm, were waving from the front porch. Clare thought she caught a wink from Laura, but couldn't be sure.

Gil got behind the steering wheel and reached over to clasp her hand in his. "Ready?"

"I'm more than ready, I'm eager."

Gil laughed. "Then let's go." He steered the Mercedes away from the curb and slowly headed for the intersection.

"I'm glad we decided to stop on the way back," Clare said, "though I felt a tad guilty about keeping that from Laura and Dave."

Gil looked her way. "I'm sure they suspect anyway.

Dave asked if I was taking the long or short way to New York and he had a big smile on his face. He also reminded me that the fall colors in the Litchfield Hills will be spectacular." He paused a beat. "Personally, I think I'll still prefer the scenery inside the car."

His suggestive grin reminded her of last night at the hotel. They'd talked for hours. At first they replayed the scene at the Carelli house, with Gil filling in the gaps about his impromptu visit to Stan Wolochuk and later, meeting Fran Dutton at the hotel. Then, reinforced with a drink from her minibar, Clare broached the subject of Rina Thomas and most of all, the words she'd uttered in the park that night. Words that could not be taken back.

But midway through her explanation, Gil had drawn her into his arms and gently kissed her eyes, brimming with tears. His kiss had been meant to comfort her—and it had—but when she'd tilted her face up to his and given a wobbly smile, something had flared in his dark eyes. There was a sharp intake of breath just before he'd placed his lips firmly on hers. Then they'd sat, wrapped in each other's arms, for what seemed like hours until he'd whispered, "I can't tell you how frightened I was that I might lose you again." His eyes were shining and his smile tenuous, as if uncertain of his next move—let alone his future.

"I'm here to stay," she'd answered. "Well—hopefully not in Twin Falls, but in your arms. With you."

They'd laughed together and for the first time in seventeen years, Clare felt a burden lifted and removed. There hadn't been much talk after that, except for the low contented sounds of two people coming together at last.

And the lovemaking, Clare thought as she sneaked a glance at Gil, steering the car out of town, had been spectacular. After she'd fallen, spent, back onto the pillows and lain staring up at the ceiling, basking in a glow that

Clare knew would envelop her, like an aura, for weeks to come, Gil had leaned over and whispered, "That was even better than the last time."

Her husky laugh had rung throughout the room and was stilled only by his lips coming down on hers one more time.

"Whatcha thinking?" Gil suddenly asking, cutting his eyes from the windshield to her.

"About last night."

He groaned. "Don't do that to me. I have to drive."

"Okay, I'll wait. But I saw this pretty little bed-and-breakfast on my way here and it's not very far."

His grin made her catch her breath. She wondered if either of them could wait even that long. When she spotted the Thanks For Visiting sign, she pointed to it.

Gil winked. "The pleasure was all ours," he joked.

"At least now it is," she added, reaching out to briefly clasp his hand.

He smiled. "Now and always." And together, they drove out of Twin Falls.

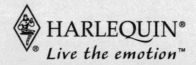

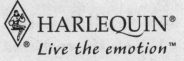

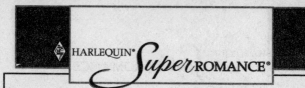

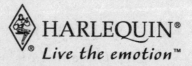